"JACK, WHERE ARE YOU?"

No answer. Amber's voice echoed down the dark corridors, not only unanswered, but she feared, unheard. She stumbled to a halt. The darkness pooling about her was deeper than night. She could not see through it. She could smell dankness and mold, street dirt, and her own fear.

"Amber."

It wasn't Jack's voice, but one she knew even better. *Don't let him find me. Please, by all the gods, don't let him find me.*

"Amber." Closer now. "Amber, It's time to kill." And then he began to move away. He said, "I have the word, Amber. All I have to do is say it."

The need to breathe clawed at her throat until she could no longer think.

"Amber?"

The voice was now farther away in the darkness. Surely, he hadn't seen her, didn't know for sure that she was here. She was clothed all in black, blending with the darkness.

But whether he sensed her there or not, the voice had done its work. Now she remembered why she was here. She'd come here to kill someone. . . .

DAW Titles by Charles Ingrid

THE SAND WARS Series

SOLAR KILL (Book One)
LASERTOWN BLUES (Book Two)
CELESTIAL HIT LIST (Book Three)
ALIEN SALUTE (Book Four)
RETURN FIRE (Book Five)

CHARLES INGRID
THE SAND WARS
CELESTIAL HIT LIST
3

DAW BOOKS, INC.
DONALD A. WOLLHEIM, PUBLISHER

1633 Broadway, New York, NY 10019

First Printing, November 1988

4   5   6   7   8   9

Printed in the U. S. A.

DEDICATED TO:

Howard, who's been there and back again and lived to tell the tale, with thanks ... some spoken but many not.

And to Sheila, for all her help and encouragement as well.

PART 1:
MALTHEN

CHAPTER 1

"No suit, no soldier. We've drummed that into you. And now, we're going to make liars out of ourselves. The purpose of this exercise," their commander said, his voice ringing off the forty-foot-high parade ground walls, "is to prove that, even if you take away the armor, you still have a Knight." He looked across the phalanx, squinting in the too-bright sun of the planet Malthen, sweating in the almost desert quality heat of the city of Malthen. "After we're done with you, it's far more than the armor or the gauntlet stingers or the laser cannons that make you what you are."

Within their rows, the soldiers stood at ease, though admittedly somewhat ill at ease. They murmured amongst themselves, listening to the broadcast from the movable platform to their fore, and closely watching the man who paced through the ranks between them and the commander, for he was their hero.

He was lean and rangy, muscle still filling out his young frame, for they were all young—the rigors of being a Dominion Knight for the Triad Throne demanded a body in its prime—but the eyes of washed out blue held a look far older than his years, dominating his angular face. He paused, throwing back his head and looking up, in spite of the too-bright sun. The movement tossed drops of water from sweat-darkened sandy hair. He frowned. He was on display here, and he did not like it. For the barest second, his eyes darkened like the storm of his surname.

Then he looked to his commander—whippet lean, wavy hair of gleaming silver, a space-tanned face, dressed to the neck in immaculate silvers.

"Where are the equipment racks?"

"They're on the way. Relax, Jack. This is just a rehearsal."

The hero made a low noise of disgust at the back of his throat and began to prowl again, much to the dismay of the short, round-bodied man attempting to measure him. Storm pointed at his commander. "If my suit's been disturbed—"

"It won't be. We've had them under guard. Don't you think I know media tricks? It won't be bugged, I promise you that. And we'll have them swept clean again tomorrow before the ceremony."

Jack Storm paused again, a fraction of a moment, and their eyes met. Nothing was more inviolate to a Knight than the suit of battle armor his life depended upon. He did not say that to his commander, however, for the man facing him also wore battle armor and the only name the commander was known by was that of his armor: the Owner of the Purple. Jack's friend and commander was so well known for the mercenary armor passed down to him by his father that he had lost his original identity.

If the waiting ranks of soldiers noted the tension, they said nothing. The coming ceremony pricked at them, too. They'd worked and trained hard and most of them looked forward to their first blooding. Not many relished being paraded on live relays for civilians to gape at. Almost as one, they shifted uneasily, waiting for their own battle gear to arrive.

Jack stopped again, two steps away from the Purple who lounged at the base of his platform. "I'm a soldier, not a hero. None of this is necessary." He started to say more, but he wasn't alone. He flinched under the tailor's measuring hologram, moving almost imperceptibly, and the round-bodied man swore.

"You'll be a soldier without legs if you don't stand still!" The little man glared at the tall one and he brandished his laser scissors. He met no resistance this time as the Purple held Jack's level stare.

"The emperor wants to review the troops," the Purple said evenly.

"Damnit, he knows what we look like."

At Jack's flank, the tailor tapped in some adjustments on his keypad. "You've filled out some more. That means another fitting!"

"Peace, Franco," the commander said mildly. "He needed it, after Lasertown. There's only three meals between now and tomorrow morning. The uniform should be adequate."

Jack looked at the tailor, amusement flickering in his light blue eyes. The tailor met the glance before looking quickly away. Bowing, he turned off the holo and hurriedly skittered across the parade grounds.

The Purple straightened up. "Pepys wants you at your best tomorrow," he said. "How often does a contract laborer become a hero?"

"I was a Knight, first."

"And before you became a Knight, a free-lance mercenary."

No, Jack thought. *I was always a Knight*. But he did not voice his thoughts, because the mercenaries followed a code that said there was no tomorrow, only today, and the Purple had accepted him on that basis. For the Owner of the Purple, Jack had no history. Instead of interrupting, Jack listened, knowing that his former mercenary friend had become a mediator, a buffer, always between the newly reformed Knights, and the Emperor of the Triad Throne. All of them had sworn allegiance to the emperor in all manner of thought and deed—except for Jack. He'd sworn vengeance. Now, as if to hide his thoughts, he turned on one heel, looking back at his fellows. "He's tripled the size of the bodyguard."

"Closer to quadrupled, while you were gone."

Storm stared at the Malthen parade grounds, but what he saw was the dead moon surface, where he had nearly died. He blinked and the dust and heat-fused parade grounds came back into focus. Would it never rain here, sweeping away the dust and misery? In spite of the heat, he shivered. He'd worked hard to become a Knight, only to lose it all when he'd been shanghaied, contracted out—but he'd fought back. And now he *was* back.

Pepys seemed determined to make a hero out of him instead of an embarrassment by adding cover-up charges to the havoc Jack had already wreaked.

Such as blowing up a Thrakian warship despite the Treaty.

Jack smiled grimly at the memory. Sound shields were up, a sonic curtain protecting the practice ceremony from electronic surveillance by over-eager media specialists. But what he had to say was for the commander's ears alone. He stepped closer to the Owner of the Purple.

"Why won't he see me?"

Purple looked at him. Humor had permanently etched its marks at the corners of lively brown eyes that belied the age his silvery hair indicated. He paused, before asking in turn, "What do you mean?"

"I mean he's talked to everybody about Lasertown but me. For God's sake, he's even interviewed you and you weren't even there."

"He's protecting you, isn't he? The man's emperor, Jack, not a damn garbage processor."

"What I have to say isn't garbage. He *has* to know what happened, not only to me but to everyone under the dome—he has to know what the Thraks are doing. He has to know what I saw."

The two men stood, nearly nose to nose, an old man with young eyes and a young man with old eyes. Jack shifted, angry but uneasy over being at odds with his commander.

"He's the emperor," Purple said quietly. "The Sand Wars brought down old Regis, but Pepys is determined not to make the same mistakes. He'll talk to you when he's ready."

Jack started to say more, but his next words were drowned out by the noisy arrival of the equipment racks and he turned, almost lovingly, to the rack which held his own armor, opalescent Flexalinks hanging rigidly from its hooks.

The sunlight became fiercer, its reflection arrowing off the equipment as the Knights suited up.

"We shall demand retribution."

The ambassador of the Thrakian League lounged on his slant board and eyed the general pacing in front of him. "You shall do no such thing. If I am able to obtain an invitation to the ceremonies, you will be expected to show decorum."

"Decorum!" General Zlakt halted. His faceted eyes glared at those of his ambassador. "The being destroys a ship, and we are made chitinless by the likes of you!"

The ambassador waved an arm. "May I remind you, general, that we were in the process of annexing a mining colony on the fringe of Dominion territory. We will not be given a chance to explain our motives. We are dangerously close to losing the treaty on the basis of your hasty orders."

"And we are no closer to Lasertown than before."

"No. And it's my understanding that the site suffered considerable damage and is of no use to us anymore, as it is. I'll not have you jeopardizing all I've worked for these last twenty years because of a warrior's rage!" The ambassador sprang up from the slant board, bounding over to face the Thrakian general.

The two confronted each other, genes of an ambassador opposed to those of a warrior.

The general made a low, guttering sound from deep within his chitin. Then he said, "That warrior rage served you well during the Sand Wars."

"No doubt of that, Zlakt. But the Triad Throne has a new emperor and it is not likely we can push forward our advances like that again." Ambassador Dhurl retreated a step. He swirled the end of his robe about and over his shoulder. "You may never admit it, but we ambassadors are soldiers of a kind. It is my skill he will respond to."

"Not if he thinks you spineless."

Dhurl pulled his face into the mask of undefeatability. Zlakt, watching him, felt the barest flicker of admiration. Even as he was a general, here was a true ambassador.

"Emperor Pepys does not underestimate us. It is my job to see he does not. As for the loss of the Lasertown site, the matter is done with. There will be other opportunities to grapple with our old enemy."

"Perhaps. Then you will not ask for anything to be done to Jack Storm."

"No," Dhurl said. His voice thickened. "Not yet. I will make a formal protest but expect nothing to come of it. Have you seen the armor?"

"Not yet."

"I am told it's been coated with norcite. An interesting combination, don't you think?"

General Zlakt drew himself upward tightly. "More than interesting," he answered, "if the beings but knew what they had." He saluted. "By your leave."

Dhurl sighed. "Of course, general." The ambassador waited until the general reached the door of the embassy dwelling. "And Zlakt—"

"Yes?"

"Don't do anything foolish. I will not tolerate it."

Zlakt ground his mandibles but did not respond. Without waiting for further dismissal, he left the ambassador, slamming the door shut behind him.

The slant board wavered in the aftershock. Ambassador Dhurl regarded it for a moment, then pulled his face plates into the mask of domination and retired once more.

The palace halls of the Emperor's wing stood shadowed, as if late at night, inviting visitors and assassins. Both visitors and assassins would normally have been turned away by the security cameras, floor and wall sensors, heat sensors and even the odd psychic or two tuned in at World Police. But now the Emperor was not at home. Having invited guests and knowing that the uninvited would be there as well, he had retired to a more secure building outside of Malthen.

A solitary figure, already privy to the pattern of the maze that formed this wing, took the opportunity presented and glided along the corridors. Dressed in black, the opportunist paused now and then to avoid the invited guests and passed them by without even being noticed, despite all the cable and wiring and camera work the media was laying down for the following day's events. With scarcely a sound, the opportunist continued to penetrate the security system, finally reaching the doors to Emperor Pepys' study and pausing there. The bedrooms were not of interest. The computer room was.

A clatter in the outside corridor sent the opportunist to the nearest shadow, where she held her breath, waited, and listened.

"I don't care who you have to bribe, I want that tape. And I want that tape pirate who calls himself a free-lance journalist brought in and hung by the balls. He's patched in to me once too often. I want an exclusive, without excuses, on that man of Pepys'."

The intruder knew that crisp, baritone voice almost as well as she knew her own. He must be standing right outside Pepys' door!

"We'll do what we can, Randolph, but be reasonable—"

"Being reasonable didn't get me where I am today. Let's see if we can't find this hero before they trot him out for public viewing. I want to see if he's got any warts."

The second voice made a small gargling sound at the back of his throat, then asked, "Are you still working on the estrangement angle?

Footsteps, a pace or two and then back. "Why not? Pepys is staging a media show ... one he expects us to relay live, but I don't think the broadcast will be as self-serving as he expects. I don't intend to overlook his desire to be elected House Speaker for the Congress."

"Shit, Randolph, we can do without the controversy—we've got to be able to leave this planet, remember?"

"That's my job." The deep voice hit a baritone note and held it for a moment, almost as if a bell tolled. "The Thrakian League will be boiling all over us tomorrow, protesting the recent events. Pepys wants a whitewash by pretending to lay out all the data, but he's not going to get it."

The girl in the shadows put her head back to the cooling surface of the wall behind her. She steadied a hand, palm down. Not only did she know the voice and the powerful journalist who owned it, she knew the man they searched for. Knew him intimately. And knew that Scott Randolph could do nothing but harm to him if they found him.

The computer room became unimportant, for the moment. She'd gotten here once, she'd make it back again. She pushed herself away from the wall and crossed the quarters to the double doors outside which stood the broadcaster and his crew.

Randolph's deep tones rumbled again. "I've got no guts to the show unless I find that hero."

There was a pause, then the second man said, "Don't bullshit me, Scott. You're still looking for a lead on your lost Knight story. You got suckered on that one—when are you going to admit it? We've been chasing that ghost for years."

"It's no ghost! I know that." There was an edge to Randolph's voice, but even if it hadn't been there, Amber's attention would still have been frozen by these words. "My source is reliable."

"Your source is a *ratt* head. I've been your technical director for too long not to notice that the rumors crop up whenever he needs the credits."

"Maybe. But if there is such a man to be found—I can't let that go."

"You can, but you won't. You don't want to admit being scammed."

"Look, Dykstra—if you had a Knight you didn't want noticed, where would you stick him?"

"In vacuum without a deepsuit."

"Or in the midst of a new bodyguard of Knights."

"Maybe." There was a pause. Then Dykstra said, "Maybe Pepys doesn't intend to have him found. Did you ever think of that?"

"Ah, my friend. Remember the pen is mightier than the sword, and the tongue is quicker than either of them. The old emperor was toppled by the Sand Wars, not Pepys."

"Regis was toppled by a shiv in the rib cage, as I recall."

A pause, then the broadcaster said, "They would never have gotten to him without help. The Dominion stood back and let it happen. And if Pepys is hiding a lost Knight, that would make my story all the more interesting. If he's here, I'll find him."

The girl in black allowed herself a fleeting smile. Not if she had anything to do with it! If Amber didn't want to be found, she couldn't be. Nor could Jack, if she could persuade him to go with her. Of that she had little doubt.

She faded into the parallel corridor, running true to the false corridor the broadcaster and his crew stood in and made her way out of the emperor's palace almost as easily as she'd made her way in.

She took care to change her clothes before going to the barracks where Jack had been hidden for the past few days. As she crossed the grounds, the huge, multiwinged palace dwarfed her, its rose stone lending a sunset glow, and she looked up, involuntarily. She'd lived in the shadow of this building most of her life . . . but lived far, far away where it had existed only as a symbol of another life, a different kind of existence beyond that of the streets. Even now, as she crossed the lawns, she avoided all the cameras and sensors she could without making her avoidance noticeable. Jack sometimes called her paranoid. Amber called it being careful. She had no implanted ID chip, so even if the system picked her up, she couldn't be immediately identified. Still . . .

The scent of him filled her nostrils when she opened the door. He'd been marching and sweating, and though she could hear the refresher shower, he'd tossed his clothes onto the floor and they were full of his scent. She inhaled deeply, glad he was there. She realized how terribly empty she would be if he had not been.

Jack came out of the bathroom, a towel knotted about his waist. "Where have you been?"

She threw him an impish grin, hiding her feelings. He had been big brother to her, but now she wanted more, and she feared what she wanted was something Jack would not, could not give. Her voice did not give her away as she said arrogantly, "Wouldn't you like to know?"

His sandy blond hair was rumpled, as though he'd just combed his hand through it, but he gave her a wry smile back. "No," he said flatly. "I don't think I would. You're usually up to something."

"Girl has to keep herself amused. You all done for the day?"

"Probably. I can't take much more spit and polish even if I'm not," he answered ruefully. "He refused audience again. I've spent all day reviewing. He won't talk to me about the Thraks and

Lasertown, or any of the review committees. Dammit, Amber, I can't do anything for Dorman's Stand, but Claron has hope—it's not Thrakian sand, it was just firestormed. But the longer we wait to start terraforming, the less chance it has!"

She frowned at him, mirroring his own expression. Absently, he reached up and touched the line between his brows. Memories of the planet where he'd rangered stung him. Once green. New. Primitive. And then charred under his very feet as he fled helplessly.

"Let's go out."

He considered her abruptness. "Can't."

"What? You think the Thraks are going to try something with me here?"

"I think that the emperor and the commander want me to sit tight until tomorrow."

She wrinkled her nose. "That's stale. Come on."

Jack strode two more steps, pivoted and looked at her, realizing he'd returned to pacing. He did not like confinement, mental or physical, voluntary or otherwise. The young woman watching him with an unconsciously defiant tilt to her head, her dark honey-colored hair all tousled, was up to something. He knew Amber well enough to know she was not cajoling him into disobeying orders on a whim.

"What is it, Amber?"

She reacted as he knew she would to that tone of voice, straightening, her chin going out a little. But her eyes widened and her voice softened. "The media's got a hunt on for you and I don't think the interviews are going to be friendly. In the long run, Pepys will be a lot happier if you and I disappear until the ceremonies."

"I'm supposed to be secure here."

"You're on the World Police's list. Sooner or

later, a reporter is going to be able to access that list, or bribe for a printout. They'll be here. The question is: do you want to be here when they get here?"

He paused a moment. Then he shook his head. "No. Wait, I'll be out in a minute."

He disappeared inside the bedroom, stopping only to kick the pile of discarded clothing in with him. Amber relaxed then, sitting down on the chair nearest the door. Once she had him out of there, out from under World Police surveillance, she could tell him what she'd overheard.

She could hear Jack stamping his feet into his boots. As she looked toward the door in anticipation of his reappearance, she caught sight of the lawn monitoring screen.

A flicker of movement at its corners. Amber froze. There was no more indication than that of someone headed this way—and whoever that someone was, he was as professional at avoiding the security as she was.

CHAPTER 2

"Someone's coming."

Jack appeared at the bedroom door, alerted immediately by the tone in Amber's voice. "Who? Can you tell how many?"

She was already at the camera controls, fine-tuning the monitor's sweep. Other flickers came to her, all barely seeable. "Four. No, five. Professionals."

"That didn't take them long." Out of habit, he looked to the corner where his suit normally hung. The corner was empty. Bogie was at the shop, being electronically swept for bugs, and would be kept there until tomorrow's ceremonies. The palm of his right hand itched. He scratched it, worrying unconsciously for a second or two over the scar where his little finger used to be.

"I must have led them here!" Amber left the camera and sprinted for the door.

"Amber, no!"

"I won't be trapped in here." A curtain of honey-colored hair swung wildly, obscured her face, then eased to her shoulder.

"There's only one way in. We can hold it, if we have to," he said, crossing the room to her side.

She bolted out from under his hand even as he started to drop it comfortingly to her shoulder. Out the door into the night, even as the lawn lights sputtered and went dark.

"Damn," Jack muttered and went after her.

He had no illusions about either Amber or the safety of the emperor's barracks. Fourteen long months ago he'd been shanghaied from his apartments here, gassed inside his own front door, chilled down and cold-shipped out as a contract laborer to the norcite mines of Lasertown. He was supposed to have been killed, but his would-be abductor had decided to double his money and sold him under a forged labor contract.

Amber had told him later, after she'd tracked him down, that the abductor had been killed by the employer he'd double-crossed. She'd not wasted time tracking down the employer—that was something Jack meant to do once his life returned somewhat to normal. As a thin veil of cold sweat broke out on his forehead, and he plunged out into the night, it occurred to him that he might have lost the opportunity.

It was not the months of deprivation as a miner, nor as a prisoner of the Thraks, for which Jack intended to pay back his enemy. No. It was for the months of cold sleep, of cryogenic imprisonment, a torture he rarely went through if he could help it.

Cold sleep had stolen away more than half his life and most of his memories from his youth. He would sooner die a hundred deaths than unwillingly endure it again. Cold sleep had frostbitten away his finger, and several toes. And cold sleep had taken him out of a hellish war most of his comrades now considered ancient history.

The Sand Wars.

Jack stumbled and went to his knees, and Amber swept him up, drawing him back against the concrete of the building, her slender arms shaking even as she drew him into concealment with her.

Amber gripped his arm tightly. "This is no media hunt."

"No."

"Jack," she whispered in his ear. "I can do it if I have to."

It. He froze then, as he realized what she meant. "*No.*"

"But, Jack—"

"I said no."

She'd been trained to kill with her mind, though the thought of it normally raised goose bumps on her thin arms. She was no murderer, but she'd just told him she was willing to, for his sake. It could destroy her psyche if she tried. He could not, would not, let her. He got to his knees as the five intruders ranged close. Even without his battle armor, he was a formidable combatant. His muscles knotted across his back. His thighs tensed as he got ready to spring.

There was a wine-dark smear about face high across the field of nighttime blackness. It came to Jack even as he sprang that he was seeing nightscope goggles—and it came to him too late that his opponent could see him better, much, much better, than Jack could see him.

By then it was definitely too late.

Jack immediately went limp, so that the intruder had to shrug off a dead weight. He rolled as he hit, kicked, and took his enemy out as the man's knee went with a sickening crack. He moved quickly then, scrambling out from under the man as he went down, felt his torso clawed at.

By then he was surrounded and he felt the sickening kick of a stunner and went face down in the grass as he vomited, involuntarily.

He heard Amber scream, amidst thuds and curses. From the muffled, struggling sounds, he guessed they now had her somewhat restrained. A hand grasped his collar and pulled him up, into a kneeling position.

The intruder couldn't possibly know of Jack's incredible tolerance for a stunner. Already, his muscles had begun to tremble back to life.

Someone wiped his face clean of the vomit. Then he was pulled to his feet. He let his weight hang as two of the intruders shouldered him. They were taking him and Amber back to the apartment. Why, he did not know. He only knew that this way, he had his hands on two of them.

Jack smiled grimly into the darkness.

Just as all the tensile strength flooded back into his arms and hands, one of the intruders said, "Jesus, this guy is heavier than he looks."

"Forget it. We deliver the message and leave."

Jack thought twice about what he was going to do to the two necks within reach. Messengers were far different from assassins. These five he might let live until they said what they were going to . . . at least until his curiosity was satisfied.

Just inside the flooding light of the open doorway, they stopped and let go of Jack. Their faces went dead white as he did not hit the floor, but stood alertly in front of them. He spun around.

The leader, dressed all in knit black from head to toe, with only the moon of a face staring back thrust a closed fist out at him. Jack's reaction was squelched by Amber's being carried in.

Amber made a stifled noise as the two men holding her, followed by a painfully limping fifth, came into the apartment. She flailed about, only managing to kick the door shut.

The leader pointed at her. "I advise you to stay quiet. The man who sent me says to tell you that Rolf won't be bound by the emperor much longer.

He says to tell you that your days of freedom are nearly over."

Her face paling, Amber collapsed within the embrace of her captors. Fury rose inside of Jack as the words killed Amber's spirit. Rolf had been the Svengali, the Fagin, who'd subliminally programmed her psychic talents for assassination. Only Rolf knew the neurolinguistics that would set her off. Only Rolf knew who'd hired him to do the programming. Jack thought they'd long been rid of Rolf.

"Leave her alone."

The leader turned back to Jack. He pulled his night lenses off and let the goggles hang about his neck, a kind of obscene looking necklace. "Just defusing the situation." He still pointed his fist at Jack. "I have a message."

"Why should I listen?"

"A friend sends it."

"Friends have other ways of getting hold of me. Friends don't attack in the night."

"This friend says you've betrayed him. He's not so sure you will listen."

"Then tell me and get out."

"In a moment."

The lamed man hobbled about, effectively gutting the security monitors inside the apartment. When he was done, he nodded, stifled a groan, and left. Now no one could hear or see or record what was transpiring.

Except for Jack. And what they'd just done to Amber, he'd never forget. And in different circumstances, neither would they. He looked at her. Her wide eyes were sunken and glazed over. She drew shallow breaths. Her skin stayed gray and she shuddered. The thought crossed Jack's mind that what the man had already said might have triggered one of her NLP programs. If they didn't say what they'd come to say and get out, he'd lose her.

He strode across the room, grabbed her up from her captors' arms and slapped her, hard. Her head snapped back, but her cheek pinked and in a second, a spirit that was definitely Amber stared back at him out of her eyes.

"Don't you ever—"

"I won't." He held his arms around her loosely, protecting her. "Feel better?"

Sulkily, she answered, "Yes."

He looked at the two men who'd held her. "I'll remember you," he said. Their breath was stale in his face. One was half bald from a laser scar, and the other had metal alloy teeth. Jack turned with Amber back to the leader, who stood impassively in his black clothes, like the assassin he could have been. "I'm listening. I won't be two seconds from now."

"Then look at this."

The assassin opened his fist to reveal a gold mesh ocular piece, a prosthetic camera. Its fine wires trailed out of the back. Bits of flesh and blood crusted its edges.

Amber gasped. "That's Ballard's eye," she said, and swayed in Jack's arms.

Jack was not immediately convinced it belonged to the middle-aged renegade of their acquaintance, who wore his gold eye like a medal, but it had belonged to someone. The shreds of flesh clinging to it told him that. Ballard had fought in the Sand Wars, too, before he'd been injured and had deserted. Ballard knew Jack for what he was. Ballard had secrets that could have been torn out of him like that gold mesh camera.

Jack looked at the intruder, who smiled.

"Now that I have your attention, I am to say

this. 'If thine eye offend thee, pluck it out and so I have done.' And this: you are betraying your promise."

Jack wrenched his attention back from the grisly prosthetic. "That's it? That's all?"

The man shrugged. "I'm a messenger. He seemed to think it was enough." Evidently finished, the intruder signaled his men, and they faded from the doorway like shadows from a nightmare. And with that, the last of the evil departed from Jack's apartment.

Amber sagged within his embrace and Jack had his hands full for a few seconds. When he had time to look up, a faint beam against his windows told him that the lawn security lights were on again.

When he looked down, Amber was staring at him beseechingly.

"What are we going to do, Jack?"

"I don't know," he answered truthfully. "I don't know."

CHAPTER 3

As Amber shook herself, Jack added, "But I know what I'm not going to do. I'm not going to sit around and wait for anyone else to show up. And then . . ."

"And then?"

"I'm going to pay Ballard a little visit and see if he's missing any vital parts."

Amber grinned then, faintly. "What if he is?"

"He may find himself missing a few more. But I can't do anything until after the ceremonies."

Amber's smile became absolutely predatory. "That's my white knight," she said and beat him out the front door.

The assassin cum messenger reported back to his employer. He entered the room with no little hesitation, for his employer was intent upon his prey and not in a mood to be interrupted. The assassin prided himself on knowing when the man who employed him was more dangerous than he himself. The employer not only commanded his skills, but his grudging respect. The man was middle-aged, his powerful shoulders bowed some-what with the weight of his years and ambitions, though no gray yet flecked his dark hair. One brow was laser-scarred, winging away. Like most men of the military, it had come from his chosen career, a laser burn that could either have blinded him or gutted his brain, but had done neither, a lucky near-miss.

Winton took his attention away from the cowering, one-eyed man sitting across from him. A plastiflesh patch took the place of one of the victim's eyes.

"It's done?"

"As you ordered."

"What about the girl?"

The assassin smiled thinly. He'd been told of the girl's possibilities and she had worried him. "You were right. What I said disarmed her totally. My thanks." And he bowed his head.

Winton shifted in his chair. "And the rest?"

"He showed little reaction. But he heard and he listened." The messenger shrugged. "I can do no more."

Winton bared his teeth. "Unless I pay you to do it."

"He crippled one of my men tonight. Even if you pay me to do it, I cannot guarantee you success. And . . . I'm told you've tried before."

"Perhaps." Winton swiveled around, riveting his attention back on his victim. "You are dismissed."

"Commander." The messenger bowed and left.

Winton pursed thin lips in thought. He looked at the man hunched in pain sitting across from him. "Your sacrifice was not in vain, Ballard." He pushed a chip across the table. "You'll find sufficient credits coded to that to buy a replacement. Perhaps platinum, this time."

"I will never see out of this eye again."

"Perhaps. Microsurgery is tedious and unpredictable." Winton stood up. "But I'd try it, if I were you. Somewhere far away."

Ballard reached out a trembling hand and clutched

at the chip. "Somewhere where Jack Storm can't find me if he comes looking."

Winton said nothing. He did not have to.

The victim looked at him as if he would have liked to have known why all this had happened, and then he turned away as if knowing Winton would not tell him. Not even if he had been dying.

Winton waited until the door closed and sealed before swiveling in his chair to the computer terminal. He opened com lines.

"It's done."

"Will it set him on the trail?" the flickering image asked him.

"Perhaps."

"Is the man who threatens us and Jack Storm one and the same?"

"If this works, we should know fairly soon. And if he is . . ." Winton's transmission trailed off.

"We have failed to get rid of him in the past." The man facing him wavered visibly. "Perhaps a different tactic. If we fail again, all that we've worked for may crumble."

Winton said nothing. He had entirely different ambitions from his partner, but revealing them would not profit him. He sat impassively.

"He will be followed."

"Yes," Winton said.

The image did not ask for reassurance. If it had, Winton would not have given it. If he said a thing would be done, it would be done.

Only three times had he failed. Two with an unknown soldier. Once with Jack Storm.

"Very well," the image said, dismissing him.

Winton cut the transmission. The com lines went dead. He sat back in his chair. Then he reached out and idly tapped out a new number. The transmission lit up, the monitor's eerie light reflected on his face.

"Yes, sir?"

"I want you to do some searching through the files. Pinpoint it to the last six months of Regis' reign."

"Yes, sir." The response was unemotional, for the being Winton talked to was not quite human. It didn't really care what Winton demanded of it, as long as it could perform.

Chillingly, neither did Winton. "What I want you to locate are some frozen slides. They won't be under biogenetics, though. I have them hidden under this code." And he told the machine generated image the code. "Let me know when you've located them. I want to pick them up."

"Yes, sir." The transmission ended. The screen went dead again and Winton sat back once more. His impassive expression slowly curdled into a feral one.

CHAPTER 4

Jack felt the sun's hot rays tattoo his back. Behind him, the lines of the regiments flashed in full battle armor. Only he stood unarmed. Bared, as it were, to the worlds watching him.

He drilled automatically, putting every ounce of strength and grace he had into his movements, aware that the more powerful suits behind him were literally at his heels—that anything his human frame could do, the suits could do quicker and more powerfully. One misstep, and he would be ground into the dust of the parade fields, an inconsequential mix of flesh, blood and sweat.

The live crowd sensed his imminent danger. At the beginning of the drill, he'd brought them to their feet, straining to watch, some looking at the monitors for close-ups rather than at the grounds below, jostling each other, their oohs and aahs as one. Jack knew that Amber stood in the grandstand, but did not let himself think about it. The events of last night had shaken her far more than she let on. If she watched now, she did so apprehensively, and he had no room for fear in his thoughts. Not now.

The lines came to a halt as their commander called out, "At ease." As the thuds of the armor going into the rest position filled the air, the Owner of the Purple looked down from his platform where

33

he and Emperor Pepys stood. Jack felt the commander's eyes upon him.

They had planned this drill, for the worlds watching them, as well as for the emperor who'd newly resurrected their regiments. It was more than a drill. It was more like a lesson in mortality.

Jack snapped off a salute, pivoted hard left, and marched forward to where his armor hung from its equipment rack on the sidelines. He felt camera relays on his every move. With movements so quick and efficient it would be difficult to follow even later, with the tapes slowed down, he took the suit down and began to put it on.

It was a risky maneuver, in that certain weaknesses of the suit—its seams and other aspects—were momentarily revealed. However, both Jack and the Owner of the Purple felt that Jack's expertise would not give away too many of the secrets. He stood, moments later, helmeted and alone, isolated, within the armor.

The crowd gasped, so quickly had he suited up. Then a ripple of applause buffeted him.

It would have been even quicker, Jack thought, as he returned to his place, had the suit still been alive.

Once, the armor, inhabited by the regenerating soul of a berserker warrior, would have quickened under his grazing touch. As the circuitry came to life, so also would have the mind and thought-touch of a being so alien to Jack's mind that it was both a curse and a blessing to share communion with it. Still, Jack had become accustomed to it . . . one of the many scars he'd carried away from the Sand Wars.

Now Bogie was dead.

Amber said no. That Bogie was dormant, in hiding, traumatized by the events of Lasertown.

Jack was not sure. He only knew that his armor had lapsed back into what it had been manufactured as, no more, no less, and that he sorely missed the abrasive, cruel, combative, and somewhat addictive contact of the berserker. *Hi, boss, we kill today?*

Even though he had faced the possibility of the day when the berserker would have overcome and devoured his host, so that he might fully live. The infestation was a parasite, mindless to the ultimate condition of its host. Jack had had it under control, bonded with it and crippled without it. He was not a killer without Bogie augmenting him. He'd ordered another suit without telling Amber what he'd done. It only made sense, but it also made him uneasy. Had Bogie even been a Milot berserker? Jack had no way of knowing for sure. He remembered a moment in Lasertown when, like Lot's wife at the destruction of her city, he'd turned back to look at the destruction of an enigmatic archaeological site and seen the mummified remains of an incredible beast ... and Bogie, through his eyes, had seen it as well. Had been jolted into silence by the vision after communicating to Jack that he felt a part of that beast. As crude and terrifying as the known was, the unknown was worse—because whatever that mummified beast had been, it was also possibly dangerous enough to send Thraks fleeing across space from their own territory. So if he did not face the infestation of a berserker in his suit, what he might face could be undeniably worse.

Jack sighed, imperceptibly. The holo screening rippled in response to his movement. "Target grid on," he said, and the pattern played across his vision. What would happen next, he'd discussed briefly with Amber. He saluted again.

"Ladies and gentlemen, viewers," the Purple said, his amplified voice carrying magnificently across the grounds. Jack adjusted his audio slightly. "You have been watching a demonstration of the movement of the human form and how the battle armored soldier translates it. Now we would like to demonstrate to you the full power of a Dominion Knight."

Jack drew in his breath. He could feel his body trembling slightly. Adrenaline rush, he thought. The gauntlets pulsed at his wrists. He felt a slight tingling. It unnerved him momentarily. *Bogie, fighting him silently for control?* He reached out, searching for that alien other side of himself. *Come out, come out, wherever you are!* He had no time for a second thought.

The next maneuver pitted him against the entire field at his back.

They had choreographed it somewhat, but not entirely, for the Owner of the Purple wanted a spontaneous show of skill and battle tactics. Jack had a few tricks up his sleeves for the melee he had not wanted to reveal. The shop had, overnight, reset the suits to demonstration power. Hits would be scored by laser light rather than laser weaponry. No one would die here today, though a few suits were likely to be crimped.

As the Purple gave the signal, Jack threw the first choreographed maneuver out the window. He was supposed to pivot, roll and fire, sending the first line of offense down.

He hit power vault, went to the side and took out the first four lines right-handedly as they milled in confusion. Obediently, they went down and stayed down as their suits registered a hit.

His left wrist tingled. Jack frowned. He finished the roll as he hit and took out the back two lines, again right-handedly. The suit responded sluggishly, as if he were a man who'd had a stroke. The left side was down. Was Bogie fighting him for control as he had in the past? Only now he refused to acknowledge Jack's presence? His skin crawled. The soft chamois patch at his back, designed to catch sweat and to keep the weight of a field pack from gouging him, fluttered against his bare shoulders. Bogie could ultimately be deadly. Or was there something else happening?

Already, he'd put down more than half the emperor's new bodyguard. It wasn't their fault. They'd practiced something different. In the confusion, he'd gotten far more of them than was humanly possible. That, at least, had gone to plan.

His side tracking screen showed a wing flank taking the initiative. Automatically, he turned and fired a light rocket, packed with little more than a show of sparks. As it detonated in the wing's midst, the soldiers obligingly went down, but Jack took no time to register it.

Using the wall of already downed suits, he was flanking the lines himself, firing single shots as he went. Still one-handed.

As he kneeled to a stop and took a breath, he nailed down what it was that bothered him.

The gauntlets tingled to signal the wearer that they were up to power.

They shouldn't have been. His right wrist sent no such signal.

His left did.

Someone had not decommissioned his left gauntlet.

The troops facing him were sitting targets, dead targets, the moment he used the firepower in his left hand. Subconsciously, he'd known what was wrong and limited his use of weaponry.

Jesus, Emperor, your new hero's a nice guy, but

can you explain why he slaughtered hundreds of unarmed men during your little demonstration?

Yeah. Right. *Bogie—let go!*

Jack hit the power vault again, letting two rushes of lines collide with each other. A hit was a hit, and the majority of those two lines went down.

Over his own breathing, he could hear the crowd reaction. Which was little. They were shocked, he knew, by the inability of the soldiers to capture or down him.

They were also more than a little frightened by the skill of the one Knight being pursued.

As invincible as the troops seemed, one skillful soldier could still penetrate the defenses and head inexorably for the emperor, as single-mindedly as any assassin.

Jack came down, running, jumping still suits as if they did not exist, headed for the emperor's platform. Behind him, the remaining two hundred troops rushed after.

As they crossed the line where Jack had used the suits as a wall, from one side of the ground to the other, the air mines he'd planted started to go off. Another forty or so suits went down. He shook violently within his armor, fighting for control. He knew the alien menaced him. He knew that Bogie was stalking him within the armor they both claimed as their own. He was running out of time!

Against the rules of the melee, he decided to go for the emperor now. It was not necessary to stop all five hundred or so ranged against him. A real assassin would not. He would merely take his opening and go for it.

And so Jack power vaulted and hit the platform halfway up, even as a lone suit came barreling desperately toward him, to stop the inevitable.

It was a beautiful, acrobatic, graceful jump. Jack

did not know the soldier personally, but he saw the winged crest on the black chest and made a note to look him up. Daring and resourcefulness combined was hard to find.

Unfortunately, Jack took him down in midair. He then scaled the platform unmenaced, gauntlets in firing position. He lowered them and wrenched his helmet off. It took a second, winded as he was, and then he kneeled before the emperor. Now the audible gasps, the shock of the watching crowd reached him.

Pepys, pale and freckled, his red hair waving on the breeze, looked down at him. Jack met the expression in his electric green eyes, and for a moment was afraid of what he saw there.

Then the fey and smallish emperor smiled and said, "For your skill, I honor you. Ask of me what you will."

"An audience, your highness. Grant me an audience."

Pepys' lips thinned and whitened. Then he forced a smile. "Done." He raised his voice. "Ladies and gentlemen. I present to you the Knight who defended the Lasertown colony in the name of the Triad Throne and the Dominion. Rise and be recognized."

Jack got to his feet and turned around. The crowd roared, filling his hearing and his soul.

His commander moved to his shoulder. Purple tilted his head ever so slightly. "What the hell happened down there," he whispered. "I didn't tell you to do it with one hand tied behind your back."

"Someone," Jack answered, while smiling to the cameras, "forgot to decommission my left gauntlet. You're lucky I didn't fry five hundred of the emperor's best." He didn't mention Bogie. Only Amber knew of Bogie.

"Jesus," the commander said. He straightened. "Thank god it was you."

They both smiled impassively and waved in acknowledgment of the ovation as the rest of the Guard got to their feet, un-helmeted and let forth with their own cheers, but the usually tanned complexion of the commander had gone a little pale.

"Well, Jack," Pepys said, in the cool of the palace, his hair still wavering as though filled with a static electricity of its own. "You have what you want, though you may regret it."

Out from under the scrutiny of the live cameras, Jack nonetheless felt ill at ease. He had not been allowed to unsuit, and he carried his helmet under his arm like an extra head. Amber had joined them, a quiet, pale Amber dressed in a sober blue gown. The Owner of the Purple had excused himself long enough to set up a detail from among the Knights Jack had left standing and operable.

"Emperor?" Startled, Jack looked at the man.

Pepys showed his age in the slight sagging of his always ironic smile, and the flabbiness under the arms that wiry men sometimes get, for he hadn't much muscle anyway. "We haven't had time to talk since you returned. I want to impress upon you and remind you that, although I've publicly and privately said otherwise, you were shanghaied. I have covered for your actions by claiming you worked undercover for me, but I will remind you also that your actions were not for my benefit. You did as you did for your own purposes."

Their gazes stayed locked.

The emperor smiled mildly. "I will not so freely accept your behavior next time. There are consequences and effects to every action. I have you here now so that you can view a few of them."

"And then I want you to take a short leave, so that you can settle your personal affairs, for once you return," the emperor's voice deepened and he said, so that Jack alone could hear, "your ass is mine. Understood?"

"Yes, sir," Jack got out. Amber stirred at his side and he knew she recognized the tone of his voice which the emperor, who did not know him nearly as well, did not. Amber knew that he lied.

She laid a slender hand on the suit gauntlet. He shifted his weight and looked down at her, but she was watching the entrance to the grand hall impassively, so impassively that she might not have had a thought in her pretty head.

He knew better, of course. They both knew that, even if the emperor had not given him leave to track down his captor, he would have found a way to do it. They both knew that, emperor of the Triad Throne aside, Pepys was only a pathway to what Jack really desired to do. What she had done, she did merely to distract Pepys' hawklike attention . . . for Jack was not as seasoned a liar as the emperor was. She knew that Jack might give away his intention by his expression.

Pepys watched him closely. "Your highness," Jack said. "You have not had the facts from me."

"I have examined the records and talked to, among others, St. Colin of the Blue Wheel. Do you accuse a religious man, a saint among his peers, of lying?"

"No, sir. I hold St. Colin in high esteem, but—"

"But what?"

"I saw what I saw."

"Yes." Pepys tapped his finger on the arm of his

chair. "I am mindful of that. Then tell me what you saw."

"Here? Now?"

"You asked for audience and I granted it."

The emperor had him. Had him, and knew it. Jack would not speak of high risk security in the open, though electronic shields were placed throughout the hall to prevent illicit recording, for Pepys had granted an exclusive to Scott Randolph to cover the throne room this day. This was not the time or the place. The emperor, for some reason, did not want to know. *Or perhaps he knew already*. Jack's blood iced.

"I saw Thraks threatening the dome and acted accordingly," he said, falling back on the cover they'd given him. *To hell with it*, he thought. *Let Pepys go down to ruin the same way the old emperor did. The way I would have if Amber had not saved my ass . . .*

As though knowing he thought of her, Amber said, "Who's that coming in?"

There was a commotion at the front of the hall where guests were squeezing in through the bottleneck Security had set up. He thought he recognized the dark blue robes of the Walker leader known as St. Colin, a childhood friend of Pepys and now a rival in empires, but the figure was jostled back even as ambassadorial guards stalked in.

"Those are consequences," Jack said bitterly, even as the com system announced, "Ambassador Dhurl of the Thrakian League." He swallowed against the gorge rising in his throat as the minister of a hated enemy swept into the audience room. At his side, Amber sucked in her breath.

A Thraks in full dress was, Jack had to admit, an impressive sight. A diplomatic Thraks wasn't quite as impressive as a warrior Thraks with laser rifle blazing, but nearly. And murderous, he decided, upon viewing the faceted eyes of the being striding down upon them.

Slope-backed, equally at ease on fours or upright, a Thraks was a cross between a hyena and a cockroach. Jack had satisfying memories of crunching quite a few underneath his armored boots during the Sand Wars . . . if any memory of the Sand Wars could be called satisfying. This diplomat was dressed Terran-fashion, out of a knowledge of human sensibilities. It tended to humanize him more and take away from the alien insect-likeness of his outer chitin. Nothing, however, could disguise the mobile chitin-plates of his face, plates which moved into masklike expressions.

Jack could not feel the pressure of Amber's hand on his arm, but he looked down and saw her fingers pinched white around the knuckles. Gently, he laid his gauntlet over her hand.

Thraks were not a pretty sight under the best of circumstances and certainly not when in as intense an emotional state as this one. Randolph's camera crew focused on a tight shot. Pepys' protocol advisor stepped close to the emperor and Jack overheard the wizened, gray-haired man whisper, "We've got trouble. The mask signifies honor that has been damaged, and redress needed, as well as social representation of the highest order."

Pepys looked from his aged counselor to Jack. "In other words," Pepys said dryly. "They want Jack's hide."

"Something like that, yes. But . . ." and the counselor paused. "I doubt they expect to get it. Otherwise, he would request a private audience."

"Ahh." Pepys blinked and turned his catlike stare away from Jack.

The Ambassador from the Thrakian League came to a halt a respectful distance from the Triad Throne. He presented a bow, very sketchily, Jack thought and realized the ambassador was communicating the fact that he considered himself an equal to, or even above, the man he was now addressing. From the careful lack of expression on the emperor's face, it was evident Pepys had just realized the same thing.

Jack shifted. Without his helmet on, the armor was hot, unable to air-condition itself efficiently. The audience hall seemed close. Sweat trickled down his back with a maddening slowness.

"Your munificence," Dhurl said, and his synthesizer implant seemed a little louder than necessary, "I have begged for an audience with you concerning a most unfortunate grievance, one which I am told you claim awareness of, and yet have not sought redress with my League over. I refer, of course, to the unhappy incident at the mining community of Lasertown."

The corner of the emperor's mouth twitched. Amber inclined her head toward Jack's shoulder.

"He can't say much, not with Randolph's cameras still recording."

Pepys looked at Dhurl. "I beg your indulgence, Ambassador. I have petitioned your offices for conference twice since the facts have come to light. You have, unhappily, been unavailable."

The mask shifted ever so slightly. A mandible worked. It was eerie seeing the silent voicings followed up by the synthesizer. Dhurl had had surgery to be able to make the throatings of a human, but unfortunately he did not have the larynx strength to vocalize loudly enough to be heard. "Then it is favorable that we both are now available."

"Indeed. A treaty of twenty years is too valuable to be given up lightly."

Dhurl waved an arm. "Our treaty is as sound as ever. I only wish to be given the opportunity to express our unhappiness over the unfounded destruction of one of our ships—an accident, I'm sure—a ship that was sent to your colony upon receipt of distress signals. Our commander logged in messages indicating that the dome was giving way and, after receiving permission from his superior officer, attempted to conduct a rescue mission."

Amber shifted unhappily. She looked at Jack. "That's not what happened," she mouthed.

He smiled briefly back at her. The ambassador's version was entertaining, if not factual.

Pepys said, "It is reassuring that our allies are as concerned over the fate of our colonies as we are, however farflung they may be. Unfortunately, I cannot confirm the distress signals, as the communication center was destroyed by the revolt of the contract laborers. You have my apologies, Ambassador Dhurl, and my sincere condolences to the crèches of your dead, for my agent's actions. Your ship, however, was thought to have been overrun by revolutionists and it was assumed that it was being brought in for a bombing run that would most assuredly have destroyed the already weakened dome of Lasertown. Out of anarchy comes chaos, damaging to all life. Strong alliances such as ours must be nurtured to avoid future incident."

Dhurl paused. His mask slipped a little. "And the accountability of your agent?"

"He did as well as he could, under the circumstances."

"He destroyed a ship and all its crew."

Pepys' expression grew hard. "Then next time, my dear Ambassador, I suggest you send a transport ship to the rescue, instead of a fully weaponed warship. Your intentions will be less questionable."

The Thraks drew himself up to his full height. He replaced his mask and said, "And then, next time, as you request, Emperor—our intentions will not be questionable at all."

"Good." Pepys made the effort to smile. "Have you any other petitions we can discuss while we have the meeting time?"

"There is the question of Bythia, your majesty. My superiors request that you consider the possibility of ceding it to our League. We have received a plea for that action."

Jack saw the violent blush start from the emperor's neckline and work its way up. Pepys stood.

"We will discuss that privately, Ambassador, in the future."

The Thraks made a sketchy bow. "Assuredly." He left, without having been further dismissed or released.

Jack watched as the crowd in the audience hall parted for the ambassador and his guards, thinking that if the Thraks were interested in Bythia, so was he.

"What is it? What happened?"

"I'm not sure," Jack answered slowly. "But I think the Thraks just announced their next move." He did not like what he had just heard. Was the Thrakian League, after a twenty year halt, once again ready to cut a swathe across the solar systems, turning verdant planets into sandy nests for their young? The thought balled in his chest, making it difficult to breathe smoothly. Had he just heard the beginning of another Sand Wars?

Pepys gathered himself with an effort and beckoned Jack near. He hesitated, then took Amber's hand off his arm and answered the summons.

The emperor was still somewhat distracted, but he said, "I've done all I can for you, Jack."

"Your highness . . . what about Claron?"

"Claron?" The emperor frowned.

"You have a committee studying the feasibility of terraforming it. This is not a security risk, but an ecological matter."

"And one which merits my careful consideration. This is not a day for hasty decisions."

Jack's heart sank. He was not to win this day, no matter what he did. "Thank you, your majesty."

"You have your leave, and then I want you back in my service. The Thraks have just promised us more trouble than we want to handle, and I can't spare a man. Is that clear?"

"Very clear, sir," Jack answered, thinking that, of all the people in this palace room, only he knew full well the implication of what the Thrakian ambassador had said. Only he was a veteran of the Sand Wars.

CHAPTER 5

"What makes you think it was Bogie?"

"What makes you think it wasn't?"

Amber wrinkled her nose. "I heard what Purple told you. The official investigation says the weaponry computer went down—a fraction of a second—probably due to a power surge, because all the media cams were being jury-rigged for the ceremonies, and it just happened to be your suit going through decommission when it happened. So the computer and the techs missed the gauntlet."

"Right." He felt her body stiffen a little, and the walk became a little less companionable. "Listen, Amber. You know I can't hear Bogie anymore. He won't respond."

"Maybe he's dead."

"You said not. Changed your mind?"

She shook her head, tawny hair rippling with the movement.

"I don't think so either. But maybe he's going through another stage. And if he is, and if it means a power struggle between us over who controls the suit, I can't let it continue. I've ordered new armor and I'm leaving Bogie behind."

"Why don't you just rip the chamois out and be done with it."

"What?"

"You heard me. That Milot officer the Thraks

had at Lasertown— what's his name—K'rok—he told you the berserkers either laid eggs or regenerated. You told me yourself it could be the chamois you put in on Milos. Just rip it out and burn it up, if you're that scared."

His face felt hot. "I'm scared all right. I'm scared of Thraks, and if there's anything out there big enough and mean enough to put Thraks on the run, I'm scared of it, too. But there's no reason to think the beast I saw at Lasertown is the same."

"Bogie thought so. And it would explain why his regeneration cycle is different. Otherwise you'd have been chewed up and spat out long ago."

"Then I'd be a fool to destroy him. He might be the only clue we have to an enemy even the Thraks are afraid of."

She jabbed at him. "You won't do it, anyway. You're even more scared you'll find out you've been talking to yourself."

She'd hit home, and from the sudden expression on her face, she knew it. Amber cleared her throat and tried to change the subject. "How long are you going to be gone?"

"As long as it takes." Jack looked down at Amber. Her face was tilted downward in thought, watching the pathway to her apartment a little too closely, and he wondered if she'd been in his guardianship long enough to lose the brittle street facade she'd worn for so long. "I'll be back soon; the emperor made that clear."

She slapped her palm onto the door lock. "I don't think you should go at all—without me, anyway. You need me to tap your sources."

"I'll be able to access what I want to." He followed her inside and watched her dampen the World Police monitors effortlessly. "I had a good teacher, remember?"

"The best," Amber returned defiantly. She stood and looked at him, her whole body on edge, weight shifted, chin out, hand on one hip.

She'd filled out in the last two years, filled out very nicely. He let the sight of her fill him, flowing into every nook and cranny of his memory. Tawny hair, amber eyes, skin with the natural blush of youth ... long legs and a firm bustline that begged—

Jack pushed his thoughts to the back of his mind. Not yet. And especially not tonight. Maybe when he got back ... but he wouldn't approach her now. Not to have her and leave her. Amber meant more to him than that.

"Seen enough?" she said testily, and he felt himself blush under his Malthen tan. She pinked in return and looked away. "I didn't mean that."

"I know what you meant."

She didn't answer right away. That bothered Jack more than her abrasive sarcasm. He said, "The Purple will be watching out for you. Rolf can't get close enough to hurt you."

She still didn't answer, but looked away, and to Jack's astonishment, tears brimmed in her golden brown eyes.

"He can't touch you, Amber."

"Maybe," she said finally. She balled her hand into a fist and scrubbed ferociously at telltale tears. "You have your dreams. I have mine."

She faced him then. "I didn't want to have to say this to you, but I'm going to. I'm the only one. Maybe Bogie's not gone, Jack. Maybe you've just shut him out because you don't want to hear him anymore. Maybe you've lost that part of your mind ... and if you have, it's not Bogie that's eating you up. It's you. You're doing it to yourself, with your nightmares and your hates and your fears. Go look for yourself while you're looking for the rest of your past."

Stung, he said, "Amber, I—"

She shook her head. "Go on, get out of here. You've got an early transport. Just remember, if you disappear again, I'm coming after you!"

Jack forced a grin. "I'm counting on that."

She turned her back quickly, denying him a parting hug, and so he left quietly, locking the door behind him. He returned to his quarters in the barracks and entered without even turning on the lights.

His duffel was packed, and Bogie was stored on his equipment rack. He ran his hand down an opalescent sleeve. Maybe Amber'd been right. Maybe he'd gone deaf to Bogie instead of losing him. Or . . . maybe he'd gone schizo. Maybe it had been himself he'd been talking to all these months. In which case . . . Jack shook himself violently.

He went to the bathroom, found a vial of mordil and sucked down a dose. It was bittersweet, the taste lingering on his tongue, promising a night without dreams.

He set his alarm for before dawn, to be in time to catch his transport and lay down to get what little rest he could. He drifted quickly into mordil-locked slumber, but nothing could prevent the dreams.

For Jack, to remember the Sand Wars was to be locked in cold sleep dreams, in a military debriefing loop that only death or awakening could free him from.

It was pleasant at first, seducing him with the idealism that led him from his agrarian planet of Dorman's Stand to enlistment. He didn't mind that . . . he had few memories left of home, most of them destroyed by the debriefing loop that had waded through his mind, kicking aside the unimportant, looking only for those memories of the engagement on Milos. The loop would normally have been unimportant, intended only to be impressed for a few weeks at a time ... not for seventeen years. It was not the debriefing program's fault he'd permanently lost most of his childhood and some of his sanity.

He blamed the Thraks for that.

He'd survived boot camp nicely and come out of it as a lieutenant, with his own squad of Dominion Knights under his command, although the sergeant was a grizzled veteran and ran the unit better than he did. But he'd taken to battle armor as though it were a second skin and he'd won his promotion fairly. He prided himself on being a good lieutenant second, a good Knight first. Jack would never forget his first view of Milos.

It hung in the heavens, another water planet, teeming with potential. As the shuttle's decaying orbit eased them in closer and closer and they swept across the continents, Jack could feel his chest swell with excitement and hope. Even barren rock peninsulas didn't discourage him—he was a farmer. With irrigation and evaporative farming, he knew how to coax the green out of a planet. Only sand defeated him. He could not miss the beige and rust continent, like a blight on a crop, and he pointed it out to Sarge.

"That's where we stop the bugs. They won't get any farther here than that."

Sarge spat to one side, catching it in a disposable cup. He rolled a weary eye at the Thrakian damage. "Don't get your hopes up, kid. They say the Milots are worse than the Thraks."

"They invited us here!"

"Yeah, didn't they, though," the veteran said and squinted out the shuttle window, saying nothing more. He only opened his mouth to spit and Jack sat back, forgetting to warn the sergeant that chewing stim wasn't allowed in transport.

But the sarge didn't spit. He pointed at Jack and mumbled something, something about eyes and began to claw at his.

As Jack screamed in horror, the veteran plucked out his eyes and held them out for Jack to see.

The transport rocked. A klaxon went out. The systems computer came on-line, announcing, "Emergency landing. Emergency landing."

Jack scrambled for his suit, thinking that this wasn't real; it couldn't be real, nothing like this had ever happened to him before. The shuttle bucked around him and with every shudder, a man fell off, sucked out windows that shattered one by one with a crystal belling that nearly deafened all of them.

The sight of his battle armor beckoned from a rack at the far end of the shuttle. Jack clawed his way there.

He reached for it. The gauntlets went up, independently, grappling with him. The helmet hung on a hook next to it, window glaring balefully at him.

"Bogie! It's me! Let me in!" Jack shouted over the shattering of windows and the hooting of the klaxon.

The white armor fought him clumsily. Then, through the open portal of the neck, a fringed frill emerged. Jack's breath clogged in his throat. He staggered back, as a saurian head pushed its way forth, expanding, rearing, and the suit stretched with it. A Milot berserker!

The lizard warrior slavered and reached for him.

The gauntlets pinched shut round his elbow, crushing bone and viscera, dragging him close. Close to fetid breath. Close to warty scales and a black, oily tongue that hung out its gaping jaw. Too close—

Jack bolted from the nightmare of sleep. He fought awake enough to wipe a thin veil of sweat from his forehead and lay with his eyes open, staring at the barren gray ceiling of his room. He hadn't forgotten that, he thought. He'd never forgotten the horror of a full-grown berserker bursting out of armor after it had consumed its wearer. No one who'd ever seen it could.

But even that horror was not sufficient reason to abandon platoons of men to the tender mercies of the Thraks.

Jack chewed on his memories of betrayal.

But he had forgotten how green most of Milos had been when they'd first landed. Not the cultivated, patchwork greens and crop colors of his home planet, but raw green, a primitive planet inhabited by nomadic barbarians. Different from Claron where he'd done his rehabilitation, but in some ways the same.

Jack took a deep breath. Sleep and grit had piled in the corner of one eye and he dug it out. Sarge had been right. The Milots had been almost worse than the Thraks . . . thieving, dishonest, stinking . . . they'd stolen the Dominion troops blind and in the relay centers, set up to maintain armor, among other things, they often bled off fuel and power as well.

Not that Jack thought they'd deserved the fate they fell to on Milos. No one deserved to lose his planet to the sand, to the living microbes the Thraks infested it with, to protect and nurture their nests, bacteria that turned all the green to beige and rust

. . . paradise to hell. Few enough Milots lived to be conquered.

It was not the first, nor the last, planet to fall to the Thraks. Unstoppable, the League swept through the outer edges of the Dominion in a crescent path, then, as suddenly as they'd begun, they stopped. Went to Treaty with the Dominion.

What was it that had driven them in the first place? A nesting swarm? An uncontrollable urge to terraform and reproduce? Jack hardly thought so, and he'd been thinking about it for years. The Dominion had rubbed up against Thraks as early as a hundred years ago. Peace had always been uneasy, but there had never been a swarming cycle like this before.

K'rok reared in his mind. Ursine, greasy, smelly, and proud. Both he and the Milot warrior, as well as the Thraks, had had a terrible interest in an archaeological site outside of Lasertown. Jack had only had a brief glimpse of it before it had been sabotaged and destroyed—but it had looked like a crash site, complete with a mummified body imbedded in the rock strata. No more had he made out . . . he'd been busy at the time. K'rok had hinted at an ancient enemy of the Thraks—an enemy so dire that the Thraks could not withstand it and had been driven into Dominion territory. Might someday soon be driven again.

A cold chill went through Jack's sleepless frame. What kind of enemy could so frighten the indomitable Thraks, Thraks who had run over Dominion Knights and berserkers alike? He could not imagine one, and he was equally sure he'd never want to meet it.

He was just as certain he did want to meet the man who'd made sure the Dominion fell to defeat on Milos. Would meet him. Was headed on a collision course with him. A man named Winton, who was hidden somewhere among the emperor's civil servants. Once Winton had been a commander and had given the orders to abandon Dominion troops on Milos while the Thrakian League closed an almost inescapable ring about the planet.

A few troopships had been sent down, for show, he supposed. He'd made it out on one, after all his men had been wiped out. He'd made it to the safety of a cold sleep transport. It and its sister ships were attacked by Thraks while pulling out, their warship coverage already canceled by someone—Winton, again, he supposed—and only his ship had made it through.

But not undamaged. The transport had suffered heavily and all systems failed, except for the auxiliary systems on the cryogenic bays, systems which operated independently of the ship and which had been solar powered.

Jack would never know how, deep in cold sleep, he'd managed to set off his secondary power system, but it was the only thing that kept him alive, though locked in sleep, for the seventeen long years it took for the drifting ship to be found.

He'd suffered frostbite, lost his right little finger, and three toes. And his sanity, temporarily.

A small price to pay for life?

Jack still wasn't sure.

He gave up on sleep and sat on the edge of his bed.

Ballard had been an early casualty on Milos and gone AWOL. He'd bought himself that gold ocular piece to replace the organ damaged and lost through inadequate medical facilities. Amber had taken Jack to see Ballard, and Ballard had recognized Jack for what he really was. A real Knight, not a member of a hastily resurrected bodyguard. A true

Knight, unheralded by the Triad Throne and the Dominion.

Ballard's face imprinted itself in Jack's thoughts, dominating the night quiet room, a hole where a gold screen eye should have been.

Jack shook off his nightmares and reached abruptly for his pants and boots. He had no business sleeping this night when a short journey demanded his attention before the longer one. The signs were all there for him to read.

He intended to find out for himself whether Ballard had plucked out an offending eye or not.

CHAPTER 6

Amber's bad habits were not only contagious, they had some merit, Jack reflected, as he stalled the commuter car, snagged back the hard disk with the delivery address on it and rerouted it to another address without leaving a record of it. On the other hand, being circumspect about his comings and goings was beginning to feel both natural and healthy. Here in the underbelly of the city of Malthen, where the palace was only a rosy morning star on the horizon, anything less than caution could be fatal.

He got out of the car when it stopped and with a stretch moved his lanky frame out of camera's view as he coded the car to go around the corner to a lot and wait. It wouldn't be too difficult to avoid the cameras down here—half of them were already out of commission—what was difficult was not looking as though he were avoiding them. Amber made it as easy as breathing.

He felt the corner of his mouth quirk as he searched for and found the door to The Rusty Bolt. Ballard wouldn't be in here, and probably not in the first five places he searched, but it was a start. In the lawful zones, the bars had already been shut, but down here, laws were made to be broken, laser-fried, and scrapped.

This was the city where Amber had grown up.

58

No one took much notice of Jack as he came through the door. The bartender's glance flickered up and back down, where he was watching a screen embedded into the bar counter. Doings in the back room, no doubt.

Jack stood out of range of the multilensed camera that would report his visage not only to the local Sweepers, the city police, but to the inhabitants of the bar and the plastiscreened booths to the rear. If Ballard were here and if Ballard were the least bit guilty about what he'd put them through, Ballard would be leaving as soon as he spotted Jack.

And Ballard would be watching; oh, yes, the old renegade would have his weather eye out for anyone coming into the bar, if only because of his old AWOL record.

Not that he hadn't had the opportunity to reconcile himself with his abrupt abandonment of duty. Pepys had declared general amnesty about eight years ago. It was just, as Ballard had remarked to Jack once, that those vets on the amnesty roles seemed to have awfully short life spans. Ballard held the opinion that continued cowardice was in order.

Jack swept his gaze about the room once more and spotted a furtive movement in the back corner. He was there in three strides. The weasel-faced street punk looked up, the whites of his eyes rolling, and a stench on his breath, his purpled hair gelled into a wave that was so permanent it carried a feathery coating of dust.

The punk froze in the booth and then leaned back, nonchalantly.

"Ballard," Jack said.

"He's not here."

"The obvious could get you killed."

The punk's chapped face paled slightly. He put out a hand on the tabletop. Plug marks scarred the back of it. "What do you want him for?"

"Questions like that will get you killed even faster."

"All right." The punk looked away. "Try th' Black Hole over on—"

Jack was halfway out the door before he finished the address. He knew the place. He called the commuter car, tickled its innards a bit more, and then leaned back. The sky was still a dark and dirty black, but it showed signs of lightening.

The Black Hole was aptly named, a bar and gaming joint along the subways reached by a black, tunnel-like entrance. Jack had no way of avoiding cameras here as he slid down and landed deftly on his feet. No one at all marked his entrance, he'd already been looked over on the way down. He straightened his overjacket and folded his collar back down.

The smoky atmosphere stung his eyes and he could barely think over the din of the tables and players. He moved about the perimeter of the floor, keeping an eye out for the man with an eye out, as it were. Thinking of this image, Jack smiled to himself grimly. But Ballard's blue-black curled hair and burly form wasn't anywhere to be seen. Jack rubbed a hand along his slacks. The air had a greasy feel to it. He wasn't excited about broaching the privacy curtains along the back wall.

No live bartender here ... the bar was computer automated. If he'd had Amber along, she could have gotten the information he wanted from the billing banks, but it was too late for regrets now. He knew of one or two other places on his own, but the Black Hole was shedding no light for him on Ballard's whereabouts.

He turned to go, as a passing subway carrier shuddered the walls of the building. Then he spotted a trio of civilians canvassing the place much as he was, only they weren't being subtle about it.

Something about the lead man's face nagged at him and Jack knew he'd seen it before, but he couldn't remember the circumstances. He stepped back into an empty booth and made it look as though he'd been occupying it for a while. The credit cursor blinked annoyingly, nagging him to order a drink or otherwise spend some money. He dropped the commuter car hard disk into the slot. Let them take a while to figure that one out! He settled back and listened as well as he could over the booth's mufflers.

"Took you long enough." This, muted, from the corner of the booth. Jack frowned, trying to remember whether he'd seen someone sitting in the shadows or not. Memory did not serve him, but from the direction of the responses, three still stood and one sat, so there must have been.

"This isn't exactly the best part of town," the lead member of the trio responded, and with those tones, Jack identified the man. It was Scott Randolph, the broadcaster who'd worried Amber so. There were sounds of bodies sliding into the booth and the whole conversation became muddled, difficult for him to decipher.

". . . paid enough . . ."

A burst of unpleasant laughter, then, "My head's worth more than that."

"Your head's full of *ratt*. Our com lines . . ."

Another laugh. "Your lines have been bugged since you laid them . . . there're some very nasty people living in the emperor's palace. They got to Ballard. Sooner or later they'll be looking for me."

Jack's steady heartbeat jumped. Ballard! Who

had gotten to him, and for how much? Had the delivery of the eye been to flush him? He thought of what he would tell Amber ... that the gold eyepiece had been torn from Ballard. He gathered his concentration and listened again.

"—name names, then! That's what you've been paid for—"

"Drink, sir?"

Jack looked up abruptly. The servo stood at the side of the booth, demanding audibly what the screen had been nagging him visually for. "Beer," he said.

"Yes, sir." The machine whirled away.

Jack leaned his head back against the plastic screening. Randolph had lapsed into silence and a higher pitched voice had taken over, arguing the finer points of obtaining information. His attention drifted.

Then Randolph said, "I want the name of the lost Knight. You've been dragging this on long enough."

A *ratt* inspired laugh. "You don't ask for much, do you? There are lots of survivors out there, hiding."

"Not Knights."

The servo whirled back within earshot and eyeshot. "Your drink, sir."

"Quiet," Jack ordered.

"Payment or tab?"

"Shut up," Jack commanded. He listened to the sounds of weight shifting in the booth.

"Your dri—"

Jack reached out and abruptly unplugged the audio. He jammed a credit disk into the slot and snagged his beer. The servo did a one-eighty and wheeled rapidly toward the bar, its "repair needed" light flashing.

". . . unreliable source. I can't use you anymore."

A muffled burp, then, "You can't get the information anywhere else. The man's not carrying ident. The records have been wiped. I know what I know."

"And you've been feeding it to me for years, a hint at a time. I won't support your vices any longer. This is your last payment."

Someone stood in the booth. A boot heel scuffed. Then, "Meet me in the alley."

Jack put the bottle to his lips, sucking down the cold, bittersweet dark beer, and watched from the corner of his eye as a shadow left the booth.

Randolph got up also, and, his back turned to the room, looked down at his two companions, saying, "We'll follow in three minutes."

"Je-sus—"

Randolph said, "Let him go. We'll do as he says." He tapped his watch impatiently, then said, "Let's go."

What the broadcaster didn't see was what Jack saw . . . two men getting up from the far side of the room and heading for the back door to follow them out. Jack recognized the surreptitious pat of jackets as the two checked their weapons. The broadcasters didn't have three minutes.

With mixed feelings, Jack lurched to his feet. The alley was topside and the shadows had gone for the elevator shaft. He took the stairs, three at a time, wishing for his armor with its seven-league strides, breath hot in his lungs by the time he reached the top and steadied himself. He pulled his own palm laser from its thigh holster and wasted precious seconds listening.

Rain had never reached this dark concrete canyon. It choked with the stench of human waste and garbage, drugs and dust. It trembled as another subway car rocketed below it. Jack blinked as light flared, burning away the night. He heard a coarse yell and a heavy weight dropping, then running footsteps.

He stepped out into the center of the alley and fired, his own beam flashing blue-white. The laser angled off the corner edge, he heard a yelp and a stumble, and then shouts.

He made his way to the cluster of figures in the dim center of the alleyway. Echoing footsteps reached him as he joined Randolph and his companions. The broadcaster lit a mini-flare and dropped it in the street.

A man lay crumpled at their feet. Jack identified their informant. He looked away. The man wouldn't last long.

One of the companions hunkered down. He took the informant's hand in his and said, again, "Je-sus."

Jack recognized the voice. Randolph's producer. He was chunky and too white, slug white, as if he rarely saw the outside of a building. The man was sweating as he looked up.

The broadcaster's glance flickered toward Jack. "Thanks," he said briefly.

Jack shrugged. He kept his gun in hand, saying, "This isn't the best part of town," echoing their earlier statement with irony.

The producer, rattled, said, "That's what we said. Wasn't it, Scott?"

"Shut up, Dykstra."

The informant took a long, rattling breath. He got out, with a hissing, sucking noise, "Ssscot. Get down here, on your knees, beside me. I'm . . . only gonna say this once."

The broadcaster hesitated, then got down on one knee. Behind him, Dykstra's pale face was illuminated by the pink glow of the flare. The informant's face was already crimson . . . by virtue of his own blood. Jack pretended not to be listening, but his attention was riveted to the man's dying words. Scott's normally firm voice shook as he answered, "I'm listening."

"Good. The man you want . . . I have a name . . . of a man . . . who survived the Sand Wars. You'll have to . . . do your own research . . ." a hissing laugh, reminding Jack of a torn vacuum hose. "He has his own armor. . . . A mercenary . . ."

Jack's blood chilled. Who was the man going to name? He couldn't afford the exposure, but something stayed him from stamping out the frail spark of life remaining in the black and crimson hulk dying on the street.

"He's known as the Owner of the Purple, but his name is . . . Kavin. And that's all I know. All I ever knew. . . ."

The man's voice faded. Scott Randolph might have heard more, but the voice was gone to Jack's hearing.

Jack blinked in shock in the black draped alleyway, looking outward, as he heard Randolph get to his feet. From the far distance came the pulse of a siren. Sweepers, on their way, late as usual, to the bad part of town.

The Purple was not a fighter's son, as he had always been led to believe. The Purple had the same heritage he did . . . and had given no sign of it.

Betrayal twisted in Jack's chest. He swallowed and started as one of Scott's men put a hand on his arm.

"Thanks, mister, but—sounds like we'd all better get out of here."

The curtain of night curled back a little around the edges of the concrete canyon about them. Jack nodded, realizing he had a transport to catch. He faded away, walking quickly, purposefully, then breaking into a run once he reached the corner, not wanting Randolph to be able to call him back as the broadcaster said, "Wait a minute! Who—"

are you?

Who, indeed, Jack thought, and ducked into his commuter car. Who were they all, the orphans of the Sand Wars?

CHAPTER 7

St. Colin of the Blue Wheel came down from his meditation tower and dropped heavily, due to his years and his worries, onto his overstuffed couch. His secretary started to hurry in, but came to a stop and then respectfully backed out as Colin waved him away. Biggle reminded him of an overfriendly creature.

"Leave me alone," he said. "I want to think."

And then, as the soft padded steps of his male secretary faded away and the door shushed behind him, he smiled with irony. He had had to leave his meditation tower in order to think.

Colin swung his feet up on a table, an antique table of burnished oak which was reputed to have come from far away and long ago Earth itself. The vibrations of the wood, still imbued with a spark of its origin, thrummed. The saint felt it. Had always felt it. Would always be in tune somewhat to the vibrations of the worlds, and he never gave it a second thought, not completely aware that others did not feel the same.

He plucked a piece of lint off his dark blue trousers. His prayer coat had fallen open and he noticed that the edges of its sharply pressed hem were somewhat worn. He wondered to himself if he, too, had become somewhat worn.

He must have. He needed to think clearly and

precisely about recent events and yet logic eluded him. All he had was a vague misgiving which grew sharper day by day. Pepys had kept him at arm's length yesterday and he did not like the way his old friend and rival had also kept Jack Storm away.

It was not right. Nor was it prudent. Pepys would surely have wanted to know what had happened at Lasertown from the man most involved, but Colin knew from his spies at court that the emperor had never called Storm in for deposition and that he had refused calls from the Knight. And, legally, the Walkers could not call for testimony until the emperor had. That was not good for them. Jack was one of the last men to have seen the Lasertown archaeological site intact. What did he have locked inside his head that even Colin was unaware of?

Colin rubbed his forehead and sat back on the couch, resting his head on its back edge. He was a Walker, named for his calling that sought physical proof that his Savior had indeed gone on to walk other worlds, preparing them for Man, and for eventual entry into Heaven. He lived in hopes that he might someday see that proof. Never mind the Messiah mythology that almost every civilization independently evolved. No. He searched for something more.

He looked at the ceiling without seeing it, seeing instead the Knight and his somewhat dubious Lady at court yesterday, remembering a dangerous and yet strangely honorable man. Did Pepys know what he had in Jack Storm? Colin doubted it. The Knights were buried in all of Pepys' machinations and plots, and the saint truly doubted that the emperor thought any more of Jack than he did of any pawn.

A definite mistake.

Storm. Colin blinked. His spies had not been able to unearth any records of Jack Storm, or of anyone with that surname.

The man sighed heavily. Storm. It was more of a prophecy than a name.

Goren watched the day room closely. Four of his current patients were enjoying the solar, bathing in the mineral waters or resting, relaxing among the greenery. One sat off to the side, talking animatedly to no one, but the look on his face was one of peace and contentment.

The rehab tech smiled slightly, the corner of his mouth drawn to one side. He liked day room duty. The observation was informal and usually he could chart optimistic predictions on his keypad. The duty was light. He did not even frown when his monitoring companion tapped him on the shoulder.

"I'm going to take a leak. Watch the corridor screens for me, will ya?"

Goren nodded absently. As the security guard stood up, stretched, and lumbered out of the room, he only flicked a sidelong glance at the other monitors. The interior of the hospital hub was a closed area. No one went in or out unexpectedly. He did not expect to see anyone nor did he.

With his twitch of a smile, the rehab tech went back to watching the man who talked to no one. Wouldn't it be something if he suddenly realized he was talking to the air? Goren relaxed. He liked to fantasize about breakthroughs that had little or nothing to do with his skill ... or lack of it. He leaned back in the swivel chair, fingers idly tapping out his observations.

It was then that a flicker of movement on one of the security screens caught his eye. Goren snapped straight up in the chair, looked, and then looked again.

Someone walked with catlike confidence down the main corridor, pausing now and then to read the computer trail etched on the floor for the med carts. When he came to a directory, he stopped and scrutinized it momentarily.

Goren's fingers froze over the keypad. He should have reached for the alarm, but didn't. He couldn't see the intruder well enough ... well enough to determine if he was an intruder, or an inmate gone for a walk. If he'd strayed from his sector, there would be someone after him soon enough.

The tech licked lips gone dry.

The man turned and continued down the main corridor. He was headed toward the main doctors' offices and administration. But Goren did not find that reassuring—if he belonged there, the man would have approached from another direction altogether. The public sector was several hubs away. The staff and records sequestered here were not open to public scrutiny.

Goren forced a cold hand toward the alarm. His elbow creaked as he did. His whole frame had gone stiff and uncooperative. Catatonic, he thought to himself. I've become catatonic!

But even as his inner mind blatted at him, he knew he wasn't. His eyes blinked furiously as he watched the security screen, and the multimonitored figure of the man walking down the corridors toward him.

Shit! He knew that man.

Goren's body unfroze, recoiling suddenly until he found himself crouched fetal-like in his chair. He punched a finger onto the keyboard, putting the solar room observation on automatic, letting the computer take over for him. He thrust himself out of the chair and down into the maze of corridors, an energy and intensity in his movements that he had not known for many years.

He had to find that man and stop him!

He bolted out of the observation room and down the hall to the staff's secured communications room and opened up com lines as fast as his trembling fingers would let him. The room's heavy fire door closed solidly behind him even as the number went through and the line buzzed in demand.

Goren blinked as the screen came to life.

"What is it?"

"He's here. He's come back. He's in the hub and he's looking for the records office."

"Who are you talking about?" The woman's sharp-nosed face frowned, a single "I want" line of demand etching deeply between her brows. Her demeanor spoke of breeding and wealth.

Goren stammered to a halt, knowing that what she wanted most now was for him to make sense. He took a deep breath. "That stiff you pulled out of the derelict cold ship and thawed out. He's here!"

"Good god." She looked at him, her eyes gone icy blue. "And you're calling me on an unsecured line?"

"No. Give me some credit." Goren felt his cheeks burn, but he glared back. There was, after all, a monitor between the two of them.

"Well." She sat back in her chair. Goren looked keenly at her surroundings, but, as usual, saw no hint of where or how she lived. She rubbed that deep frown line briefly before straightening in her chair. "Well, he won't find anything. We took care of that."

"You're sure?"

The strength of her nose shadowed the high

planes of her finely boned face as she stared back.
The stare never wavered, but Goren's did. He finally had to look away. As he did, she said, "You'll
have to get him out of there, but don't use security
to do it. He may have been followed, if anyone
suspects him for what he is. You have the meds
there to do it . . . put him under and smuggle him
out. Do whatever you have to get him off-planet."

"Is that all?" Goren asked dryly, as if she hadn't
asked him to work a minor miracle.

"For now, yes." The monitor went dark, but
Goren put out a hand and touched fingertips to it,
seeing the outline of her face etched in fading
phosphorescence. Then he shut down his terminal.
He'd have to work quickly. He found the medica-
tion he wanted, and an unallotted cart and made
his way to the records center, knowing his quarry
would be there waiting for him.

Jack didn't know what it was that alerted him.
Maybe he'd heard the sound of shallow breathing
over the air conditioning and the NLP music that
played subliminally over the system. He only knew
that as he leaned over the files and pulled up the
dates again, scanning them rapidly and finding
them empty—*wiped*—of any reference that might
pertain to him or his treatment, he sensed someone watching him.

It could be Security. He doubted that, for any
Security in this facility would probably try to yank
him out by the scruff of the neck. Therefore, someone watching him was probably trying to decide
what to do with him.

Jack took his time. Although his heart had begun pounding in his chest the moment he'd found
out he was nonexistent—that his two years of treatment in this hospital might never have happened

—he forced himself to sit calmly. After reviewing the record for a third time, he switched to the staff. He might not exist in the records, but doctors and a certain nurse—curvaceous and warm at night, as he remembered her—must.

The first name came up and he stared in disbelief. The name was right, he knew that. It was etched in his mind. But the face was different. He skimmed the bio. Then looked up. The face went with the bio. Then, his doctor had assumed the identity of an actual staff member—but why?

Briefly, Jack closed his eyes, shutting out the knowledge that he was being watched.

Jack pulled up another name. He looked down, seeing a nurse he'd never seen before, and then he knew.

Knew that all the living he'd done in the years since he'd been taken out of that icy hell had been a lie.

Jack paused for another second, then shut the file reader down. He homed in on the watcher behind him. He pushed his chair back, hearing it scrape on the flooring. Stood and turned. Saw that there was an alcove between him and the door.

Went toward it, feeling the strength in his young body, a muscular body ever so much younger than its actual years, the tension thrilling through responsive nerves.

A shadow shifted as he passed by the alcove. Jack smiled grimly as he reached out and grabbed, and threw the watcher down like a bundle of rags, his strength transformed by his anger almost as if he still wore his battle armor.

The man in gray lay and twitched on the flooring, gasping as Jack dropped to a knee beside him and kicked away the air needle, wondering whether he was supposed to be dead now or only sedated.

"What are you doing here?" Jack asked quietly.

The tech jerked under the single hand that pinned him by the throat. He gasped. "I—I—my name is Goren."

"No," Jack said patiently. "I asked what you're doing."

"I—I don't understand."

"You know me." He frowned slightly. "I even think I remember you. Yes . . . yes. You did my final evaluation for release. I have you to thank for Claron." Not that he'd been thankful at the time. No. All he'd wanted was to get out of the hospital. He'd been shuffled around, evaded and ignored. No one seemed to want to know that someone had survived the Sand Wars. But the year or so he'd spent rangering on Claron had cleansed his soul, his mind, what was left of his memories, even though it could not give him a night without dreams. His hand tightened. "I'm so grateful, I might not kill you."

The man wiggled. Spittle edged from the corner of his mouth. His skin grayed. "I . . . I can't tell you anything."

"Why? What happened to me here? Where are my records?"

"Gone," the tech got out. "All gone."

"Someone remembers. Tell me who."

"I can't. The tech's bloodshot eyes glazed a little. "Kill me now if you want to. It would be quicker."

Jack relaxed his hand a little. He thought rapidly. It was obvious now that he'd been brought here in secret. Rescued in secret. Thawed in secret. Obvious now why no representative of the Dominion or the Triad Throne had recognized him as a veteran. What he didn't know was why and it seemed doubtful that this unimportant little man would know either. He looked down.

The tech muscled out a desperate squirm. Jack pursed his lips, breaking that grim smile of his.

"Then what can you tell me," Jack said, "to keep me from killing you very slowly."

"Only that—only that you won't find what you're looking for. That it's all been wiped out. Altered. Even your mind, your name," Goren blurted.

"What are you talking about?"

"They pulled you from cold sleep. They had you for a year before they gave you to me. Some things . . . couldn't be repaired. So it was advantageous to . . . replace them. You Knights were all supposed to be dead."

"My name?"

"I don't know it! They never told me."

"Why me?"

"You were all they had to work with. They—honest, mister, let me breathe. . . ."

Jack's hand squeezed convulsively.

Even his name was a lie.

He left the unconscious man behind on the sterile hospital floor, soiled by the puddle of urine the man had loosed in his fear.

Jack made his way quickly through the maze of corridors, this time avoiding the camera surveillance and security measures the way Amber had trained him. He moved with the precise, dangerous movements his training as a Knight had imbued him with.

That, at least, they hadn't taken from him. Nor could they have falsely given this skill to him. The training was his, and so was the armor. Alien infested and deadly as it was, it was his legacy.

The only one they'd left him with.

So be it.

CHAPTER 8

Winton was eating lunch at the civil service cafeteria, a nice, spacious club with the atmosphere of middle class luxury, when his beeper began to vibrate in his inner pocket, alerting him to a call on his secured lines. He smiled at the secretary across from him, put his fork down and pushed his chair away.

"But Winnie—you haven't finished!"

He patted his slight paunch which was hard as a rock—but she had no experience with it, at least, not yet—and smiled. "Cutting back on calories, my dear. Perhaps I'll see you later?"

She pouted. "If I can catch up on the court records. I tell you, the judging is getting so bogged down. I think we should go back to live judgments, the computers take too long."

Winton gave her an indulgent smile. "Perhaps another time." He left the cafeteria, not lengthening his stride until he reached the corridors, then fairly sprinting down the halls until he reached the drop-shaft. From there, it was a matter of moments until he reached his offices. The beeper kept vibrating, letting him know the call signal was still coming in.

Winton threw himself into his chair, operating the com board with rapid efficiency, pulling in the subspace signal. When he had it locked and transmitting, he sat back with a noise of satisfaction and bridged his fingers, to wait.

"Sir?"

"Yes. I'm here."

"The subject you had followed has returned to transport. We have a full report on-line to you—"

"I want a summary now."

"Now?" A quaver in the man's voice indicated his awareness of the expense of the subspace call.

"Yes. Now." Winton felt his lips pull into a thin line. He had his lines secured about as well as anybody could, but he knew that reports could go awry. And he wanted to know. Had to know.

"The subject came to the Cluster and, after a few days of inquiries, made his way to the Dominion Social Services Hospital."

Winton sucked in his breath so sharply that his caller thought it static and said, "Hello? Still on-line?"

"Yes. Go on."

"The subject penetrated the security systems for about an hour and came back out without incident. He then booked return passage."

"Is that it?"

"The crux of it, sir. We have a full-scale report on calls, contacts, accommodations following."

"Thank you," Winton said abruptly and cut the contact without another word.

He swiveled his chair around. Now he knew the identity of the Flying Dutchman. That elusive last survivor of Milos and Jack Storm were one and the same.

Storm was as good as dead.

He leaned forward, opening up a local line. The distinguished looking gentleman who answered responded with an uplifted upbrow.

"Good afternoon," Winton said. "Bring down a little more pressure on the Bythia issue."

"All right," the gentleman said, curiosity on his face, but discretion making him keep his questions to himself.

Winton terminated the connection. He made a last call.

"Sir?"

"Did you find those slide sections I wanted?"

"They were located yesterday, sir. My report is in your files for viewing."

"Good. Very good."

Winton sat back. For the first time that day, he smiled, and the warmth of it reached his dark eyes. He had brought down an emperor with the Sand Wars. He was not above bringing down another emperor, though he had not planned to do so quite so soon.

The Dominion was not yet angry enough with the Triad Throne. He would have to change his plans a little. Not much, but a little.

He decided it did not matter. The Dominion would look to him as he wished it to. And leadership of the Dominion itself was a far greater ambition than the paltry Triad Throne.

CHAPTER 9

A cold sleep lab was little different from a morgue. Still bodies covered with plastisheets lay on gurneys, tubes carrying fluids in and out of veins. Only the air was different. It was colder than a morgue, far colder, and the workers who moved between the rows of bodies wore protective clothing as the temperature dropped lower and lower.

Bundled behind hood and shield and under the suit, the hair rose on the back of Jack's neck anyway. He didn't like cold sleep. He liked nothing about it and even to move about the lab the way he was doing now pushed the gorge up in his throat and tapped chilled fingers down his spine. The suit, of course, was not his—borrowed, as inconspicuously as possible. As he moved along the rows, he only hoped that he was not endangering lives by pretending to check gauges and fluids, mimicking the real techs who moved along to either side of him, carefully fulfilling their jobs.

Jack paused by the still form of a beautiful woman. In cold sleep, her skin was pale, translucent, the veins a delicate tracery underneath. The planes of her face were well-defined and aristocratic. A sharply defined frown line was etched between her brows. What was she doing here? Why had she chosen the Little Death of cold sleep to travel from one world to another? She was markedly different from most of the bodies in the lab. Most were male, rugged and ill-used, soldiers and laborers who traveled like fodder wherever their contracts sent them. Was she fleeing from someone? Did she seek the illusion of youth by outliving her contemporaries? Was she someone's high-priced consort? He watched her for a long time, then noticed the nearly imperceptible movement of her eyes under the lids. Even in this sleep, she dreamed. Jack moved off with a shudder, remembering his own cold sleep dreams.

Beyond the lab was the inner office he sought. Having penetrated this far, it took a great deal of self-control to keep from breaking his cover and entering it, but he steeled his will and waited, cruising up and down the rows of deathlike forms, waiting for his time.

To come this far and not find what he sought would be more than a waste. It could cost him his life. And, as he thought this, the corner of his mouth twitched upward ever so slightly. As to that, he'd come even farther than Amber had and he wondered if she'd be impressed when he told her. *Only if he'd come back with the information he wanted,* Jack thought.

A muffled buzzer rang through the lab. The workers had finished checking the rows. They turned and left quickly, Jack trailing them to the corridor. They passed on, he stayed behind, pressed against the walling as the security camera panned the area, missed him and traveled on. Jack stayed very quiet as he accessed the viewing area of the lens. It gave only cursory coverage . . . for who would want to penetrate a cold sleep lab?

No one, unless, like Jack, they knew that many of these bodies were not here of their own free will, but as victims of kidnapping. Their papers and permits falsified, more than flesh was frozen here. Freedom of will, if he wanted to be dramatic.

He took a few quick steps, then eased back out of the camera's sweep. As he waited for it, he shivered inside the suit and realized the temperature was dropping rapidly. He did not have much time to work his way through the lab. Now he understood why the workers had evacuated the area so quickly.

Eyes on his objective, Jack fought down his fear of being caught here, of being chilled down without preparation, and approached the portal to the innermost office hidden beyond the lab, protected, he imagined, by a legion of the sleeping dead. The portal opened to his questing touch, for who would it be locked against?

He moved inside. The air immediately felt warmer and his shivering stopped. A mild fog rose inside his visor. He reached up and pulled it out slightly to allow the air circulation to even out the temperatures. As he looked about he saw no cameras. Jack smiled to himself. The inhabiter of these dens wanted no recordings of the activities here. He did not wonder at that. He wondered, instead, who he would find on the other side of the office walling since the operation's original creator was dead. Huan Ng had been killed for chilling Jack down and selling him as a contract laborer instead of terminating him.

Well, Jack was back and he was mad.

Jack wasted no time kicking the door in. The lab operator at the console across the room turned half-around, snapping, "What do you think you're doing? Final chilling is in process. Get that temperature leveled off or we're going to have dead meat on our hands."

"Then I'd say you have a problem," Jack answered smoothly as he pulled off his hood.

The woman swung around. She was not beautiful. Half-Oriental blooded and half-redhead, the freckles were incongruous on her dark skin. Her almond shaped eyes widened. Her hand stabbed out for the beam that would call in Security, but Jack caught her by the wrist.

"I wouldn't do that if I were you."

Her eyes narrowed. She sat back in her chair, her wrist pulled in his grip, but he did not free her. "What do you want here?"

"Just a few answers. I could want more, but I haven't the time to waste. About fourteen months ago, I was processed through here as a contract laborer."

The woman's lips thickened momentarily. Then she forced a smile. "I was not the operator here then."

"That I know. Your father was—or perhaps your brother. It doesn't matter to me and I doubt if it mattered to you." As he talked, Jack made a few minor repairs to the control console, then released her. It wouldn't matter now if she tried to summon Security. Her board was temporarily out of commission. She coiled back in her chair.

"If you know who was in charge then, you know that he was killed for not doing his job properly—a situation I do not intend to face." Her not quite brown hair was heavily overcast with red, and she wore it in two thick braids, pulled back from her round moon of a face. She was not pretty in any sense of the word, reminding Jack of a spade-headed viper, sizing up the strike zone. "My father ran a lot of contract laborers through here."

"I'm different," Jack said. "I'm the one he got killed for."

Her eyes darkened. Her gaze flicked away, then back. He followed her line of sight and saw the butt of a hand laser, taped or in a magnetic holder, under the top of the desk next to hers. He moved subtly, just enough to block her reach.

She said carefully, "How do I know you're who you say you are?"

"I'm a Dominion Knight."

Her breath went out in a low hiss. "So you're the bastard."

Jack folded his arms.

She spat. It pooled off to the side, not far from the hip he had leaned insolently against the desk. "I'll tell you nothing."

"I think you will. There's an empty gurney or two out there. I've been chilled down a few times in my life. Without preparation, the blood spoils. Cells disrupt when the temperature drops. The hypothermia of waking is nearly impossible to counteract."

"You wouldn't!"

"Wouldn't I? It makes no difference to me. I've got the lab suit. Your workers won't be back in until next shift, to move these bodies out and new ones in. You won't be discovered for hours. By then, it will be too late. And, maybe by then, I'll have accessed your files and found what I wanted to know."

"Father would never have put anything like that into his files."

He stared at the woman's angry face. He shrugged negligently. "It's up to you."

"I will suffer my father's fate if it is known that I told you."

"Perhaps. If I'm clumsy. But I'm not, or I wouldn't have gotten this far."

He blocked her view of the gun. She hesitated,

drawing herself up in her chair. The viper getting ready to strike, Jack told himself in warning. He braced himself slightly.

Then she relaxed visibly. "It makes no difference," she said. "I'll tell you what you want to know. My father was hired by the Green Shirts—you will not have heard of them before, probably—they wanted to take out a member of the emperor's guard to show him that he was not as invulnerable as he thought himself. Emperors are made, not born, in these centuries. It was Pepys who was attacked, through you."

Jack absorbed her words without emotion, not doubting her, but wondering if even she knew the whole truth. When she had finished speaking, she turned her back to him and began to monitor the lab once more.

"That's all?"

She flashed him a triumphant look over her shoulder. "That is enough. Having heard of the Green Shirts, you're as dead as my father. Only, you do not yet know it."

He left the labs without being challenged once. The workers parted to let him through, and he realized she had called ahead, giving him a free exit.

She must have a lot of faith in the Green Shirts, he thought, peeling off his insulation suit and leaving it in a heap by the front portals. Enough that being a martyr appealed to her.

CHAPTER 10

"Jack. Where are you?"

No answer. Her voice echoed down the dark corridors, not only unanswered, but she feared, unheard. Amber stumbled to a halt, twisted and looked back, but the darkness pooling about her was deeper than night. She could not see through it. She could smell darkness and mold, street dirt, and her own fear.

"Amber."

It wasn't Jack's voice, but one she knew—and feared—better. Amber sucked in a breath so cold it burned her chest as she held it. *Don't let him find her. Please, God, by all the gods, don't let him find her.*

"Amber." Closer now. Coming inevitably toward her. She stopped breathing altogether and felt her heart hammer in her chest.

"Amber. It's time to kill, now."

Right next to her! Soft voice in her ear, warm breath tickling the shell of her chilled flesh, stirring the fine hair along her neck. By biting her lip so hard that blood sprang forth, she kept herself from jumping, crying out, betraying herself to Rolf.

He could not see her if she could not see him. She told herself that several times as she waited in the dark. Long seconds crawled by. Her chest swelled with rank air and ached for fresh.

The man moved away. He said, with laughter in his voice, "I have the word, Amber. All I have to do is say it."

He didn't know she was there. How could he? He had no idea where she was. The last time he'd seen her, she'd been with Jack, who had only been a mercenary. For all Rolf knew, she could be a roadie, following Jack from assignment to assignment.

How would he know where she was?

But she did not doubt that he did. Rolf was more than a pimp. He had access to a network of underground information that never made it into the master system.

The need to breathe clawed at her throat until she could no longer think.

"Amber?"

The voice was now farther away in the darkness. By stretching out her arm, she just might see her wrist. She, too, was clothed in black. She touched her fingertips to her face. A black mask muffled her cheekbones.

Now she remembered why she was here. She'd come here to kill someone.

Amber tilted back her head and screamed.

The noise woke her up, shaking, in the half-lit illumination of her room. The sheets under her pressed damp and rumpled lines into her body. She put a trembling hand to her mouth to still her cries . . . and drew it away covered with blood.

Amber savagely slapped her hand down on the light switch, flooding the room. She sat, curled up in the bed, surrounded by the rankness of sweat and fear. Damn Jack. Damn him and his bad dreams anyway. Now she was having them.

When the trembling left her limbs, she lifted her face from its resting place on her knees, a dimple in her skin where her pointed chin had dug. "Dreams," she said again. "Dreams that can kill."

There was something about Jack, had always been something about him, and she hoped she would always see it in him. He might be a soldier, but he had roots in the earth, in the life that earth could hold and nurture from world to world. He had told her it was because he'd once been a farmer's son and then a ranger, but she thought it was something purer that managed to shine through him. Like the sun. And the only clouds that ever shadowed it were those of his dreams—and now she was dreaming.

Was Rolf out there somewhere, rapping on her psychic keyboard? Tapping her soul? Could he, somehow, someway, still use her as an assassin?

Amber abruptly swung her feet off the bed and stood up. There was only one man she knew and trusted besides Jack, and that man had more than a little experience with souls.

Jack looked across the vast complex of the emperor's grounds. He hadn't been gone that long but the view seemed to have changed, or perhaps he had. Amber had accused him of being a coward, of being afraid to enter his armor and draw Bogie out. Perhaps he had been. He had the new armor on order, but knew now that he would never use it. The last hope of knowing who he was and regaining his past might lie within the old armor, in the being slumbering there. The techs had played games with his memories, but they hadn't known about Bogie . . . and Bogie had been alive on Milos, even back then, and so just might retain that shred of his consciousness that could tell him who he was.

All he had to do was wake Bogie and hope to

control the berserker soul long enough to find out who he was. Before Bogie regenerated enough to become a true parasite and devour him a bit at a time. It was a gamble, but then, what choice did Jack have? What choice had he ever had?

He flashed his palm print at the security gate and was let in. Sulfur-colored lights glowed over the barracks. The grass had been watered earlier. It made damp sounds under his feet until he reached the pathway to his private officers' quarters. The door wasn't locked firmly when he opened it, and he smiled, knowing Amber was waiting there for him. Jack stepped inside the doorway.

He froze as the men rose from their resting positions, but the flash of their uniforms made him pause, waiting, because these people weren't supposed to be the enemy in this part of Malthen, though Amber thought otherwise. The World Police devices on their shoulders winked on their epaulets.

"Captain Storm, good evening. We've been waiting for you since we received word you'd docked."

He dropped his duffel just inside the doorway as he said, "Thank you, gentlemen. What can I do for you?"

The man in charge of the trio was a big, lean man and his nose had been broken at one time. He evidently had liked it that way, for he wore it now as if it were a badge of distinction, not having had cosmetic surgery to restore it. "I'm Captain Drefford. The emperor has asked me to debrief you on your findings."

The door closed at Jack's heels, a shield against his back. He looked from Drefford to the two escorts who stared blandly back at him. He noted that the second one to the rear, wore a black caduceus in addition to his WP markings. A medical interrogator.

"My leave was for personal reasons," Jack answered, wondering what was going on here. "If Pepys wants to know what I found, I'll be glad to ask for an audience."

"Your leave," Drefford said, with a faint and ugly emphasis, "was on the emperor's behalf."

"He gave me leave to go."

"He ordered you to go," Drefford corrected. "And it is perhaps best you don't remember what you learned. Mavor." He crooked a finger and the medical interrogator came forward.

The smallish, dark-skinned man smiled. "It's best you have a seat, captain. The floor can be hard when you topple."

If the door had been open, Jack would have bolted. As it was he made to shrug as Drefford and the third man caught his arms, but they had him too closely quartered as Mavor came forward with the air needle. Jack did the second best thing. He lowered his chin to his chest, took a deep breath, and ordered his mind to perform the mental exercises he'd learned long ago as a Knight of the "Pure" wars—training which Amber had later reinforced for him—and thought of a time when an emperor would not have treated his own man in such a way.

He woke with a dull pounding permanently lodged in his head. In the grayish light of early dawn, Bogie hung from his equipment rack like a golem, a mechanical homunculus. Jack scrubbed at his eyes. The drugs had left a brackish taste in his mouth, and thinking that, Jack sat up quickly.

He remembered! He had not been intended to, but he had. And then he remembered that Mavor had gotten very little out of him . . . nothing about his visit to the rehab center, only about the cold sleep lab and the Green Shirts, because Jack had had to give them something . . . it had been turning him inside out to retain anything.

Jack staggered into the bathroom and put his face in the washbasin, standing crouched over it while he splashed cold water, then rinsed his mouth and spat. When he stood up to look at himself in the mirror, it was with a grim expression of satisfaction. But he said nothing aloud, knowing that WP had probably bugged the apartment, too, and he would have to have it swept later. He'd be able to cover that action of his.

But now he would not be able to take further action against the organization that had kidnapped him and sold him into contract labor. That information had been taken from him and he should no longer be able to remember.

Jack winced as he scraped a razor over his face. Could he trust the emperor to take advantage of that information? Would there be vengeance taken for him? He could only watch silently and carefully to see.

As he straightened, to a pounding at the back of his head, the general com line sounded.

"Guard alert. Guard alert. All available personnel report. Assassination attempt in the west wing."

Jack paused long enough to grab his hand laser from its wall cabinet. He looked longingly at Bogie, knew he didn't have the time to put his armor on. The west wing . . . the emperor's personal recreation wing! He ran across the grounds.

WP lights had come on, flooding the gray dawn with white-hot light, bleeding the pink buildings out. He could see the tall, slender, silver-haired man forming trios and sending them out. The

Owner of the Purple—no, Jack corrected himself—Kavin, and he felt again the keen edge of betrayal. If he had been a Knight, why did he not fight for the complete resurrection of the Knights, with all the ideals and codes . . . or did Pepys know what he was harboring as his right arm?

As Jack fell in, the Purple's brown eyes sought him out. Always laughing, the expression in those eyes, unless things were terribly, terribly wrong. The expression was somber now and as their gazes held, Jack wondered if he had told WP about Kavin. He could not remember.

"Captain," called the commander. "Good timing. The floors have been secured, but I need a detail at the North-Six exit."

Jack nodded briskly. He pointed at two he knew. "Farrel and Davidis. Come with me."

Farrel, short and wiry, had gone through Basic with Jack. Davidis, tall, chestnut-haired and incredibly young looking, was one of the new Knights. Jack knew him only from the parade grounds. Both were fit and fast-thinking men and he did not hesitate to have them with him. Farrel was in his armor, carrying his helmet, but Davidis like himself had only taken time to dress and grab a weapon.

The sixth floor north exit was in bleak shadows, on the far side from the WP lights, and the moment Jack craned his head back to look at it, the hairs prickled at the back of his neck and he knew what his friend had done to him.

If the assassin were looking for a way out, this was the way he would come. Jack had no doubt of it.

"Shit," Farrel said. Neither, it appeared, did he.

Davidis only asked, "How are we getting up there?"

"We're climbing," Jack answered. He motioned

for Farrel to affix the grappling hook carried in his belt pack. A WP alarm shut down all systems, trapping the perpetrators inside, but also effectively hindering entrance through the doors and elevator shafts. Jack wondered briefly if the emperor had been home to greet his callers. If so, he was locked in with them.

With a retort, the wrist barrel fired and Farrel's grappling hook and line arced into the air. It anchored just off the balcony of North-Sixth's doorway. Jack smiled thinly. Just where he wanted it.

He signaled for Farrel to notify the commander and he went up first, hand over hand, feeling the pounding of the drug-induced interrogation hammering at the back of his head. Davidis scrambled up behind him and, as told to, took a crouched position where he could lay a cross fire in front of the doorway. Farrel came up the side of the building as though he were moonwalking, but his face was slightly flushed inside the armor's neckline. He landed and, at Jack's nod, notified the Purple they were in position.

Jack heard the Purple's muffled response, "Systems coming on. Get ready."

Davidis' exotically dark skin paled a little. Jack heard the thrum of power, and the North-Six door blew.

Two figures just inside, hugging the portal, began to edge out.

"Hold it right there," Jack said.

They froze. Then, the man in faded blue trousers, with a magnificent dark blue robe over them, stepped forward. "Don't shoot," he said. "We haven't done anything."

Jack straightened up as he recognized the voice of St. Colin of the Blue Wheel. A lithe figure cowered in his shadow.

"What are you doing here? There's been an assassination attempt."

"I know," Colin said in his deep, ringing voice. He'd been a handsome man once, and his face showed the ruins of it. He looked back over his shoulder. "There's a dead man back there, in the corridor. I think it's that broadcaster, Scott. He seems to have gotten in the way."

He could hear the tramp of WP boots in the corridors behind. He motioned for Davidis to go "at ease," and it was only then the shadow stood up and came forward.

Amber gave him a stricken look. "I didn't do it, Jack, honest to God," she cried, just as the WP caught up with them.

CHAPTER 11

If he had not been behind Scott in that alley in under-Malthen, he might have wondered. It was clear though that the journalist had had enemies, and this was but one of the outcomes. But he did not even blink as Amber stared at him with anguish in her face. Scott, he knew, had been living on borrowed time.

All he said was, "I know."

Colin's mouth dropped open slightly, then the saint clamped his lips tightly shut and put an arm about Amber, drawing her close for support. His expression met Jack's just before the Knight turned to meet the WP. The look of approval jolted him slightly.

The WP man saluted and then spent the rest of his detail to cordon off the murder scene. "Captain Storm, welcome back."

"Thank you," Jack answered, with a blank expression. Drefford was working late tonight, he thought, as he looked past the man. He was not supposed to recognize the WP officer. "I have two here who escaped harm. How is the emperor?"

"Fine. His inner portals closed as soon as the alarm went off. Although," and Drefford turned on his heel, "the embarrassment of having a guest killed is bad enough. St. Colin, I'm Captain Drefford. Do you know the victim?"

"Yes, indeed. That's Scott Randolph, the broadcast journalist. He was here for dinner last night, taping an interview with Pepys."

Drefford nodded briskly. "I thought as much. But, the physical evidence, it's helpful getting ID from someone who saw him get hit. We'll have forensics verify it."

Jack watched as a plastisheet was laid over the amorphous crimson blob in the corridor beyond. "Has the assassin been found?"

"No," said Drefford after a pause. "We have evidence he went out over the roof, however. If we're lucky, he's on camera."

"And if you're not?" asked Colin harshly.

"Then Pepys will have to be very careful for a while." Drefford rubbed the bridge of his nose. "We'll get word of who it was soon enough. Then the Sweepers will pick him up for us, never fear, your reverence. Why don't you take the young lady and go downstairs to the lounge? We've some unpleasant work to do here." He paused, then looked at Jack, Farrel and Davidis. "The bodyguard isn't needed any more either. I suggest you report to your commander and tell him we have the situation under control."

"Good idea," Jack said, as if the WP officer hadn't rudely brushed them off. "I'll escort the remaining guests down just in case your information is incorrect and the assassin is still in the wing."

Colin gave him a sidelong, amused glance as the two fell into step with them and moved down the corridor, past the assassination scene. Jack saw Amber tighten her lips as they walked past the walls still running with blood. She put her chin up and tossed back her tawny hair and Jack was glad that the saint had his arm about her.

Once out of earshot, Jack signaled for Farrel and

Davidis to run on ahead and report back to the Purple.

Colin chuckled. "Well, Jack. It appears that court and power intrigue agree with you."

"Never."

"Jack," said Amber softly. "I swear to you—"

"I know. Don't worry about him."

Colin tightened his arm about her shoulders. "She has to, Jack. That's one reason she's with me tonight. I came here hoping to lay some demons down and ran right into one."

They stopped as one just before the elevator shaft, and heard the smooth hum as it approached.

"What do you mean?"

She pulled herself away from Colin's secure hold and held herself tautly. "I mean that I don't know that I didn't do it."

"But you told me . . ."

"I know! I meant that I didn't do it on purpose. . . ." Amber's voice trailed off, like that of an exhausted child.

But she wasn't a child any more. She was no longer the street smart teenager he'd taken away from Rolf, he reminded himself, and desire for her was almost as much a part of him as his concern for her.

"We can't talk about it here."

Colin nodded wisely. The door to the elevator slid open and he drew Amber in with him. Jack followed.

She faced him. "Where then? When then?"

Jack looked at Colin over her head. "Perhaps you should go to church," he said, with a slight quirk of his lips, and saw the saint return the smile in agreement.

Jack never got that far, however. Word was waiting for him in the lounge that Emperor Pepys desired his presence in the audience room immediately. Colin gave Jack that unperturbed look of his.

"I'll look after her," he said. "She's been scared enough."

Jack half-bowed and watched the saint guide Amber away into the early morning light of what promised to be a blistering day. He wondered just what she had told Colin.

"Jack! It's good to have you off leave. I trust it was a successful one."

Jack frowned slightly, then nodded. "I seem to have things resolved," he said, knowing he could not answer any other way without arousing the suspicion of the WP. He looked to his commander, the Owner of the Purple, who stood elegantly at attention and patterned his own stance after that of his friend.

Pepys' red hair moved on end with its own static electricity, as he swiveled in his chair to look at the face of first one and then the other. The emperor looked wan and tired this morning.

The wiry man said carefully, "I called you both here this morning to tell you that you failed."

The Purple inclined his head slightly. "I am sorry, Emperor."

Pepys waved a freckled hand. "Don't interrupt! But, nonetheless, that's not why I called you here. The fault is mine. I sent the bodyguard detail away last night."

Purple's head snapped up. Jack watched him closely. This was news to both of them. "Why," the commander said carefully, his right hand pulling slightly at his jacket flap, "did you do that, sir?"

"I did not wish to be spied upon for dinner." Pepys shuffled his feet. He'd dressed casually for the morning, but already looked rumpled. "Scott was a friend as well as an enemy, and we wished to dine alone. Without the WP or the Knights taking in our conversation. Unfortunately, it was the death of Scott." Pepys sighed. "I hope he can forgive me someday."

"Scott was like you, your highness," Jack said. "He thrived on the challenge of being powerful."

"Yes. Well. Possibly." Pepys ran his hand through his hair, attempting to pull it flat, but only increasing the static electricity. Individual strands rose and wavered about. "He had a story he wanted to tell me that he did not get a chance to finish. It began with a name. The name of John Wesley Kavin."

The Purple blanched, his space-tanned face becoming incredibly pale.

The emperor sat down heavily. "No," he said, looking in the other direction, far away. "I didn't think he was lying to me. This leaves me with a dilemma. Suddenly, you have a name and a history, Commander Kavin. Do we announce it? Celebrate it? Or do we ask you to resign and fade away anonymously? What of your history? Do I have the right to ask for it, or must I fear a traitor within these walls?"

The Purple cleared his throat. Jack could feel the tension in his body even though he was standing two feet away from the Purple.

"I suggest, your highness, that you give me a name, if you wish. But as to my history—it is unrecorded. No one but you will ever know that I fought in the Sand Wars and survived Dorman's Stand. I was not enrolled in the guard, then. I was a stowaway on a staging freighter and when my brother died, I stole his armor. No one has ever heard that story before today. And I don't think either of you," the Purple looked at his emperor slowly and then at Jack, "I don't think either of you will betray me."

Jack had no words, his mind reeling. This man had seen his homeworld fall to the Thraks.

Pepys had placed his hands on the arms of his chair, and now they trembled. "My god," he said. "You must have been little more than a boy."

"Yes," Kavin answered.

The emperor rubbed his brow. "So be it," he said. "I will announce that, because of your meritorious service to me, whatever trangressions you have in your mercenary past have been pardoned, and your anonymity is no longer required. Nothing else need be revealed. Captain Storm, will you be my witness?"

"Yes, your highness."

"Good. Then it's done. I'll have it put in the morning releases. You're both dismissed. And, commander—"

Kavin turned back.

"Yes, your highness?"

"Don't let me have made a mistake."

"No, your highness." The commander bowed smoothly and upon straightening took Jack out of the audience room with him.

They faced each other on the landing outside the palace. Purple smoothed back a wing of his silver hair.

Jack found himself saying, "I don't know if I can get used to calling you John Wesley."

"That's Kavin to you," returned his friend. "I haven't been called J.W. in . . . oh . . . twenty-five years or so."

They stood, nearly toe to toe, and the tension

between them was undeniable. Jack ached to be able to tell him that he had been a Knight and to ask of his colony's last days, but he couldn't.

"It's good to have you back," the Purple said, finally.

"Thank you. Did you know St. Colin and Amber were in the building?"

"Of course. I didn't know that it was Pepys who called off the detail, but I kept a watch, anyway. I saw them go in. I sent you to North-Six because that seemed to be the most likely exit, and I knew you'd want to be there if Amber had been taken hostage." Kavin smiled, and this time his eyes reflected his usual humor. "I'm told, however, that the WP let him escape over the roof."

"Let?"

"Shoddy defense up there. I'll be talking to Pepys about it soon, but not right away. I don't want the WP to think I'm stepping on their toes."

"Of course not."

Kavin hesitated. "You're back on duty, then?"

Jack nodded. "I seemed to have gotten whatever it was out of my system." He paused. There was a time when he might have confided further in his friend, but now . . . Kavin was clearly the emperor's man, and Jack could not forget what other of the emperor's men had done to him last night.

"Good. I'll have the duty roster posted in about an hour." Kavin clapped him on the shoulder. "It'll be nice having a name again," he said, before he pivoted and marched off.

Jack watched him go. He thought of K'rok, spared by the Thraks because of his fighting prowess and, although he wore the yoke of their command, he'd made it clear to Jack that his first objective was the revival of his race.

Dorman's Stand had been even more of a massacre than Rikor or Milos. How then, did John Wesley Kavin, little more than a boy, live to talk about the day? By what good fortune had he lived long enough to become a mercenary with a suit of armor considered antique?

He shook his head and struck off across the grounds to his quarters. If he was lucky, he had a few hours of sleep left to help him work off the travel fatigue. But there was nothing that would help him work off the uneasiness of the past two weeks' events.

CHAPTER 12

Jack ignored Amber who sat cross-legged in the middle of the floor, critically eying the sable colored armor hanging on a second rack in the corner of the room. Jack had Bogie opened along the seams, turned almost inside out, and was probing the circuitry to make sure everything was in order. He could do it at the shop, but liked his privacy when working on the white armor. "I didn't think it was any of your business," he replied briefly, frowning over a power line. He looked to see if the fiber optic cable was attached properly and, sure enough, the chip wiggled a little. He tapped it into place delicately.

"Not any of my business?" Her voice seemed high and a little strained. "Or is it because you don't trust me any more?"

"You told me you didn't kill Scott. I trust you." Jack looked toward her. "The WP comes in and wipes my mental slate. What I'm not supposed to remember, it's better you don't know."

She gritted out, "How can anybody treat his men that way?"

Jack looked up. "I don't know that the order came from Pepys."

"Who from, then?" She sucked in her breath suddenly. "Winton has that much influence with the WP?"

"Maybe. We don't know he doesn't. I haven't been able to locate him."

"The implications boggle the mind. What about Scott? Why do you think he was eliminated?"

"He could have been in the wrong place at the right time. Or, he could have been the target. I don't know."

Amber stared at Bogie's replacement hanging in the corner. "Going to replace Bogie?"

"No. No, I'm not. I thought about it, but he's probably the only chance I've got to regain what I was."

"What do you mean?"

Jack paused, searching for the words. He had had little chance to talk with Amber since he'd gotten back. "I was never meant to be brought out of cold sleep alive. I was found by accident. They took me out and hid me, and they tampered with what was left of my memories. I don't know if the snatches I do remember are mine, or what they tried to implant in me."

"What do you mean?"

"I mean that no one was meant to survive Milos."

"Who found you, then?"

"I don't know. But my records weren't at the hospital. They've been wiped clean. My doctors had assumed identities. Why me? Because I'm a Knight who survived—or because I'm someone I can't even remember anymore."

"But you dream, and you remember when you dream."

"That's right, and that means whoever revived me botched the job. If I'm no good to them, I'm a liability."

"Winton?"

"Maybe. Or maybe someone else. God knows the Triad Throne has enough enemies."

"What are you going to do about it?"

"Nothing yet. I haven't got enough information." Jack straightened up the suit. "But I do know that Bogie was with me on Milos. Living then, even though we didn't interface yet. It's possible—just possible—he was alive enough to have contact with me and I just never realized it. He may even know who I really am, what my name was, where I came from."

She sucked her breath in. "You're not even Jack Storm?"

"Maybe. Maybe not. Some things feel so right to me that I don't think anyone could have changed them . . . I know I was a farmer's son from Dorman's Stand." He grinned ruthlessly. "They couldn't take that from me, although now I think they might have tried!"

"And all this time you thought it was the debriefing loop from cold sleep that wiped out your memories."

"And it may have taken many of them, and the rehab center took advantage of the damage to implant a new persona."

"But why? Who did it?"

He met her expression now, and this time her eyes did not look away. "I don't know why. Possibly to protect them, or me, or maybe I've even been programmed the way you have."

"But your dreams—"

"I've been in contact with Bogie, remember? He may be feeding back into me what he remembers me feeling from Milos. Anyway, I won't be trading him in. I can't. God help me, but I've got to keep using him."

She tucked a strand of hair behind a delicate ear. Jack felt a feeling wash over him then, an irresistible urge to kiss her, and was glad there was a room and an assortment of tools between them. He cleared his throat.

"You've got to help me, Amber. You've got to help me wake him and then control him."

Her lower lip trembled a little. "I—"

"What's wrong?"

"Nothing. I'll do whatever I can. After what happened at Huan's lab and then here with the WP, I don't know who's the enemy anymore." She stood up again. "I've got to go. Colin is waiting for me."

"You're with him a lot, lately. Going to convert?"

She wrinkled her nose, her somber mood fleeing. "Street scum like me? Not likely. But his secretary, Biggle, is doing a lot of lobbying in the palace, getting on Pepys' nerves. I'm sort of filling in. I'm good with computers, remember?"

"What you can do with computers can get both of you nailed by the Sweepers, saint or not. Maybe I should warn him."

"Really." She paused at the doorway. "Jack . . ."

He was already peering back into the suit. "Mmmm?"

"Oh, nothing. Forget it. Start working on your meditation again, if we get Bogie awake."

"I am. And I want you to start working on yours. I'm altering the gauntlet weaponry system a little . . . putting a stun in. I'm thinking that we need that option of my knocking them down and you probing them, if you can."

She turned a little and, or was it his imagination, whitened. "You know I can't—"

"You can try."

"And what if I fry their brains?"

"I don't think you could, if you worked on refining your talent."

She shook her head vigorously. "Forget it! I've already told you, it's all or nothing."

Jack flexed his shoulders to ease a muscle that threatened to cramp as he leaned back into the armor. "Nothing," he said, "is all or nothing, whether we like it or not."

But she didn't hear him. She'd already fled the apartment.

Colin looked at the com screen impatiently. The oval, good-natured face of Biggle looked back at him, eyes wide in an ingenuous expression. "Biggle, for god's sake, that's why I have you there. To make a continuous impression on Pepys. We've got to get permission to go into Bythia. There's no reason why the Walker religion should continue to be denied access. I have a memo right here that states a rabbi was assigned to the embassy last month. If a priest and a rabbi can be there, a Walker can go in. I don't want you to drop the subject just because you think it's a sore spot with the emperor."

Amber, curled up in a lounge chair nearby, looked up from her keypad long enough to grin at the tone of exasperation creeping into Colin's voice. She didn't like Biggle personally . . . he oozed. What, she couldn't put her finger on, but she disliked oozers of all sorts whether it was evil or innocence or anything in between.

Colin sighed. "Think of yourself as a drip of water and Pepys as a rock. Sooner or later you're going to etch in your influence."

"Yes, your reverence." Biggle's image flickered as he turned away and then turned back. "Perhaps I can catch him unawares."

Never, Colin thought of his old friend Pepys, but he answered politely, "Perhaps."

"The emperor is under a lot of pressure from the Dominion Congress."

"Oh?"

"They've doubled their budget and expect the Triad to make up the deficit."

Colin tapped a finger on his desk. That would account for a lot of strain in relations.

"And the Thraks are still mad at him, too. Ambassador Dhurl has requested another audience."

"Really? That'll be the third one this month."

Biggle nodded. "So maybe I can catch his highness when he's distracted."

Colin thought, *don't count on it*, but he smiled at his secretary. "Just remember, persistence. And logic. Please don't forget logic, Biggle."

"Yes, sir." The com screen flickered and went dark, buzzing a second longer before going silent.

"I like the water and rock bit," Amber said.

The saint smiled at the girl. "You would," he said. "I've seen you employ the same technique."

She shrugged. "Whatever it takes."

"Does it work with Jack?"

She unfolded her legs and looked uneasy. "Sometimes."

Colin rocked back in his chair and wondered a moment. Then he said, "How are you sleeping?"

"In my own apartment!"

The saint, in spite of his years and sophistication, flushed slightly. Then he rumbled, "That's not what I meant, young lady, and you know it. I want to know if you're still having nightmares."

"I think so."

"Don't you know?"

"I—I can't seem to remember what I've been dreaming anymore. But I wake up, and the bed's all torn apart, so I know . . . I know they're not peaceful."

Colin frowned. "I think perhaps I cannot help

you any more, Amber. I think you're going to have to seek—"

"No one's going to mess with my mind!"

"Someone already has," he pointed out. "And you're going to be susceptible to whatever NLP Rolf has implanted you with until it's ferreted out."

"I—I can't. Really. I'm sure if I do that he's also put in a Trojan Horse."

"A what?"

She looked at him. "A delayed bomb, of sorts, of psychic suggestions. If anyone messes with what he's set up, I'll be destroyed, mentally. It's inside, closed up, until triggered. It would be like him to do that to me. So, I guess . . ." her voice wavered and faded away.

Colin crossed the room and took her up in his arms as if she were still a small child. "Oh, my dear," was all he could think of to say to her.

Biggle, on the sidelines of the audience room, watched as the Thrakian League's ambassador strode in. He was always impressed by the Thraks, impressed and horrified in the same breath. He watched the chitin face plates of the alien move into a hardened mask and wondered what it indicated. The expression was horrific, like that of an ancient Kabuki, but he did not have the expertise to know what was meant by it.

"I demand," the ambassador said, "immediate retribution. We have fenced long enough, Pepys. The dignity of our peoples requires this."

The red-haired emperor leaned forward slightly from his audience chair. Even on the dais, he sat barely taller than the Thrak stood. "Retribution for what, my good ambassador?"

"Your memory, like your honor, seems to be a

frail thing." Dhurl paused, not unaware of the gasps and the sensation he was creating throughout the hall. "I have a warship and crew destroyed by your guard."

"And we have had this discussion before." Pepys, however, seemed to retreat slightly into his chair. His fingers tapped its right arm thoughtfully. "If I were to offer retribution, what might the Thrakian League be willing to accept?"

"Money would only seem an insult after what has already taken place."

"Naturally. But there must be some redress?"

The ambassador moved back on his hind legs. Biggle watched in fascination as the face plates moved slightly, and the mask altered. "We wish assurances that an incident of this kind will not happen in the future, or else our very Treaty stands in danger of being destroyed."

"I have already given you that assurance, based on your assurance that such actions of yours be tempered as well."

Dhurl waved a talon. "And there are other considerations. Lasertown was an outlying fringe territory, where lines of responsibility and obligation blurred. It would be best that other such territories are not placed in a like jeopardy."

Oh-oh, Biggle thought as Pepys suddenly leaned forward. *Here it comes, whatever it is.*

"And what territories might we be discussing?"

"Bythia for one, Emperor. As you know, we have received requests through our embassy there that they have asked for secession from Dominion and wish to be sequestered under our guidance."

Dhurl might have some of the nuances of the language wrong, but not the impact. Biggle noted that the tension in the room literally hummed.

Pepys scratched his jaw briefly. "I've received no such requests through my embassy," he said.

The two beings regarded one another. Dhurl shifted yet again. "Perhaps," the Thraks suggested, "your representatives hesitate to reveal the truth to you."

"And perhaps," replied Pepys very softly, "you are lying."

A gasp. An intake of breath around the room, one that was held.

The Thrakian guards pulled in closer to their ambassador. Dhurl made a diffident movement. "Then I take it that secession is not to be allowed, as a part of redress, *or otherwise*."

"You take it correctly, Ambassador Dhurl. The Bythians are free planeteers, but we will not allow them to be invaded if we can help it."

"So be it," said Dhurl. He spun on his beetlelike legs and strode out of the audience hall, and Biggle did not need to read the masklike expression to know something of terrible import had just passed between the Thraks and the emperor. He waited until the media had followed the ambassador out and then pressed forward.

Pepys wore a distracted, unhappy expression, but turned as the secretary approached the foot of the dais. "What is it, Biggle?"

The Walker raised a solicitous hand. "Perhaps, your highness, on the subject of Bythia, I can now obtain permission for a Walker team to become part of the embassy?"

Pepys' green eyes bulged a little, but then he forced a laugh. "Very well, Biggle! There will be little enough left for your team to explore as it is. Go on, get out of here, and tell St. Colin he's a bigger fool than he thinks he is."

"Thank you, your highness!" Biggle bowed with an ecstasy of feeling.

The emperor waved him away. "You don't know what you've done," he said. "Now go!" He pushed himself up from his chair and left the audience hall abruptly, his advisers scurrying after him.

Biggle, his heart full, pushed his way toward the public entrance to the hall. He longed to be the first one to break the news to His Reverence and it would be nice if the young lady were with him also. Biggle had feelings of lust and yearning for the young lady and he had hopes of having her look on him with favor. He had a powerful position as secretary to the saint. Many young women had fawned on him for less.

Maybe now she would look on him less scornfully.

Biggle licked his lips and hurried toward the public com room. He turned down the distant corridor, thinking he was alone, and then stopped suddenly as he found out he was not. "Ah!" he said. "You're here, after all? Great news I have to tell you. Wait until you hear what I've done! Congratulate me!" Flushed with his success, he opened his arms and moved forward in a bold embrace.

He made a sound of astonishment as his chest flowered crimson, and then he collapsed, but he was dead before he hit the tile floor.

CHAPTER 13

"There's not a kill mark on him," Jack said, pacing, not looking at either Colin or the girl.

"I know, I know," Amber answered him.

"And forensics is telling us that Scott just exploded. They can't tell what hit him, there's no burned flesh or chemical markings. It's as if the man just decided to . . . explode. And now Biggle."

"I know."

Colin raised his eyebrows and gave Jack a look which the other ignored as he continued pacing. When he came to a stop, he said, "You didn't do that, did you?"

Amber sat engulfed in a chair, her legs drawn up under her, tawny hair curtaining her face from his survey. She didn't react visibly, but the older man did.

"Now see here! She was with me both times, yes, but there's absolutely no reason to think she would be capable of such a thing!"

"Not could be, but would be. That's the key," Jack returned. "And, unfortunately, we have no way of telling who she's been programmed for. If there's a list engraved inside that pretty head, it's hidden from view . . . you know it, and I know it. It doesn't make any difference what you say to Pepys now, the emperor is going to have to consider Amber a suspect."

"But why? There's a perfectly logical reason why we were coming into the public wing ... Biggle had called me. He told me about Dhurl's audience and we decided we wanted to see the show ourselves. Amber's finding the body was sheer coincidence."

"Maybe." Jack looked down at the chair, at the mane of hair hiding the pale face and mellow golden brown eyes, eyes which were the windows of a soul he valued ... and now was growing to fear. "Did you sense he was there? In any way?"

She shook her head. A miserable sound escaped from her, a sob or a muffled moan. Jack sighed in spite of himself.

"Go to pieces on us now," he said, squatting down so his face was roughly on a level with hers, "and we might as well stuff you down the Disposall and save Pepys the trouble."

She peered at him. "I'm almost sure I didn't do it."

"What?"

She turned to Colin's outrage. "I'm not sure anymore. I didn't like Biggle, your reverence. He was ... greasy. He thought he knew exactly why you liked me and why I'd accompanied you to Lasertown and why I was keeping you company now, and he wanted some of that, too. He would make inferences when you weren't around. So I might have—I might have killed him—just because I didn't like him or the way he tried to handle me. Or I might have killed him because he's an influential man, powerful, like you, and I was programmed to do it."

The saint ran a thick, square hand over his balding head, chestnut and white strands ruffling in its wake. "Or you might not have killed him at all! I resent the implication that I could be standing next to a murderer and let it happen without doing anything at all."

"What could you do?"

"Stop you."

"Then maybe you'd be dead, too," Amber said flatly.

Jack stood back up. "And then, of course, there's always the chance that the emperor will consider you a suspect," he said to Colin.

"Me?"

"You were there both times and maintaining your position as the head of an empire such as yours has called for drastic measures in the past."

The two men looked at one another. Washed out blue eyes in a plain-boned face met angry, deep brown eyes.

"I hope," St. Colin said heavily, "You are referring to the historical past."

"Naturally."

"Ummmm." The older man moved away, shoving his hands in his pockets. His dark blue tunic robe rippled with the movement and fluttered behind him like a banner as he began to pace. He could not easily forget how he'd first met Jack when Pepys had assigned him to investigate a militaristic movement within the Walker organization. He'd not worked with Jack on the investigation, but when he'd been picked up and taken hostage by the militants, Colin found himself rescued in a very professionally-run maneuver that prevented what could have been a bloodbath. Now, Colin admitted, he was deluding himself if he thought he had rooted out all the dissidence in his fellowship. He found he had completed the circuit of his room and was back in front of Amber, who'd uncurled in her chair and now sat up, watching him, a defiant expression on her gamine face.

He reached toward her and brushed a tangle of hair from her eyes with a gentle fingertip. "He's right, you know. Pepys could be after me as a suspect as well as you." He heaved a great sigh. "That only leaves us one choice, Jack."

The Knight stirred as if he'd been waiting for that signal to activate him. He nodded. "I know. I want you to stay with Colin, no matter what happens."

She leaned forward in alarm, at the sound of his voice. "What are you two talking about?"

Colin said gently, "The only way we can prove you're not suspect is to find out who you've been trained to kill. As I understand it, there's only one man who knows that."

Amber stood. "No! You can't go after Rolf, he'll kill you this time—Jack!"

But the man had already gone out the door, leaving Colin to put his arm about the grieving girl.

Rolf had no illusions about his life in Malthen. He was fast, smart and mean and kept his edge as long as he was all three of them. As long as he had that edge, he had everything he wanted—nearly. Limitations chafed him.

He strode through the streets in the early morning, scouting the crowds of beggar children who surrounded him like a scummy, early morning fog. He looked for that instinctive quickness, that talent of knowing quarry from predator, that deftness his best pupil had had.

They scurried out now. One or two slunk back upon spotting him ... they knew him, but the others didn't ... there was always a new crop of children from failed farms outside Malthen, or the factory techs, or religious cults gone morally bankrupt overnight. Whatever the cause, they were always there, their eyes gummy with hope and their grubby fingers twitching at his pants pockets. Rolf smiled as he felt their touch now, for he wore his clothes sleek and tight like a pelt, a second skin, and he felt their intimacies as clearly as an electric shock.

Still smiling, he growled down at the crowd. He grabbed an insolent hand and twisted it back on its pale wrist as the child attached to it cried and went to her knees. Her companions froze in shock. "Get away from me," he said. "Unless you want to be missing a hand."

They fled. Instinctively, they knew the smile to be false and the growl reality.

Rolf enjoyed frightening children and for a snatch of a moment, the smile grew. Then it faded. Never, it seemed, would he find another child with the talent and potential of Amber, and that was a limitation on his future wealth that he could not tolerate. With Amber, he'd had everything to look forward to, once he'd identified that elusive quality of hers.

As he strode toward an all-hours bar, he chewed the bitter curds of having lost her—as a roadie to one of the emperor's mercenaries, no less, which would make taking her back a tangled and difficult proposition. As yet, he'd not figured out how to do it without murdering the mercenary outright. As the months went by, that plan grew in his mind like a dark, but satisfying, fungus. He wanted nothing more than to kill the man, anyway, and if he could convince others it was necessary, he might have allies who could overcome his difficulties. Yes. He might well draw in some very powerful allies to help him.

He entered the bar. It was dark and quiet, except for a minor discussion in the far corner. Rolf frowned. He disliked trouble. He had most of the Sweepers in this sector paid off, but it was never wise to attract attention. The discussion chilled quickly, as Rolf found a booth and sat down. He tapped in his order for a fruit and dairy drink, breakfast, and sat back with a flex of shoulder muscles so developed they almost obscured his neck.

Rolf liked being in shape. It gave him the power to be as cruel as he wished. He liked to hear squeaks of pain and pleading, and to see tears welling in his victim's eyes. An eye just pooling with a first teardrop of pain or terror was a truly beautiful object, luminous, shimmering with soul that no robot or other animal could reproduce. And he had created it. It was a moment that fled quickly, disintegrating into bloodshot messiness, but he was a true artist and loved his creations.

Except for Amber, of course. After those first few months, she'd never cried. Tough, like him, or she had been. True gutter slag.

Rolf swelled uncomfortably with lust just thinking of her. He'd never been able to touch her—no, that's how he'd found out about her potent defenses—but there'd never been a girl who'd excited him as much as Amber. She'd be grown now. Less desirable, but still alluring.

When the servo waiter came by, the machine found Rolf in a truly foul mood and suffered a dent for its slowness. It gyroed awkwardly back to the kitchens.

Rolf took his time with his breakfast, pondering

the day's business. He had little working at the moment, so it pleased him when the com line at his booth rang. He keyed it on.

"Good morning, Rolf."

The monitor, irritatingly, stayed dark. Rolf pursed his lips and shoved aside his beverage. He disliked anonymous callers who knew his name.

"What is it?"

"You can't see my face, but I can see yours—and I would suggest that it would be very wise of you not to show your temper with me. I'm here to help you. I understand that there is a man who took one of your operatives, a man you would like to dispose of, carefully."

As rare as people of Amber's talents were, Rolf's eyes narrowed suspiciously. This caller's suggestion was too close to his own thoughts to be taken guilelessly. "What do you want?"

"Only to help you get what you want."

"Name your price."

"Ah. Nothing's for free, is it? No, my price is what you yourself want, Jack Storm's death. He's coming to you. I've pointed him in your direction."

Rolf tensed in the booth. "Armored?"

"No."

The man relaxed somewhat, though an odd muscle in his right thigh twitched a few times reflexively. "Where is he expecting to find me?"

"Why, right where you're sitting now."

Rolf's arm jerked, the beverage container careened and splattered halfway across the room. "What?"

Laughter rang out from the dark monitor. "Relax, my friend. He won't be there for a few hours yet. You'll have plenty of time to be ready. Is it a deal, then?"

"Maybe."

"Maybe?"

Rolf smiled at the anger in the other's voice. He turned his own monitor off, saying, "Thank you for the information," and cut the com line. He would kill Jack Storm, all right, but not before extracting the information from him he needed to track the caller down. Rolf intended to pay his disrespects in person, next time.

Jack entered the Closed Circuit carefully, squinting to equalize the brightness of the street and the dimness of the bar. He had his hand on his gun as he went through the door, having watched the establishment for an hour or so first, and seeing no one else go in or come out. He'd been set up and knew he had, but also knew that it was likely Rolf was personally waiting for him. As the portal let him through, he dropped to his knees, rolled and came up in the far corner, avoiding the automatic stunner that flashed in his wake.

He let out a burst that half-melted the portal and jury-rigged circuitry flash-fired into nonexistence. Jack dodged behind a table, carrying it with him as a kind of shield.

"You're too late. The minute you walked in, you were too late." Broadcast and distorted, Jack could not read Rolf's position from his voice.

He cleared his throat. "It doesn't have to be like this."

"No, but this is the way I want it. I will have Amber back. This is the best way to do it."

"I only came to talk to you about Amber."

"Oh?"

Jack saw a movement from the corner of his right eye. He abandoned his shield with a sliding dive and watched it laser-burn behind him. He took up residence beside a more solid and hopefully burn-proof booth.

His eyes refused to adjust to the lighting. Jack cursed himself for the disability . . . he'd probably sunburned his eyes watching the too bright pavement for the last hour or so. He brought his gun close to his chin and checked the charge. Then he saw it. The servotender. Still on automatic, looking for its customer to bother it into ordering or to collect credits due. It wheeled along the floor, avoiding the smoke and ash table and made its determined way to a far corner.

It had homed in on Rolf, Jack knew. With a smile, Jack got to his knee. To disguise his awareness of Rolf's location, he called out, "I want you to let Amber go. I don't know how you triggered her, or if you did, but—"

"Oh, so that's it. People dying a little suddenly in the imperial palace? Wonder if you've got more than you can handle on your hands?" Rolf laughed. The sound system battered the waves of cruelty about Jack, but Jack cradled his gun and sighted carefully, waiting for the little servotender to wheel to a stop.

"I want you to see Amber. I want her deprogrammed."

"Really? Is there a lot of money in that?"

"Maybe. Maybe just staying alive would be enough for you."

Another laugh buffeted him. The servotender hesitated in the dark, far regions of the bar. Jack saw a privacy barrier hanging above the booth. He sighted along its fastenings.

"Amber's on automatic," Rolf said. "Maybe you'd like to know who's on the list . . . because that's the only way you'll save them, by getting to them first and killing Amber. I can stop her, if I want to. But I don't. The only thing I want to do right now is terminate you, Jack. With extreme prejudice."

Jack fired. The privacy barrier toppled, and there was a scream of anguish below it.

Jack rose. He crossed the bar. At the barrier's edge, he could see the crushed wheel of the servotender peeking out. He pulled the barrier off.

Rolf lay beneath. Jack kindled a table lamp. Its glow flickered off the crimson stream flowing from the corner of the man's mouth. Regretfully, he saw that he had miscalculated. Instead of stopping Rolf, he'd mortally injured him.

Jack rocked back on his heels.

"You don't have much time," Rolf said. A broken wheeze stopped him.

Jack reached out a hand automatically, then drew it back. "Neither do you."

"Then it doesn't matter." The man's bestial black eyes blinked rapidly. "I won't collect the final payment on Amber's terminations, however. So I'll take this as payment instead . . . the joy of knowing she's out of control and you've got no idea what to do about it, and neither does she. It'll be hell for th' bitch and she deserves it. Try to help her and you'll destroy her. You don't know the NLP."

"Are you in pain?"

Rolf's eyes narrowed at the switch in the conversation. He grimaced. "Not much."

"Then maybe you should be." Jack hunkered closer and put the barrel of his gun on Rolf's kneecap. "Tell me who her targets are and how to stop her."

The dark eyes widened with a knowing kind of fear. "Random, at first," he said, recognizing his enemy as a man capable of inflicting great pain. "To build up her strength. Then, St. Colin of the Blue Wheel. Then—" he collapsed with a bubbling, gurgling rattle, and then was quiet.

Jack removed his gun. It was too late for that, now. He looked at the dead man. He might have lived, if Jack had sent for the medics. Somehow, Jack didn't feel guilty. He stood up. A door slammed to the rear of the bar. Time to leave.

Then, he thought of Amber and St. Colin. Alone together. Allies . . . target and assassin.

He wondered if he could make it back in time.

CHAPTER 14

Pepys looked along the length of his public hall. Large wall screens displayed the throng waiting to talk to him and listening to those who'd waited before. Cameras broadcast those views not only within but without the palace, all over Malthen, and Fornex and Ipswich, the other two planets that comprised the core of the Triad Throne. Even now, as he lifted his chin to look, he could see out of the corner of his eye, a wiry, fuzzy-headed man lifting his chin to look. . . .

Pepys sighed. He was caught now, as caught between the Thrakian League and the Dominion and Bythia as he was caught on the cameras. He was truly caught on the horns of the dilemma and now the problem with Colin did him no good. He wasn't worried about Colin himself. The man was too soaked in spirituality to have been involved in the assassinations, but the girl—the girl was some-thing else. Her association with Storm worried at him like an Ipswichian sand burr and was about as easy to deal with. Could she be the killer? She was trackable when at Colin's side or at Jack's, but WP noted that she was a veritable ghost oth-erwise. Her comings and goings had been extremely circumspect. It was rumored she'd come out of under-Malthen, and that made Pepys rub a worry line across his forehead as though he wished to abrade it out of existence.

Which he probably did, fussing about his age as he did. He worried about his mortality as he waited for Colin and the girl to arrive for their meeting in his private chambers ... the most compassionate thing he could order and totally against the wishes of the WP. Pepys made a mental note that the WP was getting a little out of hand. But the assassin had to be found, and quickly, for there was no knowing who the next target would be. That was why he'd chosen the private chamber for his discussion with Colin, for Pepys had it shielded as well as he could against any kind of attack, and he had his psychics tuned in to read the thoughts and emotions of the two he was bringing in.

Not, Pepys snorted to himself, that a damn one of the psychics could actually read thoughts. Their powers had never been all that had been promised. His voice scans were probably more accurate in picking out emotional inconsistencies. Still, he was not a conservative about matters such as this. Anything would be given a try.

The Dominion representative speaking before him droned toward a halt, and Pepys took a deep breath, perpetuating the image that he'd been deeply immersed in the man's speech. This was all a formality anyway. He'd already decided to foot the deficit in the budget as it served his purpose well. Then, when the Dominion began to totter, he would step in as a strong and responsible leader. The Triad Throne would be merged with the Dominion Congress

A stroke of genius.

The representative halted, mopped his brow with a silken handkerchief, and smiled.

Pepys nodded wisely. "I will give your proposal all due consideration," he answered, "and make my response tomorrow. In the meantime, know that I'm not adverse toward your needs. The Dominion and the Triad Throne walk hand in hand, more than just providing the armed forces needed, but also advice in times of trouble."

The representative looked at him with wide, startled eyes, hooded his expression immediately and bowed before leaving. Pepys smiled. The man had just realized he might have parlayed his Congress into a very precarious position indeed . . . but too late to reset the game board now.

Now all he had to worry about was Bythia and the Thraks . . . and the damnit-all Walkers.

As if in response to his internal turmoil, St. Colin entered the hall with that blonde girl on his arm.

Pepys felt a muscle at the corner of his eye tremble. He disguised his weakness by smiling widely and standing. "Colin, right on time. Young lady," and he noted that she paled in his presence but showed no other sign of fear. "Let's retire to my chambers and get this tiresome business over with. We'll have recorders on, it won't be necessary for the WP to be there."

He stepped off the dais, his bodyguards fading discreetly away from him into the crowd, for all that battle armored men could be discreet, and led the way to his chambers.

Jack waited impatiently at the gate for authorization to get in. The WP guard looked at him critically, but then the computer/printer spit out a small badge and he handed it over.

"Authorized," was all he said, but he gave Jack a measuring look.

Jack had no doubt that Captain Drefford would be told as soon as he set foot in the elevator. He attached the badge as he entered and punched up the public audience hall.

So far all had been calm. The lift moved gently, vibrating under his boots, and Jack watched the digital count of floors and wings go by, moving horizontally as well as vertically. The door opened none too soon. Jack stepped out and got his bearings.

Amber and St. Colin. Where they here already? And if they were, was Amber still under control? Jack flicked a strand of hair from his eyes and found his forehead fringed with nervous sweat. He hesitated a moment, and then heard the scream echoing throughout the shell pink obsidite halls.

Jack turned and ran toward the sound. A man walking in the other direction rammed into him, shouldering him, and Jack recoiled from the contact, determined not to be slowed, for he recognized Amber's voice in that scream. He skidded to a halt outside the emperor's private chambers just as all hell finished breaking loose.

Amber was on her knees, Colin's head pillowed in her lap, his body curled in pain, a drop of crimson leaking from his nostril. Pepys stood over them, his hair electrically alive in a halo of worry.

"Jesus," Jack said, bracing himself in the doorway against the intrusion of other Knights and the WP.

Amber looked up. A sob caught the first word in her throat and then she stammered, "Is he dead?"

Pepys leaned over and caught the crabbed up fist of Colin in his hands and took a great deal of care smoothing the fingers out. "No," he said to Amber. "He's still got a pulse. The medics will be here any second." Then, "What did you do to him?"

"Me? Nothing! It was you, talking about the murders, and then with all that arguing about

Bythia, and their savagery, and the Walkers . . ."
Amber's voice trailed off as she realized she'd accused the emperor, and she ducked her face away, looking down as she stroked Colin's agonized face.

Drefford had shouldered his way in, and now he said with satisfaction, "The recording room and your monitors report a great deal of emotional and psychic stress, sire."

Pepys let go of Colin's hand, watching the older man labor for a breath. He did not answer.

Jack turned on his heel, remembering as if in a haze a black-suited assassin holding out a gold ocular piece in his palm. Why would he be remembering that, and why would he be remembering it now?

Then he felt his shoulder where he'd been bumped in the corridor. "Sweet Jesus," he whispered, and knew that he knew who the real assassin was.

Amber looked up. "Jack?" Her lips trembled. "I didn't—"

"I know," he said, shutting her up. The meds pushed by him and he let them into the room.

A sable-armored Knight patted the man down before letting him kneel by St. Colin. He peeled back the eyelids and read the retina pattern through his instrument, then did a few other cursory checks. He sat back on his heel. "This man's had a stroke. Let's get him out of here."

Amber relinquished St. Colin's form to the gurney and stood, wiping her hands. "Will he—will he be all right?"

"The sooner we get a biochip in to clear away the clot, the better," the medic told her as they took the fallen saint away. "But the damage looks mild."

Pepys beckoned to the two WP men standing

there. "Take her in for further questioning," he ordered.

Jack took Amber by the shoulders and moved her behind him.

Pepys frowned heavily. "May I remind you, Captain, that your oath is sworn to protect me."

The corners of Jack's mouth pulled up in a bittersweet smile as he remembered lying to give that oath. Amber leaned slightly against him, and her slight form was cold. "I saw a man in the corridors, running out, as I came in. I've seen him before on the grounds. I'd like to check him out, sir. I think the corridor camera will have caught him. I know your highness would want every circuit checked out."

The emperor's face flushed, his freckles becoming ugly blotches, and Jack could tell he did not like being caught in indecision. Then he said, "Very well." He turned and left, the curious onlookers falling away from him like waves breaking away from a rocky shore.

Amber pressed close to his back and he could feel her trembling there. "Oh, god," she said. "I did it, didn't I?"

"I don't think so," Jack said. "But proving it is another matter."

Pepys was still shaking with fury when he reached his private wing. He snatched off his robe of office and threw it on the ground before his valet could reach him. Winton stood there waiting for him.

"Your WP let another killer into the palace," Pepys said venomously. He let himself drop into a chair.

Winton bowed and stayed low, keeping his gaze on the flooring, though he wanted badly to see the look on the emperor's face, a precautionary measure like watching a cobra to see it spread its hood before it struck. "Is your highness well?"

"I'm fine. But the leader of the Walkers is not. Struck down in his prime, while we were arguing. How, I don't know. It appears to be a stroke, but—I won't tolerate it, Winton. Your security department thrives on secrecy, but it is not doing its job. That's why I resurrected the damn Knights."

"And were they of any assistance?"

"No."

Winton straightened. "Then the fault is not entirely mine."

Pepys' cat-green eyes glared at him, attempting to drill holes, and failing. "Perhaps," he said, finally. "But Captain Storm has requested the chance to investigate the incident."

Winton held himself very still. He dared not push one way or the other.

"I don't want him to," the emperor stated.

"Another assassination at this date might prove awkward. The Dominion—"

"Blast the Dominion." Pepys grabbed a paperweight from his end table and held the flawless crystal ball between his shaking hands. "I gave them the money to finance their armies. I have them, even if they don't know it yet."

"Then, may I suggest you do what you've been considering all along. The situation on Bythia demands your immediate attention. Send in the Knights, along with a full complement of the other militia. Even Jack Storm can hardly be two places at once."

"No," said Pepys, considering. "Damn you, Winton. You're forcing me into full confrontation with Colin if I do that. It's been a long time since a religious empire has struggled with a financial or political one, but it's due. Colin has the magnetism, if he has the ambition."

"I thought you said his reverence had been struck down."

"But not dead! Not dead, Winton! And his recovery should be extremely quick. He will fight me tooth and nail on Bythia; he has to, the Messiah mythos is in full bloom there, and he will not let the Triad Throne's presence disrupt what might just possibly be the event his whole religion has been waiting for. If we go to Bythia, he will, too, and that's just what I don't want."

"Or," and Winton smiled, "he could die in the civil uprising."

The emperor's private rooms grew very, very quiet.

CHAPTER 15

Jack rubbed his sleep-wearied eyes. The recorder got a few frames ahead of him; he blinked and fast reversed it until he could catch up. It was in those frames that he saw what he wanted.

The man who'd come to him as a messenger, pacing St. Colin and Amber as they followed Pepys from the audience hall to the private diplomacy chambers. The man reached up, touched St. Colin briefly on the shoulder—nothing more menacing or deadly than a clasp.

And yet he had air-needled a clot into the man's bloodstream with that touch. Jack licked his parched upper lip, thinking. He had to have. It was the only way Jack could think of to have had a stroke come on so quickly. This was the third time he'd been over the recording. He knew this was the man who, hurrying away, had bumped him in the corridor.

Sheer luck. Five corridors leading away from the action, and Jack had been in the corridor chosen as an escape route.

It would not clear all suspicion from Amber, but it would help. He tapped out a request to have these frames duplicated, adding them to the tape he'd already had made of the corridor where he'd run into the man.

Sensors had already told him that this man, like himself, carried no ID chip implant.

The world, it seemed, was full of unidentifiable rogues.

He wondered if the assassin had any connection to Winton.

Jack stretched and then looked about the small WP viewing room. He got up and flexed his shoulders, working out the kink between his shoulder blades. The room was littered with disposal cups, reeked of old coffee, and yet held nothing. All printouts were carefully secured away. All tapes. All sensor readings. The room was not the casual lounge someone wanted it to appear. And because it was not, Jack wondered if it held some of the answers he so desperately wanted. He strode across to a bank of footlockers.

He also wondered if Pepys knew what a tenuous hold he had on his own World Police Department. The department ran like a finely tuned machine, had no doubt run like that for Emperor Regis before him, and would for whichever emperor followed.

"Captain Storm? No, don't turn around. If you do, I'll be forced to kill you on the spot, and that will do neither of us any good."

Jack froze. The tense spot between his shoulders tightened further as if it could sense the target focus there. "What do you want?" He stared into the beige plastic door in front of him, eyeing a reflection that showed him only that another man stood behind him.

"I have a warning for you. The Green Shirts think it's time to remind you that you should be dead, that your job is to be a soldier in Pepys' hire, and nothing more. And if you think that you know all there is to know, think on this: do you remember the man Stash?"

"Do I?" Jack coughed out a bitter laugh. "He

nearly killed me in Lasertown." And Stash had destroyed the artifact site just outside the mines that both Thraks and Walkers desired so much.

"If you had access to WP files, you would find out that Stash had been a WP officer."

Jack felt an itch to move, and dared not. The itch grew maddening as he said, "Who sent him to Lasertown? Who did he cross?"

"No one. Pepys was not lying when he said he had an agent in Lasertown. He only lied when he said it was you."

"And I have your word on this."

"The Green Shirts have found out they have been manipulated."

"Welcome to the real world," Jack said. "What makes you think I'm going to believe you any more than I'd believe anyone else? I'm a Knight, sworn to protect and defend the emperor."

"Once, the Knights were sworn to the Dominion. Which allegiance do you think is more trustworthy?"

"Get to the point. If you have anything else to tell me, spit it out. Give me something I can use or leave me alone."

"Then one last bit of information. Claron was burned because a man named Winton ordered it, after hearing that a lost Knight was recuperating there. But there was a second reason. A Thrakian sand nest was growing, hidden, on one of the smaller continents. He got official permission to act as he did."

Jack clenched his teeth on anger so swift to boil up in him it sickened him. "Give me proof!" he said, and his voice husked in rage.

"You'll find the proof on Bythia if you can gain permission to go there. We owe you nothing now. Now we are back to square one, and you are merely a soldier between us and our target. Guard him well."

"Who are you?"

Silence behind him. Jack waited another hair twitching second, then pivoted swiftly.

The room was empty.

He looked up. The camera eye swept across him and he knew their whole conversation had been recorded. He could do nothing about it—could not reach it to destroy it.

Others would know what he'd just been told. Ultimately, the emperor himself would. And what, Jack wondered, would be the consequences of that?

Amber sat. Her muscles had long ago frozen into numbness. When she moved, it would be with agonizing stiffness and pricks of feeling returning. If she moved. She sat, her thoughts turned inward, examining herself, recoiling from what she found, and wondering if she had become a murderer.

Like some tall sentinel standing in the corner, the white battle armor hung from its equipment rack. Jack was gone, examining records at WP. In his absence, the armor appeared to watch over her meditation.

She had thought and thought and thought until it felt as though her eyeballs bled. She could find nothing within her that she hadn't put there through her life's experience, nothing that could have been Rolf instead of her. But she knew it had to be there. Knew it did! She'd been programmed to kill.

Kill, boss? Do we fight today?

Amber snapped her chin up. Her eyes watered and she moved to rub them, first one and then the other, and looked about. There was an undefinable shimmering about the armor in the corner. A chill ran down her spine. It was almost close enough to touch. Amber thought about the warrior spirit that resided within the armor, the spirit growing into an infestation which would kill to live, so that it might live to kill.

She shivered and ducked her head back down. Bogie was dead. Or if not dead, dormant. With a deep breath, Amber went back into her meditations, searching for the truth, even if it destroyed her.

The right gauntlet twitched. It moved toward her, palm down, in silent benediction.

Bogie strained toward the radiant warmth of the being sitting in front of him. He liked Amber, though Jack was Boss. He bathed in the psychic energy shining about him, tortured though its frequency was.

He was awake once more.

Winton moved quickly through the hallways, taking hidden doors that few knew about, putting as much ground between himself and the security room as he could. He wiped a sheen of perspiration off his upper lip. He could have killed the man and been rid of him ... but this way was better. Now he might well be rid of both Jack and Pepys. Once Jack acted on his instincts and the monitoring tapes were made public.

He smiled coldly and pushed forward into the bowels of the palace where his own kingdom might be found. He'd given Jack a push that Pepys would never be able to divert.

CHAPTER 16

Colin lay in his bed and stared at the ceiling of his bedroom, a little unnerved by the resounding silence of his quarters, especially now that Biggle was gone. He gripped an exercise tool in his right hand and worked on pinching it shut to bring back the strength that had been there only days ago. Open and shut. Shut and open. Despite the fact he was working only the one hand, a sheen of sweat covered his entire body, dampening his robes and the bedsheets. When he relaxed, he did so with a gasp of gratefulness.

The overhead screen upon which he fixed his gaze with an almost religious fervency spoke. "That is very good, sir. You have almost regained complete tensor strength. Are you done?"

Aching in every fiber, Colin licked his lips and tasted the sweat dripping down. "Yes," he said softly. "For now."

"Very good, sir." The screen darkened as the therapist signed off.

Colin undid the collar of fabric and sensors binding his right arm and shrugged the cuff off the bed. He was too tired to do more, and he lay back, staring at the dark screen.

"St. Colin?"

Wearily, he keyed open the com lines. "Yes? What is it, Margaret?"

His second in command, Reverend Margaret, smiled at him. The monitor screen was not flattering to her strong, squared off face, nor her years, but, he reflected, she presented as honest an image as anyone. "I'm almost done interviewing candidates for your secretary. Will you be well enough tomorrow to conduct final interviews?"

"I'd damned well better be," Colin answered. "I'm falling too far behind in my work as it is. I still don't understand why you won't send the girl out. Amber knows what she's doing even if she isn't a Walker."

Margaret's lips tightened. "Sir? She's the one who attacked you."

Colin waved his hand, weakened though it was. "Ridiculous. I know her too well."

"Perhaps." The visage wavered slightly as Margaret touched a hand nervously to her brunette hair. "I let in a visitor downstairs a moment ago, he should be there . . . he insisted."

"All right," Colin grumbled. He cut the call off, and then recognized a sound from the shadowed corner of his room, a shifting of weight. Fear gripped his aged heart for a second then, the same kind of fear he'd felt when his thoughts had exploded in a blinding headache at the palace, his body had crabbed in a spasm of pain, and he'd fallen to the floor. He took a deep breath and pushed the panic away. "Who is it?" he called out sharply.

"Don't be afraid, old friend. It's me."

Colin coughed. "I'm not afraid, Pepys, and I don't have many old friends who skulk around in corners. What are you doing here? Taking time off from the palace?"

Pepys laughed, too shallowly and too quickly,

and moved forward, sitting down on a hassock near the bed. "The scathing wit's not been damaged."

"No." said Colin, finally. He punched a button to bring himself upright, and stared at the emperor. "Nor much else."

"Good. I wanted to come sooner, but your Margaret's a better guard than most of my Knights, and at least as formidable."

Colin eyed his friend. The emperor did not look good this night. The freckles liberally sprinkling his pasty skin looked warty and troublesome. The fine, frizzy hair drooped as though all its electricity had completely discharged. There were purplish sags under the cat-green eyes. He decided that Pepys had not been sleeping well. "You can relax," he said. "The percentages are that the attack was directed at me, not you."

Pepys' pupils widened, then contracted. "I said nothing . . ."

"You didn't have to. But there has been ample opportunity to go after you, if you were the assassin's target. No . . . he aimed for me and he got me."

"Or she."

The saint shook his head. "No. No, in spite of what you may wish to think, the girl had nothing to do with it. She may even have helped me. I hemorrhaged very little in spite of the damage. I don't think that was meant to be."

"Do you think she has some latent ability as a healer?"

Colin snorted, then answered, "No! I think she got my head elevated and my blood pressure steadied as quickly as any medic could. For God's sake, Pepys. Are you still looking for a miracle worker?"

The emperor leveled his stare at Colin. "No," he

answered finally. "I think I've found him." He stood abruptly. "I've had the charges dropped against Amber. There's been contradiction in the evidence, and we've no real case against her. You'll need all your talents and then some to go into Bythia."

"What? You're giving us permission?"

"I gave it to Biggle just before he was struck down. But I'll tell you now what I cannot say at the palace. If you want to go in and investigate, you'll have to take your army in with you to do it. Don't petition my permission; I can't give it. Just take your fighters as well as your cleric philosophers and go."

"Why—"

"Because it's the only way we'll keep Bythia from the Thraks. I'm sending in a small force as well, but you might as well know what I've gone to great lengths to keep from you and your intelligence. They're savages and they're tearing each other apart and in the middle of it is a Messiah mythos that should make even you happy."

"What?" Colin's sweat had chilled, and he shivered at his friend's clipped tones. "Is that why the place is so important to you?"

"No. It's important because it's on a warp curve and anyone going through that region has got to pull out, renavigate, and go back in. If you're going to pull out of warp drive, you might as well stop and visit, do a little trading, and make it worth your while, eh? But because of the curvature, navigation has to be realigned, there's no choice. Space doesn't 'fold' evenly there."

"And that's why the Thraks want it, too."

Pepys ran a hand through his hair. "God only knows why the Thraks want it, too. They're even more acquisitive than I am. The blasted planet can hardly be farther from where they've done the most damage to the Dominion and I'll be damned if I can figure out a motive."

Colin grasped a corner of his sheets and wiped his face though most of the sweat had already cooled to a clammy coating. He looked back. "What do you want of me?"

"I want your assurance that we won't, in the end, be two kingdoms fighting against each other."

"I have no kingdom but the Kingdom of God."

Pepys swore explosively, then pinched his lips shut tightly. When he spoke again, it was in a strangled tone. "I judge you by myself, I have no choice, but I tell you this—I will not hesitate to choose myself over you if I have to, saint or not."

Without breaking the stare, Colin returned, "And I have already chosen God over you."

The emperor stood tensely another second or two, then turned away. He had nearly reached the doorway when he turned back. "See you on Bythia," he said.

Colin nodded. "Good-bye, old friend. And try to get some sleep."

Winton, sitting in front of his console, swore. The old fox had outmaneuvered him again. But at least he had advance notice that the Knights were going to be sent out with the Walkers. Storm might yet play into his hands . . . yes, every cloud had a silver lining. He reached out and keyed on his com line and waited for the impersonal features of the other to focus.

"Yes, sir?"

"Are my slides ready?"

"Yes, sir."

"Good. Penetrate the staging area. The Knights are preparing to ship out. Take care of their armor."

"It will be done."

Winton terminated the com. His grim smile grew wider. An old nemesis of the Knights was about to rear its ugly head once again. He would leave nothing to chance this time.

Last time, the wrong man had become emperor.

PART II:
BYTHIA

CHAPTER 17

He came out of cold sleep swearing, words slurred, but their time-honored slang unmistakable nonetheless, and the nurse attending him frowned and put her warm hand on his still cold forehead and shushed him into quiet. He lay under her hand and trembled uncontrollably, unable to turn away from her gaze, locked into it as though it were a homing beam and she was bringing him back to life.

Not that he had been dead, no, though he'd rather have been dead than locked into cold sleep dreams.

Jack blinked and with that movement, the nurse seemed to sense her duties were done. She removed her hand and walked to the next bay. He could hear her quiet murmuring to one of its occupants, and then her footsteps moving onward. His chilled down body continued to warm under the netting and somewhere in the crèche where he couldn't see it, he knew the dialysis lines were cleansing and gently warming his blood. He stared up at the coffinlike lid the nurse had released and felt the thrum of the orbiting ship vibrating.

His eyes blurred. No fever or reaction this time, and for that he was grateful. Down the line of the transport, he could hear a man retching, and his own insides ached in sympathy. There was a sharp sting at the back of his right knee ... the dialysis shunt being removed and the incision being swabbed. The restraints crawled back and he could sit up, if he wished.

Short term cold sleep transports were like meat wagons. His crèche was not a single bay; there were four of them packed shoulder to shoulder, although Jack seemed to be the first to revive. He sat up and threw his legs over the ledge, fierce pins and needles lancing his calves as he did so and unbidden tears springing to his eyes.

Pretending it was still the cloudiness of sleep, Jack fisted them away. He took a deep breath and stretched, feeling the same pins and needles cramp across his back muscles, then prickle away, a sensation much like having an outbreak of hives. The sheet fell off him as he sat motionless, his mind still half caught by cold-sleep dreams.

He could still see Pepys in his mind's eye, standing over them before they marched to the prep labs, giving them a talk about the duty ahead of them.

"For Rikor," he'd said, and Jack's diaphragm had contracted then with emotions for a dead planet whose name he hadn't heard in two decades. Rikor had been the first planet to fall to the Thraks, its colony and history gone to sand now. "For Rikor and New America, Calafia, and Milos. For Dorman's Stand and Blue Cluster I and Opus. We must convince the young Bythians of the dangers of courting the Thraks and of fighting among themselves. I am sending you, my Bodyguard, to guard them from themselves as you would guard me from harm."

"Hot shit," a recruit had mumbled at Jack's side. "We get to go to war!"

Indeed. Now Jack wondered only if he would be fighting Bythians or Thraks.

And if it became an out and out war, would the Knights be abandoned once again?

The ship shifted. Jack braced himself on the bay's ledge, then stood. He reached up among the overhead lockers to the one marked with his name and insignia and pulled out fresh clothing. His fingers were still slightly cold and even the stored clothing felt warm to his touch as he held the dark Blues between his hands for a moment. Then he dressed quickly and made a reservation at the gym for a workout. The sooner he got cold sleep out of his system, the better.

He went by way of the equipment hold, just off the shop, where the racks swayed with armor, each squeezed in tightly to the next. He would have preferred to ship Bogie in his own trunk, but space here was a precious commodity and there had been no allowance for the extra weight and dimensions of the carrying trunk. Jack fought off a shiver. He felt as though he'd left the suit exposed and vulnerable to tampering, but the transparent cages showed no signs of entry since they'd been packed at the dock and loaded. He checked the lock, intuition pricking at the tiny hairs along the back of his neck, felt nothing, and turned away.

Wake up, damn you, wake up. Tell me who I am.

Perhaps it would never be as important again who he'd been, as who he was going to be. Or where. On Bythia, he might find the damning information he needed to shame Pepys into terraforming Claron. The Green Shirts had all but accused the emperor of the ignominious act. This time he wouldn't be stopped. He looked forward to being melded with Bogie's warrior spirit again, mowing down the enemy.

Like women, he thought. You can't live with it, and you can't live without it.

And thinking of that, he thought of Amber.

They woke Amber after reaching Bythia and settling into the new quarters set aside for the Walker prelates. She awoke in a bed chamber, too warm in the crèche blanket she was wrapped in, her dark honey-colored hair damp with sweat, as a cool, exotic smelling breeze wafted over her. She sat up, shedding the blanket.

There were no windows in this inner room, off a courtyard, and no walls, just graceful columns holding up the roof. Amber got up, felt a little wobbly, and leaned against one momentarily. The courtyard was tidy though covered with greenery and flowers planted in swirling patterns of color, which drew one naturally to the fountain in the center.

She knew she was on another world when she saw the rearing creature whose horned forehead formed the water spout. She'd never seen anything like it . . . saurian and ugly, yet graceful. Her head whirled. She tilted it back, and, looking up, saw the rolls of gauzy curtains that would be lowered for privacy in the evening. A flicker of gray-green across the curtain . . . she caught a glimpse of a darkened, winglike thing fluttering through the air, a pink tongue lashing out, and then a lizard scampering back to safety among the curtain's folds, an insect wing still poking out from the corner of his mouth. Everything was so different from Malthen.

Bells tinkled. Turning, she saw another, heavier, curtain lifting to one side. The bells implanted in its hem jingled to herald the approach of another, and St. Colin's smile met her gaze.

"Awake at last?"

"And hungry!"

"Hungry! Is that all you think about?"

Amber's eyes lowered and she examined the floor contritely. "No." But it was among the first. She'd learned hunger the hard way, in the gutters and back alleys of under-Malthen. She looked up. "When can I talk to Jack?"

"It'll be another couple of days."

"You mean we got here first?"

"Yes. A cold ship moves a little slower. We'll be busy, don't you worry . . . I have preliminary field surveys to set up, then reports to examine, plus I have to get these offices staffed." Colin paused. "there's a war going on here, but it's a way from this city yet." He took a deep breath, and Amber could tell his thoughts before he spoke them. "The air even smells different, doesn't it?"

Amber nodded. She hugged her last swaddling blanket about herself, a little afraid at being so far from Jack.

"Better shower then. They use real water here, but the plumbing is a bit odd. You'll figure it out for yourself. Oh, and there're house lizards running about—"

"I know. I saw one."

"Just so you know. They evidently keep the insect population down. We'll have a vaccination schedule set up later this evening." He turned to go and, framed by the softly tinkling curtain, stopped at her words.

"Colin . . . I want to thank you."

His head turned to face her. "For what?"

"Believing I didn't do it. For bringing me along, so I wouldn't be too far from Jack."

He smiled gently. "I don't have to be thanked for believing something I know. I know you, Amber. Hard when you want to be, soft as honey when you don't want to be. You weren't the assassin that struck against me. And if you hadn't been there, I've no doubt the neurological damage would have been massive. I thank you. As for Jack ... I don't think either of us wants him to get too far out of reach. There's something about the man. . . ."

As she smiled, he ducked back and left, his words trailing along after him. "Shower and dress quickly. Follow your nose to the dining room!"

Amber showered warily. The feel of water raining upon her body brought back old memories of another world she'd shared with Jack, a world of much rain. She and Jack had nearly died there at Rolf's hands. She thought now that she had been torn when she'd heard about Rolf's death. Torn between despair and satisfaction. Despair because he was the only one who could have undone what had been done to her and satisfaction because there was no one she'd rather have seen dead, unless it was the ghostly Winton who haunted Jack's past and future.

She toweled off. There was a sound in the outer room, a sound that was both unfamiliar and menacing. Amber darted through the door. She was not even aware of what she was doing until it had been done.

The tiny green lizard dropped from the curtain, limp and lifeless, its jaws open in agonized death, eyes popped from its skull and blood running in a river from the empty sockets. It fell at Amber's feet.

She began to shake and recoiled from the carcass which had once been limber and graceful but was now twisted into rigid death. Amber forced herself to stand still. She eased a bare toe forward and nudged the carcass. Yes, it was dead. No doubt about it.

She wondered if it had been a house pet. Bending swiftly, she pinched it up by its tail and threw it out into the garden, unable to face questions about it if she left it in her room. With a corner of the discarded shroud from her cold sleep, she wiped up the blood which was not crimson but more of a pinkish orange. She returned to the bathroom, looking for the Disposall. There was nothing in the sink or pipes or drains remotely resembling one. "Oh, shit," Amber said. Then she smiled grimly, tore off the bloody rag and threw it down the toilet. She flushed it, hoping that she wasn't stopping up the primitive system for the whole household.

It wasn't until she sat down on the low bed that she began to quiver all over. It wasn't her fault she'd killed it—she'd heard the unfamiliar rustling form the curtains in the other room and she'd reacted before she even had a thought about it.

Amber raised her face from her hands. She looked up at the plastimirror across the room, small and oval, barely big enough to frame her head and shoulders. She scowled. "Right, bitch," she told herself. "It scared you. But if it scared you so bad, why didn't you just pick up a shoe and beat it to death? Why did you shoot it out of midair . . . with your brain?"

The enormity of the situation silenced her a moment. Then Amber got up and dressed swiftly, carelessly, stopping now and then to press the back of her hand to her mouth in horror.

The smallish man worked in the kitchen, washing unfamiliar vegetables and keeping an eye on the even more unfamiliar meat roasting on a spit. A series of well-angled mirrors on the roof were doing the roasting, beaming down a concentrated stream of light not unlike that of a laser. He'd been told Bythia was new, relatively uncivilized and unchallenged, but what he'd found here so far belied that. It was as though, having tried the more technical methods of doing something, the Bythians had retreated to the more natural. The roast being done, he shuttered the mirrors.

He chopped up a large orangish root and dropped it into a kettle of boiling water, wincing as the steam scalded his hand. He was not here to make judgments on the intelligence surveys of his employer. He was here for one purpose and one purpose only: a realistic assassination attempt on St. Colin of the Blue Wheel. For what reasons, he had not asked. Nor did he intend to succeed beyond an attempt. The death of St. Colin would not put into motion the particular wheels of his own ideological plans. Therefore, a paycheck was just a paycheck.

And he was in the process of earning it when a willowy young lady stepped into the kitchen's doorway.

He paused in midsprinkle, his hand filled with spices and herbs poised over a savory vegetable casserole in its individual dish. That she was beautiful, he noticed immediately, that she was human followed on its heels. He relaxed slightly though he was careful not to let her see the spice mixture he now had fisted in his hand. He recognized her as the secretary Colin had kept running for the past three days.

"What can I do for you, memsa?" he asked.

She smiled hesitantly. "Dinner smells good. Are you the cook?"

"'One of them. The other is out tonight." He felt uneasy. He had not wanted to be caught until the dish was presented to Colin. Otherwise, the implication, as Winton had explained it to him, would be lost. "I will be serving in a few minutes."

"That's all right. I came in to help. We're working in the library and Colin said you wouldn't know, and we didn't want the food sitting around and getting cold. Is that for Colin?" And she reached for the poisoned casserole.

He froze.

She took a long inhalation, and then she stiffened, too. "What's in this?" she asked casually, and he knew her tone of voice to be entirely too casual.

"Shit," he said, as he reached for a carving knife.

Amber moved quickly, shifting across the room before he could take aim. He stumbled as he felt a blinding flash across his mind, through his thoughts, and wondered if he'd stumbled through the cooking beam. Then, realizing he'd shut it down and couldn't have, and at almost the same instant that he'd not live to collect his last paycheck, he hit the floor.

She stood poised over him one last second before letting out a sharp cry of fear and agony.

She'd killed again.

Amber grasped the little cook by the ankles. She closed her eyes for a moment, gathering her thoughts. She couldn't let Colin see this. And Jack's ship was landing that night, he'd be here soon, just to check in. Amber's hands snapped open as though sprung. She quickly went over the body for ID, money, jewelry, anything to identify him. All she could tell from his outward state was that he was not Bythian, and he was definitely dead.

She pulled a tiny scrap of microfiche from deep in the lint of a pocket. Without even taking it to the reader in the corner, where the cookbooks and household lists were stacked, she groaned. She knew what it was. An ID chip. Amber held it up to the skylight, afraid to take it to the reader which would read it, all right, and leave a record of what it had seen.

The infinitesimally small letters were barely perceptible. Amber frowned. She was not sure she'd seen what she thought she'd seen. She didn't recognize the emblem. With a muffled noise of self-disgust, she threw the chip into a sack of leavings that passed for a Disposall. Then she grasped the ankles of the little cook.

She couldn't leave him here. There was only one thing she could do with him. Wild beasts ranged the city gates at night, scavengers of the garbage dumped there. The garbage was already neatly sacked. All she had to do was arrange a small accident for this cook. Perhaps he'd fallen from the city walls when slopping the scavengers.

Or perhaps one of them had gotten bold enough and torn him down.

Amber shuddered at the idea. When she had enough momentum for the body to slide smoothly after her, she reached out with her right hand and snared the slop bag. She'd have to dispose of the poisoned casserole too. It wouldn't do for the assassin to succeed posthumously. Colin wouldn't notice her being gone for long minutes yet. The saint went into almost ecstatic meditations in the library over the field survey records. She had time, if she had the nerve.

And she had to have. She'd never survive another investigation. Never.

With another heave, Amber got the body over the kitchen sill and outside into the night.

She never noticed a man watching the Walker

dormitories from across the grounds, his body shadowed in the corner.

Drefford smiled grimly to himself. He made a note on his keypad to contact Winton as soon as his watch was over. This was the break they'd been waiting for. Meantime, he aimed his pocket camcorder and filmed the entire sequence.

CHAPTER 18

It was dark in the hold. Dark and cold. Bogie struggled with his growing awareness, trying to amuse himself by tracing the suit circuitry that was far more complete and intricate than his own circulatory and nervous system. He waited for Jack. Jack completed him. Jack gave him warmth and salt and water . . . life. Bogie worried a little then. He also wanted blood and other nutrients from Jack, but had kept himself from burrowing inward for it. He sensed he could harm Jack in that way.

In a split second of amusement, he encountered another life. Bizzare and deadly. Growing rapidly. In a split second, Bogie found himself fighting for survival on a plane that was little more than microbiotic. He felt himself pulled down and rended. He fought absorption and death desperately and wondered where Jack was, and what would become of him if he lost.

"Jeeze," Sergeant Lassaday said, looking at the view screen. The three-sixty view of Bythia swooped about them as the ship came in on a decaying orbit, and the planet's surface loomed closer and closer. They skimmed below the clouds, and the movement of the ship, buckling and vibrating against the atmosphere, shook them all.

Lassaday had been Jack's D.I. for the emperor's

revival of the armored bodyguard. He was bald as an egg, tanned deep space brown, with heavy bags under skeptical black eyes. Built like a squat, granite mountainside, the sergeant stood with his feet slightly apart, braced against the transport's movement. He peered avidly at the view screen, then swore again.

"What is it?" Jack asked.

"They've lied to us again, bucko. That's fracking what." He turned to one side and took a heavy drag off a drugstick, blue-gray smoke trickling out of his nostrils.

Jack looked back to the screen. Coming in at this speed, he couldn't see much of the landscape. Brown and green and blue flashed by him, around and past him. "Tell me."

The sergeant measured him with a look. "Th' hills," he said, "Bucko. Look at the hills. Even the high mountains."

Jack frowned. "I don't—"

"Rounded," Lassaday said. "Not a sharp peak among them. Th' wind and th' rain's been at 'em too long. Snow and ice, too, likely. This is an old world, an old, old world . . . and I'll give you my nuts if that warring civilization down there is much younger."

Jack closed his eyes a moment. Then he opened them and straightened. "Form an opinion after we land, sergeant. It might be more accurate." He left the man's side, but a low, humorless laugh followed him.

"Yes, sar," the sergeant said.

The scent of blue-gray smoke touched Jack mockingly as he left the viewing hold. He made his way to the equipment hold. It had become a nervous obsession for him to check it several times a waking period, sometimes more. He couldn't tell himself why he did, except that it had become nearly impossible for him to function if he didn't. Frowning, he entered the hold, unhappy at being at the mercy of his compulsion. He leaned over the lock.

A faint red light blinked, showing the integrity seal of the lock had been broken. Jack backed up a step and swore.

Someone had opened the lock.

He forced himself forward again and looked keenly through at the equipment. Nothing appeared damaged or tampered with. No suits were missing, although Jack would not have been surprised at that, considering the black market on battle armor. Nothing seemed amiss.

Perhaps it was that which bothered him the most. Sabotage, to be successful, had to be undiscoverable. If anything had been sabotaged, it was successful at this point and there was little he could do about it.

Thinking this, Jack turned away. If he were considering sabotage, then he had to consider that someone among them was the culprit. Who would he pick? Who could he suspect? No one, as yet. His fist balled, then opened. He would tell Kavin. The Purple should be aware of it even if nothing else could be done. When they rigged for the first time, he'd have his men look for damage.

He came up sharply in the corridor as he ran into another knight. The young man looked up, his white-blond hair cut short in front and long in the back, thick, spiked white-blond hair and eyes the deepwater blue of a bottomless pool. This was the man who'd made the desperate, last-ditch attempt to stop him at the demonstration.

"Captain, sir," he said and came to a stiff halt.

"At ease," Storm murmured. The man's name came to him. "Rawlins, isn't it?"

"Yes, sir."

"What can I do for you?"

"Commander Kavin," and the younger one stumbled a little over Purple's newly found name, "is looking for you."

"Good. Where is he?"

"In the Officers' Lounge, sir."

Storm's mouth twitched at that. The lounge was a closet someone had cleaned out, thrown a few chairs and a table in, and dubbed that. Its only advantage was its proximity to the liquor storage area and the galley. Cold beer made a short run to the lounge. The only way to get it quicker would be to sleep next to the storage kegs. He nodded. "Thank you, Rawlins. I'm on my way."

There was a light that flickered deep in those endlessly blue eyes. "Sir!"

Storm brushed past him, then paused. "What is it?"

"I know it's early yet. Purple—ah, Commander Kavin—told me you'd be picking your team when we landed and found our quarters but, ah, well, sir, I'd like to be your second lieutenant, sir." The young man's face fairly shone as he said what was on his mind.

How long had it been since he'd run up against such blind idealism and excitement? Storm stood a moment as though held in thrall peering into a mirror, looking at himself twenty-five years ago, but his youth would be a poor copy of this boy—his own hair much darker blond, almost muddied, and his eyes sun-faded with squint marks at the corners from too much wind and laughter. Then he shook himself mentally as he realized that Rawlins eagerly awaited his answer. He nodded. "I'll think about it."

"Very good, sir. That's all I can ask." Rawlins saluted again.

Storm moved past him in the corridor and on up to the lounge, his mind clouded with faint memories—and he paused for another second, poised in the cubbyhole's doorway, as he wondered which memories were real and which had been implanted.

"Damnit, Storm, don't just stand there, you're blocking the beer run. We've got this down to a fine science and the timing is to the millisecond." Kavin shouted good-naturedly at him over the tiny round table that brimmed with empty glasses. "Glad you could make it."

The commander swept aside a few disposables to make room for Jack. Others had been there and left and now only the two of them were there, along with the invisible beer runner, somewhere in midshuttle.

"What is it?"

Kavin leaned back in his form hugging chair and put both heels up on the table. His silvery hair gleamed in the low power illumination of what had been intended to be a closet. But his brown eyes weren't dim. He'd had a drink or two, that Jack could tell, but he'd never known the commander to get drunk. Kavin eyed him. "How long have we known each other?"

"Long enough, I'd say."

"The mercenary code. A man protects your back once and that's all you have to know about him."

Jack grinned and set his own heels up. "Something like that."

"You never asked about what Scott told the emperor."

"I figured you'd tell me if you wanted me to

know." He shrugged. "If not, I already knew enough about you."

Kavin smiled as the beer runner ducked in with two ice cold bottles and left. Jack had a fleeting thought that they were lucky to live in a time when ship's gravity could be maintained throughout an entire flight. They popped the caps off and clinked the necks together.

"To soldiers."

"To soldiers," Jack echoed. He took a long drink. "Only once did I ever wonder about you," he said to his commander.

"Oh, yeah? When was it?"

"Where were you when I got hijacked to Lasertown?"

Kavin's smile went lopsided. "I followed you," he said. "I got as far as Ng's cold sleep lab and killed the son of a bitch for his troubles."

"What? I was told his employer did it for botching the job."

"Probably would have. I beat 'em to it. Couldn't get him to tell me where you went, though. Sorry."

They tilted their bottles back again. Jack felt better than he had in a long time.

"Thanks," he said.

"Don't mention it. You'd have done the same for me." Kavin slapped his bottle down and sat up, suddenly alert.

"What is it?"

Kavin shook his head.

"What is it?" Jack repeated.

"Listen."

He did. Then he felt it ... the vibration of the ship's orbit. They were coming in gradually—it would be another hour before they hit dirtside, but now he felt the inconsistency of the motion.

Barely perceptible. Only veteran mercenaries like Kavin and himself might notice it.

"Shit. We're in evasive maneuvers."

"Right. What do you say we pick a few of our best and brightest and suit up?"

The ship shuddered. Jack looked at his friend. "That was a burst. I'd say you're a little late."

They surged to their feet. Kavin activated the intercom just inside the door sill.

"The following personnel meet at the suit lockers. Lassaday, Abdul, Pickett, Hernandies, Peres, Sax—"

"Rawlins," Jack suggested.

"And Rawlins." Kavin's voice had just finished echoing throughout the corridors when the general quarters alarm went off.

Jack and Kavin were already halfway to the equipment hold. They took a running leap through a closing bulkhead, somersaulted back onto their feet. Jack slid down the last corridor, his commander on his heels. Lassaday was already there, lock ripped off the crate.

Storm looked at it and knew that whatever evidence he had of tampering was gone. He put the idea out of his mind and reached for Bogie, splitting open the seams and suiting up as the hold filled with the Knights called for, the veteran and the novice, all of them without question reaching for their battle armor.

Abdul came in last, sweat dotting his brown skin from the exertion of opening the bulkhead manually and reclosing it. He flashed a grin at his commander and said, "Jesus, boss, they're firing at us."

"That we know." Lassaday stumbled, getting his other leg into the armor. "Tell us something we don't."

"Awright, sergeant. It's not the Thraks—it's the Bythians. One of the splinter factions, just south of the equator. That's why we ain't been hit yet. They're poor shots."

Jack paused, helmet in hand. Little twinges of power warming up arced at his wrists. "The Bythians?"

"That's right." Abdul's voice faded as he shrugged into his armor. His face popped back out. "They might not have done it yet, but their technology is good enough to at least try knockin' us down!"

Lassaday shot Jack an almost feral look of "I told you so" which Jack cut short by donning his helmet.

Primitive barbarians with tracking and deep space technology. He bit his lip and keyed on his holograph and com lines.

Kavin faced him. He wore the latest in armor now, but its grayed skin had been overglazed with a faint mauve tone, in deference to the battered antique which had been first his brother's and then his. Jack could not see the face behind the sunscreened helmet visor, but heard the voice clearly.

"Shall we try the drop tubes?"

Jack felt the adrenaline surge. He hadn't been to war in two decades as a Knight of the Dominion. "Yes, sir. I'll get the com and tell them we want coords." He switched frequencies while Kavin stayed on the main line. He was telling the others, Jack knew, what they were going to do. The new recruits had practiced this. One or two, as former mercenaries, had even done it. It was, Jack reflected, like making love: never as good or as scary as the first time. As he waited for an answer, he watched the others shrug into their field packs, containing parasails and other essentials.

"Bridge here."

"This is Captain Storm. Commander Kavin says we're not going to take being fired upon. Give us coords, and bring us in. We're using the drop tubes. I want you to finish your landing pattern after we've dropped, and send back a troop hovercraft for us, got that?"

The pilot sputtered a moment, then said, "Yes, sir!" with a kind of fierce joy. The ship rocked even as he keyed off.

The drop tubes were little more than jury-rigged. Ten of them lay ready and the nine Knights loaded in. Jack felt the pressure lock flex at his end of the tube and sensed, more than felt, the inward lock circulating. He could see nothing in the drop tube. His outside cameras were unable to function, and his face was locked into a forward only view by the helmet.

But he could feel. And he could hear. Someone wordlessly murmured a low chant.

Lassaday said, "Shut up, Abdul."

Silence then. Someone sneezed. Jack felt himself smiling. His body tremored in compulsion, the anxiety of a well trained athlete waiting to be sprung into action. He felt his heart pound, then settle into a steady beat.

And, god help him, he felt Bogie.

Boss. It grazed him, flickered across his mind briefly, like an internal breeze, cold and chilling where it touched.

"I'm right here, Bogie," he answered mentally.

Nothing. It was gone. He searched after it, but the elusive spark stayed out of his reach.

Jack hadn't had time to strip down to the clothing he usually wore in armor, and his shirt was soaked. If he had time, he'd pull his arms out of the sleeves and rip the shirt off—

The bridge broke in to the circuits, saying, "Launch in twenty seconds, gentlemen. Good luck."

The drop tubes shifted, angling their trajectory. Jack felt like bracing himself, but it was useless. He was already being held in the tube's embrace.

"Ten, nine,—"

"Oh, shit," a young voice broke in.

"Seven, six, five—"

"I'll give my nuts to the first lad to make a kill," Lassaday said.

"Who'd want your nuts?" he was answered derisively, even as the tube shuddered, and they were slung into the air.

The sky was plum-colored. It swept past his visor in a blinding panorama, as they plunged through it. Propelled by the tubes, and weighed down by the armor, they plunged toward earth with a whistling intensity. Jack put a hand up to his parasail rigging and counted with Kavin as the commander said, "Target in sight, ready the pull-ropes, and guide yourself in. Prepare to do it one-handed, we're going to go in firing. Steady now . . . OPEN!"

His field pack jerked viciously as the parasail came out and caught the wind. Around him, other armor came to a swinging halt and then aggressively took the breeze, and they rode a thermal in.

Jack had four light missiles on his gauntlet. "I've got them on my grid, but they're slightly out of range."

"Let's salute them anyway," Kavin answered.

He fired two quickly, covering their descent, for the rookies were making no move to fire. Kavin's armor stalled and dropped behind and above them.

"Got a problem, Jack. They're too green to drop in well."

"I understand." Jack did. There were four suits

of armor hanging back . . . too inexperienced with the parasails or maybe just too scared to go in. He spotted Rawlins below and underneath him, diving in recklessly, too low and too fast. Same problem, different reaction. Jack squeezed his parasail rigging together, partially collapsing the sail and going in after him.

With a whoop, Lassaday's mottled green armor joined them and Jack realized the sergeant figured they were going down aggressively. The plum sky exploded into crimson and black, the explosion buffeting Jack. The Bythians had retargeted onto them.

Lassaday muttered, "Get that son of a bitch first."

"I've used two of mine. Have you got the stingers to do it?"

"Got one, son, and that's all I need." Lassaday's parasail careened away from them.

Kavin came in over a circuit that suddenly rang with static. "God damn, what are you three kids doing?"

"Taking out the enemy," Jack said grimly. He said to Rawlins, as green hills came up under them, and he could see the enemy lines, "Get ready to collapse your rigging. Start firing as we go down, remember to hit and roll, and for god's sake, remember you've got a suit on!"

Bythia was beautiful. He had time for that one thought, as Lassaday's stinger arced toward the enemy installation and the horizon exploded in dirt and flames, metal shards and wood chips. *Earth, air, fire, and water,* Jack thought. *The elements of life—and death.* He opened up his right glove, pointed and let go the laser burst as infantry rushed them. The parasail rigging tore away as it was supposed to, and the suit plunged to the ground.

Grunts, all around him, as they landed heavily, the armor taking up the shock as they rolled and then came back up on their feet. Abdul forgot about the suit translating his muscular action, and overcorrected, somersaulting across the field, tearing up landscaping as he went. Lassaday buffeted him to a stop and righted him. Kavin's armor bounced gracefully next to Jack's, but they were wide of the landing perimeter. The two of them turned and found several hundred infantry surrounding them.

They never had a chance. Jack and J.W. went back to back without a word, and raised their gauntlets.

"They don't know what they're facing," Jack muttered.

"Keep on target," his friend and commander answered grimly.

"They're carrying projectiles, but I don't see any anti-armor."

"Keep on target!"

Jack's brows dripped with sweat. He ducked his head forward, wiping it off on the targeting grid. It blurred a little, but at least he could see now. The infantry closed in, tightening the ring.

"They mean to take us out," Jack said.

"Power up," was Kavin's answer.

"NOW!" They both cried simultaneously as weapons they recognized as deadly trained in on them. Laser fire silently bled across the air as they pivoted back to back in a precision dance of death. The Bythians went down in a bloodied, smoking heap, charring their death into the forest floor. The two Knights stepped over them and formed a wing with their seven companions.

"All right," said Kavin grimly. "Let's quit playing

around. Hit your power vaults, I want to be on 'em before they know we can run."

Jack toggled the switch and the suit hummed at his fingertips. They ran, taking the ground in fifteen foot strides, bounding across the plain, at the lines and quarters of the Bythian encampment beyond the hill. He could see a sudden bustle of activity. Shell fire exploded before them.

Lassaday laughed. "They can't get our range!" Even as the tough little sergeant exclaimed, a dark shell arced the sky, aiming right at him.

Rawlins made a clean shot, exploding the shell in midair. The three of them ran through a rain of metal and flame. Out of the smoke and darkness a machine came roaring at them. Jack vaulted over it, pivoted and blasted it with his next-to-last stinger.

"What was that?"

"A tank, I think. Or something like that. They're homing in on us." Jack didn't finish his sentence, as a line of the house-big machines reared above them. Dust and ash filled the plum-colored sky, along with the view of unstoppable traction treads.

Kavin, Rawlins, Peres and Jack vaulted. Jack landed on top of the machine, wrenched its turret off and spewed enough laser fire inside to barbecue either inhabitants or circuitry. As the tank ground to a halt under him, he saw one go up in smoke, another roll helplessly to its side, and a fourth undergo the same treatment he'd given his.

As Jack jumped down, he reflected that he'd probably killed more than a hundred so far and had yet to see a Bythian's face. He'd not been looking, any more than he would have looked to see Thrakian faces.

He licked his lips and hesitated a moment. He

saw a line of soldiers up on the ridge. Kavin and the others were charring a flanking maneuver.

He had to leave them something, even if only to carry the tale of a slaughter. He saw a massive battery of machines that could only be the last of their artillery works. He pointed and fired his last stinger at close range. The roar muffled his systems and he could not hear for a few minutes.

When the smoke and dust cleared, the Bythians, the living among the dead, were facedown on the blasted hillside in fear and surrender.

Kavin stepped forward. He wrenched off his helmet and took a deep breath of war-choked air.

"Gentlemen," he said. "Welcome to Bythia."

CHAPTER 19

"The troopship is setting down at the South Quarter," Colin said, sticking his head into the library, returning after being called away by one of the prelates.

Amber's attention immediately dissolved from the aerial maps she'd been examining. "Jack?"

"He's supposed to be on it. I'm going out to meet it—the local high priest will be there to scourge it."

The girl frowned. Bythians were a strange people, alien in thought as well as sex to her. She stood up, drawing her hand through her hair to separate the tangles gained during long hours of study and to tuck loose strands behind her ears. "What does that mean?"

"It means," Colin said, ducking inside and grabbing her hand, "that I get to see something I've only heard about. The scourge is supposed to be a cleansing ritual."

"I still don't understand why they didn't come in on the transport with the others," Amber complained as Colin steered her toward the outside.

"I'm told they had a skirmish at one of the trouble spots." Colin added, "Rumor says the Bythians fired at them coming in. Kavin just couldn't wait to get his armor on."

"They were fired on coming in?"

170

"That's what I heard."

She paused as they went through the heavy tapestry that concealed the main doorway. At her back, a hundred small bells shivered from their passage as the full force of Sassinal, Bythia, hit her.

It was in the air, dancing in every breeze, the light, exotic scent of another world, even in the plum-colored horizon which would curtain the night like port wine when the sun went down. She smelled grasses and flowers, and trees brushed close to the concrete and stone villa, giving off new fragrances with every touch of their leaves.

Amber wondered briefly if the Bythians smelled as she did, or with greater or lesser capability. Did she smell to them? Or did the ever present war so color their perceptions that only fragrance could distance them from it?

Colin tugged at her hand, his deep blue robes shaking impatiently with the movement. "Come on, girl, I don't want to miss this."

Remembering that religion was rightly the passion of the saint's life, Amber uncurled into action and joined him as he strode away toward the South Quarter. She fought not to squint under the curious glances of the Bythians as they passed them in the wide streets. Polite and cool, but ever so curious, with their sideways eyes and colorful markings, the people of no-sex (or was it just one sex?) brushed by. Their dry skins oozed a musky fragrance barely hidden under the scents they affected. More than once, Amber ducked away as though jolted as she smelled—what was it? Anger? She thought it must have been. Tattoolike markings they seemed to have been born with swirled over every inch of visible skin. They walked upright but with a sinuous grace no human could hope to emulate, and they wore delicate, fluttering strands of cloth instead of hair.

Like strands of silk, finely woven and almost as thin as the breeze they bannered on, the cloth fluttered from turbanlike headdresses. No two were alike; indeed, as Colin had told her, no two Bythians were alike unless one were an offspring of the other, and then the youngling would be a miniature version of its parent, with the exception, perhaps, of its headdress.

And so they wove through the crowd, Jonathan, their bodyguard, running to catch up with them, and Amber wondered which citizen of Sassinal it was who had seen her murder the cook.

At her thought, her jaws clenched and throat tightened until she could scarcely breathe. She'd thought the assassin dead and gone, but his body had been found torn to shreds outside the city walls, his fist still closed about the deadly herbs he'd been about to kill Colin with—and forensics had shown he'd been alive until the surfas, the wild scavengers, had gotten to him. Amber's eyes clenched shut a moment in agony.

She'd thrown him over *alive*.

But she hadn't known! And even if she had, she might have done it. Knowing that did not make her feel any less guilty or ashamed.

And the message that had arrived secretly for her that morning worsened the ordeal past bearing.

She'd been seen. But by whom and what did they want from her? She was divided by her need to search the streets for eyes that might meet hers and her fear that she would find that being. For if she found the blackmailer she knew she would have to kill again.

Jonathan, puffing as he jogged in his great black boots and voluminous Walker robes, his hand-carved cross bouncing up and down on his chest, began to slow. The young reverend rolled an eye at her and Amber smiled in spite of her fear and guilt. "Out of shape, Jonathan? What did you do, eat your way to Bythia instead of sleep?"

The dark-haired man blushed, his face already reddened. He was a big, square man with a small, round belly that might expand with his years like the girth of a growing tree. Or it might not.

Colin laughed and squeezed Amber's hand. "Don't tease," he said, but his admonishment was offset by his own laughter.

They slowed as the low, thunderlike rumbling of the hovership coming in over their heads made conversation impossible and began to whip a wind about them.

Colin looked up. "There's Storm," he said.

Something in the tone of his voice made Amber turn and look at the older man.

They squeezed into the South Quarter with what seemed half the population of Sassinal. The merchants and free miners were out in force, cheering the arrival of fellow humans with a lusty enthusiasm. Bythians left them a wide passageway, giving off scents, as Amber wondered if the fragrances were fear, respect, or hate again, and then realized the emotions were probably as individual as their skin markings. Each a separate nation unto its own, she thought, and fell in behind Colin and Jonathan as they edged toward the landing platform. Her own guts clenched in fear. Which one of them knew what she'd done, and would she be revealed to Jack and St. Colin? She'd never be able to explain to Jack this time.

The bizarre sight of the High Priest made Amber forget her fear and catch her breath in wonderment. He stood at the edge of the platform (he, she thought, though such a sex did not exist), his head-dress pluming above, silken robes revealing his plum-swirled gray skin. About his wrists and trousered ankle cuffs were miniature headdresses, giving him "feathers" at ankle and hand. She had never seen skin tattoos the color of the Bythian sky. Was this what gave him the distinction to be the High Priest or was it something more? He was involved in a chant, with his hands moving like graceful birds in sign, but he stopped suddenly, and turned to look at them, and a deadly silence fell over the crowded South Quarter.

What had it been? Had he smelled them? Amber's stomach clenched again. *Holy shit*, she thought. *He's looking right at me. Can he smell what I did?*

There was no doubt. Those jewel-toned eyes of bright emerald were tangled in her own gaze and for a moment, Amber felt as though he could reach in and rip her soul right out of her skin.

It occurred to her that perhaps that was what she needed. Her head became light, and the ground moved dizzyingly under her feet.

Jonathan said, "I think he wants to speak with you, sir."

Colin stirred beside Amber. "I hope so," he answered softly. "Can you get us closer?"

The bodyguard shrugged, but even as he indicated doubt, the crowd opened and fell away to let the foreigners meet the holy man. As Colin moved forward, the hovercraft shuddered to a halt, its engines began winding down, and heat roiled about those standing near the platform's edge.

The High Priest had a sloping snout nose, and like all Bythians, had his mouth built into the underside of it. He smiled though, a facial expression Amber could not remember having seen before. She shuddered, Colin's and Jonathan's bulk hiding her, but convinced the alien watched her.

The High Priest gave a contortion of a bow. Speaking in Standard, he said, in a dry, rustling voice, "Welcome. I am most pleased to be greeting with you. Are you granting absolution?"

Colin bowed back, a clumsy mimicry. "No," he answered. "I'm only here to meet friends. I, however, am pleased to meet you as well."

An unfelt breeze stirred the plumed cloth strands of the headdress. The Bythian blinked, a drawing together of his eyelids from side to side. The High Priest said only, "They have killed."

A gasp and murmur through the crowd. How fast, Amber wondered, did gossip and news reach them? How had the priest known of the defensive action?

Yet she was not surprised he did. She shifted weight uneasily on the platform. A hold door cranked open beyond. She should be looking for Jack, but the priest held her focus. She could not wrench her gaze away.

Colin answered, "In my religion, it is God himself who gives absolution. I can only give ease and advice."

The priest nodded briskly. "I understand. I can only give so much until the Holy Fire is called up."

"I have heard . . ." Colin said carefully, as though weighing his words, "of destiny calling. And scourging."

Another gasp, and a trilling through the crowd. The priest stood tensely. Jonathan made a nearly imperceptible movement and Amber realized he was baring his holster.

"Such matters," the priest said, "are not spoken

of in the streets. The Holy Fire that cleanses all souls is beyond my humble power."

Colin bowed again, saying, "I'm sorry. I did not mean to offend you."

The Bythian regarded him for a long second. Then he said, "You are forgiven. Our contacts with your people lack much. Trade this for that, but souls are always last to be given, eh?" With a dry gargle at the back of his throat, the alien turned away, facing the hovercraft.

He made a pass through the air, and a fragrance wafted out, even as the doors opened and the ramp pushed out, and she could smell smoke and oil. She saw the sunlight glint off the armor of the men waiting for the ramp to settle and she wanted to cry out for Jack, but her voice stayed dry in her own throat.

The High Priest had looked directly at her when he had said that the Holy Fire cleansed all souls. He had not meant all Bythian souls. He had meant *all* souls. She knew it.

Amber felt goose bumps on her arms and lightly chafed them with her hands, shivering in the hot afternoon, feeling incalculably dirty.

Kavin and Jack led the fighters onto the ramp. Amber felt the crowd trembling around her as they pressed a little closer to see these off-world killing machines.

The High Priest waved for Colin to join him. "Who is that in the armor of all lightness?" the alien asked.

"That's Jack Storm," Colin told him. "He's a good man. If he killed, he did so in defense of others. He once risked his own life so that many others, including myself, might be saved."

A hiss of indrawn breath. The High Priest looked to the clergyman. "Are you sure of this?"

"I saw it myself."

"And might it be done here on Bythia?"

"I don't see why not." Colin paused.

Jonathan muttered at his back. "You're treading on local prophecies, sir."

The saint nodded abruptly as though he knew what his aide and bodyguard warned him of.

The High Priest countered, "Then I am not needed here." Suddenly, he whirled, and was gone, leaving behind a perfume of such exquisite delicacy that Amber nearly cried.

Jonathan made a noise under his breath before asking of Colin, "Your reverence, what is the Holy Fire?"

"We had Noah's Flood . . . they had a burning fire."

What had Colin just done to Jack?

Amber wedged her body forward. "What did you say about him?" she asked savagely.

Colin gave her a bemused look. "I merely told him Jack was a hero." He placed a comforting forearm about Amber's shoulders. "Relax, little one. Your Jack is safe."

Fears locked in her throat, Amber stared fiercely out to the hovercraft as they descended. She watched Jack take his helmet off and look for her.

She choked. She wanted to cry, "Run while you've got the chance!"

But she didn't, and because she didn't, she would never forgive herself.

CHAPTER 20

Jack held Amber with a fierceness that made her give a short cry. "Jack! You're bruising me!"

He let her go reluctantly only to find himself confused when she held onto him tightly as though having changed her mind about letting go. She tugged on his gauntlet.

"What is it?"

"Bend down."

Tall, he was even taller in battle armor. He bent down as Kavin passed and greeted St. Colin. She pressed her lips to his forehead.

"What kind of a greeting is that?"

Amber smiled as he straightened. "I was checking for fever." She traced her fingertips coolly down his left temple. "You've been known to have trouble coming out of cold sleep remember?" She took up his hand and squeezed it.

"Careful. It might be loaded," Jack said, totally distracted as another part of him sprang to life and told him, damnit, that *it* hadn't been asleep for two months. He wondered if he blushed and hoped the dirt and sweat of battle obscured it. He looked around. Most of the Bythians had begun leaving with their High Priest. He let out a low whistle.

"What are they?"

"Who?"

"The Bythians," Amber whispered. "Are they really snakes?" She'd heard the East Quarter merchant slang for a Bythian was snakeskin.

"Only in the same way a platypus is a duck," he answered.

"A what?"

The tension between Kavin and St. Colin had drawn Jack's attention. He stepped out. "What's going on?"

The Walker bodyguard bristled visibly. Colin held up a hand. "Back off, Jonathan. I have the situation under control." His deep brown eyes, mild and intelligent, sized up Jack. "We'll discuss it at your new headquarters, perhaps?"

"I'm not a goddamn hero."

"I never said you were," Colin told Jack mildly.

Jonathan still eyed Jack with an expression Amber did not like, and he'd kept his holster bared, his palm inched toward the butt of his handgun. She made plans to distract him if Jack got really upset.

Kavin said something then, having listened with a bemused expression while the saint and the soldier had been arguing in the nearly empty South Quarter villa. "I thought you two were friends."

The Knight turned away, making a disgusted gesture with one hand, his four-fingered right hand. "I do my job, that's all. And I don't like being set up as part of some alien's prophecy."

"I don't think that will happen, Jack," Colin said. "But if it does, I'll take care of it. The Bythians are very interested in keeping us out of their affairs."

"And so you used me to buy your way in?"

"Sort of." Colin sat down on a duffel bag, as there was very little else in the way of furniture yet in the barracks. The noise and clatter of equipment being unloaded in the back made it hard to hear him. "It's been difficult for me to get a start investigating. Sometimes stirring up a hornet's nest or showing them I have a stake in their religion will do the trick. I'm sorry if I offended you, dear boy, but what you did at Lasertown *was* heroic."

"It was stupid, but I couldn't think of anything else." Jack stopped pacing.

One of the new recruits came in, whispered something in Kavin's ear, then stepped to the back of the room and stayed at attention. The commander smiled, cutting a network of lines into his tanned face. "The sonics curtain is up and operating. You may talk about whatever you wish without being overheard."

"Except by present company," Amber muttered. She dropped down next to Colin.

The Walker looked keenly at Jack and then at Kavin. "I won't mince words," he said. "What are you boys doing here?"

"We've been told to cover Dominion assets," Kavin said, and smiled.

But the Walker prelate wasn't smiling. He was angry and when Jack recognized that emotion emanating from the man, he was surprised.

"After months of petitioning the emperor and the Dominion, we now have official permission to join the embassy staff, including the ability to make field surveys of our own. I want to know if you have intentions of interfering with my work."

Kavin's eyebrow arched elegantly at Colin's words. "And you brought your militant wing with you just to polish the silver?"

"No. Because . . . it was suggested that I do so, for protection."

"Then let's just say it was suggested that we follow you to make sure your zeal for answers doesn't jeopardize Triad or Dominion concerns. I don't have orders to interfere, but the Thrakian League has suggested strongly on several occasions that the Bythians wish to sever all ties with the Dominion and join the League. We're here to protect you and anyone else human who might be caught in the middle. And, I'd say our welcome confirms a volatile situation."

Colin muttered something the others did not quite hear, except for Amber. He was too old to blush, but several of the fine veins in his fair skin had broken with age, and now crimsoned deeply. He stabbed the air with a finger. "Then why let us in in the first place? Damnit, we're being used by Pepys to justify sending you in," he said. "And I'll not take it any longer. I should have known the old fox had something in mind when he gave in so quickly. He wanted you boys here and didn't know how to get you in."

"He's stopped just shy of declaring war."

Amber gave Jack a worried look.

Kavin cut in with his smooth voice. "Then there's no doubt it's the Thraks."

Colin stood up, and the deep blues of his overrobe swirled about him. "I'll have aerial reconn of strategic areas sent over. You may find what the Thraks are doing interesting."

"What I think is interesting and what I can do something about may be two entirely different things."

Colin met Kavin's expression. The wispy headed older man smiled broadly. "Are you any less devious than your emperor?"

"I'm a whole hell of a lot less devious." Kavin duplicated the grin. "But I can try. How soon can we have printouts?"

"I'll have them tonight for the embassy dinner.

You are going, aren't you? I understood all the officers would be there."

Kavin stifled a groan, and nodded.

Colin gathered up Jonathan, saying, "Come on, my boy. We've a bit of praying to do."

Jack watched as the man left, his bodyguard in his wake. He took Amber by the elbow as she started to follow. Their reunion had been all too brief and he noticed that she looked pale and distracted. "How are you?"

She shrugged. "You should know. It's not the sleep, it's the dreams."

"Still? I'll be busy setting up shop and a staging area today. Can I see you tonight?"

"At the embassy dinner." She gave a half-smile.

Jack hesitated. "What is Colin talking about?"

"We picked up some strange stuff by accident while trying to bounce some waves off a curious rock site in the north. He doesn't know what it is. My guess is, he hopes you do. I've got to go."

"All right." He let go of her reluctantly and watched her run after Colin.

Kavin made a clucking sound against his teeth. "I don't like it."

"Neither do I."

"The Thraks have most of this city under surveillance—I saw the installation when the hovercraft brought us in. It's hard to miss that kind of handiwork."

"But not very sophisticated."

"No. It would seem not. They must be walking a fine line between bringing in the best of their technology—and not revealing it to the Bythians." Kavin walked over to Jack's side and joined him, looking out at the street where Colin, Jonathan and Amber's lithe frame could just be seen in the distance. "I'll give you a little time, and then we'll have to go into debriefing."

"All right." Jack straightened from the doorway where he'd been leaning. He located his duffel and hoisted it, before heading to the wing shown him earlier as officers' quarters. Bogie should be waiting on his equipment rack when he walked in.

Word of Thrakian involvement had sent a bristle up his spine. He couldn't help it. He wondered if Dhurl had beaten them to Bythia and would be joining them at the Embassy that evening. And, if he did, who would keep the two of them apart.

But, as much as Pepys' duplicity rankled at St. Colin, it heartened Jack. He'd not seen much concern for the Thrakian presence in the trading and war lanes since he'd awakened years ago, and there had never been a way for him to protest or call for an alert against it without exposing himself. Perhaps the Treaty was weakening enough that Pepys—even if the Dominion didn't—could recognize their clear and present danger. He'd first donned the armor to fight Thraks. He'd do it again, he thought, as he crossed into the barracks' wing where he was housed.

The armor was there. It had been hosed off since he'd shed it, but Jack insisted on doing most of the shop work himself so little else had been done. He dropped the tapestry door closed behind him and was startled as two or three small green lizards raced across the ceiling at his entry. He tossed his bag into a corner where the duffel raised a cloud of dust motes that swirled in the bright light from his window. Jack frowned. Dust was death to the suit's circuitry. He'd have to make sure the cadets got into the shop and vacuumed it down as well as they could.

There was a scoring across one shoulder. He fingered it. One of the Bythians would never known how close he'd come to knocking down a Dominion Knight, he reflected. The norcite coating flaked up at the edge of the damage and Jack knew then that, without the norcite, he might have lost the whole arm. He must have taken a shell directly and not felt it.

Boss.

In spite of himself, Jack jumped. It had been so long since that deep-toned voice had run through his mind so clearly, the inner voice that sounded like stone rubbing stone: He grabbed for that fragile link, intending to reel it in, hoping to build a rapport that would allow him to see if the sentience did exist as more than an extension of himself.

And, if it did, to see if it remembered Jack's life from before.

"Bogie—"

"Captain Storm?"

Jack whirled. Rawlins stood in the doorway, the tapestry draped across one shoulder like a formal cloak. The second lieutenant saluted, and added, "I hope I'm not bothering you, sir."

His hand trembled and he dropped it out of Rawlins' line of sight. "Just going over my equipment. The first rule of armor is never to let a tech be more familiar with it than you are. I don't want another man to be responsible for my survival."

Rawlins rubbed a hand through his shock of white-blond hair. He nodded. "I understand, sir. But you said ... survival. Don't you mean ... victory? Or performance, as a soldier, I mean?"

"That all depends on why you put on battle armor in the first place."

The young man grinned then. "I got it. Why you fight."

"Right."

"But you were a mercenary before getting into the guard."

"And I still am."

"Oh." The second lieutenant hesitated another second longer until Jack prompted him.

"What can I help you with, Rawlins?"

The deepest of blue-eyed gazes pinned him. "I didn't get a chance to ask you on the ship or tell you why I wanted to be your lieutenant. I, well, that is—I came to ask if you're the one who knows about Claron."

Another icy touch reached Jack somewhere along the base of his head, where his spine met his skull. "Claron?"

"Yes, sir. I heard that one of the Knights fought so that the emperor would hear about Claron and find out who had it burned off. I've been watching you, sir, and I think you're that Knight."

"And if I am?"

"Then I'm serving under the right man, sir. I'm proud to be serving under you. My father was one of those who lived long enough to be taken off, but he was going to send for us before it all happened. I have pictures he sent us, sir," and Rawlins slipped the top button on his dress jacket, to reach inside for holos. "We had a colonization application in, when it was burned off."

Jack did not take the pictures, but the image danced in the air in front of him, and he felt a stinging sensation at the back of his throat. He did not look at the boy, wondering if he faced another Green Shirt, or just an idealistic cadet who'd become a Knight for many of the same reasons he had. "How is your father now?"

"On disability, but he's doing okay. He and my mom have another app in for another world." Rawlins paused and a thoroughly disgusted look curdled his young features. "He says it was all politics, and that the burn-off was covered up and we'll never know what happened. But I heard, when I joined, that one of the Knights was looking for the answers, and pressing the emperor, talking about terraforming even." Rawlins' voice died off as Jack turned away.

Who had told him? Who stood in the background, manipulating all of them like waldos? "I suggest, lieutenant," Jacks said, keeping his voice as even as he could, "that you concentrate on one world at a time. You'll stay alive longer."

The holos went back into the inner pocket and Rawlins snapped off another salute. "Yessir." He grinned. "But I've got the right man, haven't I?"

Jack nodded wearily. "Yes. I guess you have."

If Kavin and Jack had had any doubt that they'd been quartered in the poor end of town, it evaporated when they reached the embassy. The villa was a four-story, tiered extravaganza that had been adapted for Dominion security. Windows had been put in, shutting out the chilling night air as well as uninvited visitors, and the stuffy interior now made do with a series of solar fans for circulation. Some things, Jack reflected, as he pulled on the neckline of his dress uniform (too tight now, and he thought of the bandy-legged little tailor who'd threatened him on the parade grounds a few months ago) were not improved by innovation. But the rest of the villa was abundant with the riches of Bythia. Fragrances hung in the air, some sweet and flowery, others dank and musky. Tapestries and artwork adorned the open spaces between the columned walls, and headdresses of antiquity with their odd silklike strands of hair and feather sat on featureless statuary. It made walking around the reception wing difficult and Jack was only thankful he'd not been summoned in battle armor. He'd be graceful but much too bulky for the villa.

Kavin caught him by the elbow. "Relax. Quit pacing."

Jack smiled ruefully. "I don't like ceremonies."

"What soldier does? Amber will be here soon—that should take your mind off things." Kavin released his arm. "Or maybe it won't. She's a pretty independent girl. I think she's outgrown your role of guardian and protector."

Jack eyed Travellini, another Knight who'd made captain in his absence, where he stood across the room. He said nothing, all too aware of the truth of his friend's statement.

"As one buddy to another," Kavin added. "I'd make a decision rather than risk losing her."

His attention shot to his commander's face. "It's not for me to make," Jack said.

"Maybe. Maybe not." Kavin was distracted by Colin's entrance, framed by Jonathan and a third man Jack had never met but knew by reputation. "Who's that?"

"Denaro. He's supposed to be the quasi-general of the militant wing."

Kavin whistled softly. "I hope our reverend can keep that one under his thumb. I wonder how many weapons he has hidden under his robes of office?"

Jack shrugged. "Not less than five he can get his hands on easily, is my guess." He watched the trio walk across the room to join them, snagging drinks from the little servo wheeling across the floor with a tray. Militant Walkers made him uneasy. He'd faced them before. Religious fanatics fought with a zeal that almost matched that of the murderous Thraks. He sipped at his own drink. "How about I handle Amber and you handle the diplomatic intrigue?"

"Think you're up to it?"

"Barely," he answered Kavin's ironic tone. He smiled as Colin came within earshot. "Your reverence. Nice to be seeing you again."

"Amber's late," Colin said. "Doing her hair up. We lost her somewhere just inside the foyer en route to the ladies quarters. She should be out in a minute."

Jack smiled at that. Amber had a deft touch with hair and makeup, as part of her activities on Malthen's streets. She could range her age almost anywhere from pre-teens to the sixties if she wished. Accenting her natural beauty, however, was the skill Jack liked best.

Colin pressed a sheaf of papers into Kavin's hand instead of shaking it. "I promised you these, but I suggest you wait until you're on more neutral ground to examine them thoroughly."

"Indeed," Kavin answered. His silvery eyebrow arched in irony. The embassy was supposed to be the most neutral ground in Sassinal or, for that matter, the southern hemisphere of Bythia. He opened his tunic seal to stow the papers away, but paused as he glanced at the top one. "Holy mother," he said.

Jack peered over his shoulder. The computer simulated photo hit him like a gut-punch. Pink and beige sand swirled out from the midst of a green belt. Kavin hurriedly stuffed the papers into his jacket's interior pocket.

"Thraks," Storm said, and his voice sounded choked to his own ears. "That's a Thrakian sand crèche. They're already establishing a foothold here."

Kavin pitched his voice very low. Jack knew that soft and deadly tone. "What do you know about Thrakian sand crèches?" the commander asked.

"As much as you do. Enough to know there shouldn't be sign of one on Bythia." Jack fought to get a grip on himself. Over his shoulder, he saw the curious expression on Colin's face and knew the Walker could neither hear their voices now nor had he recognized the phenomena from the aerial photos before he handed them over. The two Knights were in possession of intelligence sensitive material that could easily get either one or both of them killed.

"Where would you have seen one?"

Jack looked back steadily. "There are places," he answered, "where one can see just about anything in the universe."

Kavin had put a hand on his wrist and held him, too tightly. Jack did not allow himself to flinch. "I think," he said, raising his voice, "I'll go look for Amber."

"Good idea," Colin seconded. "I heard the dinner bell. The ambassador should bring us into the main rooms in a few moments. Wait a minute—there she is."

She came to a hesitant pause in the doorway, and even clear across the room, Jack could feel her impact on him. Beside him, Kavin sucked in his breath as well. She wore blue tonight, her gown undershot with tones of green, setting off the dark honey color of her hair, which she wore up and set with a jeweled band, letting tendrils plume out in imitation of a Bythian headdress. The result was more than spectacular.

"A beauty," Colin murmured, but Kavin made a low sound in his throat like a growl, interrupting, "and there's the beast," as Thraks moved in behind her, framing Amber's delicate looks with their chitin bestiality.

Their scent filled Jack's throat like smoke. He

tried to swallow and ended up coughing. Kavin thumped his back in sympathy. The other Knights around the room froze in their dress uniforms, and as Jack looked up, eyes watering, he realized that most of them did not know what it was to face a Thraks in battle.

Amber acted as if she did not know the Thraks were behind her and drifted across the reception room to his side. Then she turned to look back and as he took her hand, he saw the light gooseflesh on her arms. She hated the aliens almost as much as he did, and not entirely for his sake.

Behind the Thraks bobbled a man, dark-skinned and wrapped in white robes, his bald pate shining in the lantern light.

Colin smiled. "Dr. Quaddah!" He approached the man, saying, "The good doctor is Special Envoy here."

"Sir—" Jonathan muttered, as the saint did not notice the immediate bristling and rearing of the Thrakian contingent as the human approached. Dhurl's face settled into a hideous mask.

Dr. Quaddah dodged around the trio and came forward to grasp Colin's hands. Both Amber and Kavin let out a low sigh of relief. Jack was not sure that the Thraks would have shot Colin for approaching them, but he was not totally sure that they wouldn't have either. Meanwhile the saint and the doctor had gone from vigorous pumping of hands to a brotherly hug.

Colin broke away with a boyish grin. "Anything you want to know about Bythia, the doctor knows. I've been waiting days to meet him."

Kavin eyed Jack but said nothing. Jack read his mind as if his friend and commander had spoken. How had he known about sand crèches?

Colin brought the doctor over as the Thraks entered and made themselves conspicuous in a corner of the reception hall. Amber relaxed slightly on Jack's arm and then tensed again.

A last guest walked into the hall, his aroma wafting before him. It was sharp as wood smoke and distinctive as herbs. His headdress and feathered arms and ankles wavered as though a whirlwind surrounded him. Jack frowned and looked down at Amber.

"Who is that guy? Didn't I see him at touchdown this morning?"

"Briefly. He's a High Priest. He was there to purge you of your sins of war," she answered.

Dr. Quaddah lost his happiness but stayed at Colin's side. The holy man asked, "How powerful is he?" of the doctor.

"With all the factions on Bythia, who knows? But he's the leader of the group waiting for the Third Age and he's powerful enough here in the south, where the religion borders on the fanatic."

Colin's mild eyes grew sharper. "And what of the religion?"

"We must talk, St. Colin, but tonight is not the time. I'll tell you this . . . I have heard of things, and seen things, that can't be explained easily."

"Really," Colin murmured.

The High Priest stayed framed in the doorway, aware he was the center of all attention. Even the Thraks forgot their paranoia over the Knights long enough to pinion their attention on him.

"What's the Third Age?" Amber blurted out, and he looked down to see her face had paled and she was taking great pains not to look at the High Priest.

Dr. Quaddah's brown face was a network of wrinkles, some of humor and others of pain. He looked sympathetic. "I cannot talk here, young lady. Suffice it to say, that what you have been told of this world isn't true. These are not barbarians we face—"

Jack thought of Lassaday's assessment.

"—what is done here is done because of the errors of past civilizations and centuries. The scavengers outside the cities are called surfas. Do you know what that means in Bythian?"

She shook her head, the curls of her hair waving in mockery of the High Priest's headdress.

"Mistakes. The ontology of the word alone suggests that the creatures were manufactured, not evolved. And so the Bythians suffer them to live— even feed them, as dangerous as they are."

"Genetic mistakes."

"Perhaps." Dr. Quaddah coughed politely and turned away as the High Priest took a mincing step in their direction.

The conversation lulled until the Bythian reached them. His scent mellowed even as it surrounded them. Jack did not find it unpleasant, but at the same time knew he would never forget it if he lived to leave Bythia. *Reptilian*, he thought, as the alien's sideways slanted eyes widened a little to observe him. *To hell with the platypus theory*. It amused him a moment, to think of buglike Thraks trying to dominate a reptilian culture, particularly one as belligerent as this one was.

He took the creature's observation silently, wondering if the alien thought much the same of him.

Dr. Quaddah said, "Gentlemen and my lady Amber, may I present the Omnipotent Hussiah."

The High Priest sketched a movement too sinuous for them to mimic. Jack might have tried had he been wearing battle armor, famed for its suppleness, just to see the surprise on the alien's countenance. He saw now, up close, what he had not seen in the battle he'd fought that morning: the face of Bythia.

The mouth that was part of a snout stretched into a smile. "The young lady asks of Third Age, my hatch-mate Quaddah? Why not be telling of it?"

The doctor's dark face lightened a little. His surprise could be easily read by anyone in the room, and Jack was aware the Thraks watched them closely. "I did not think it proper to cant your religion for dinner party chatter."

The Bythian inclined his head, and the beauty of his headdress wavered on that unseen breeze surrounding him. Aura? Energy?

Kavin muttered next to Jack's ear, "This fellow puts new meaning into charisma." Jack had no answer for that one.

But the girl at his side seemed mesmerized. "I—I did not mean to offend."

"You did not," Hussiah told Amber. He blinked. "We await the Resurrection. With it comes our Third Age. Without it, the death of all Bythia."

The ambassador chose that stunned moment to enter the reception hall and announce dinner.

Jack did not like filing into a relatively closed room with Thraks at his back. He could feel his senses roaring as adrenaline began to pump, and he looked for ways out among the columns and tapestry walls. Amber looked up at him. She smiled tentatively as though she sensed his distress. If he could have noticed, he would have seen her own distress, but he was too blinded by his.

The end of the dining table had been modified greatly to accommodate the Thraks. Jack looked at it, saw that the modification had not been a hasty jury-rig, and knew that the Thraks dined here often, or at least often enough to make the arrangements permanent. His stomach churned at the thought of witnessing Thrakian dining habits.

Colin bumped his arm slightly and said, "Sorry, dear boy." Under his breath, he whispered, "There was a man in the far corner, shadowed. Perhaps I'm losing my nerve in my old age. . . ."

Jack looked sharply away from the Thraks to the opposite end of the room where shadows hid the kitchen entrance. The ambassador himself, large, jolly, dressed in formal clothes, and wreathed with smiles, partially blocked the view. Jack rubbed his forehead and, out of his peripheral vision, saw a slight movement.

Someone was there who did not belong. Why hadn't Amber, always so security minded, sensed it? Amber had always seen potential ambushes long before they happened.

Or perhaps he and Colin were just unnerved. This was, after all, the embassy.

Amber seated herself in a swirl of light blue. The shadowed figure disappeared even as Jack tried to focus on it. "Jack?" she looked up.

"Just a moment." Jack did not answer, but strode away from Kavin and the others as forcefully as he could, reaching the columnar doorway where he stood under a fan, feeling its tiny breeze wash across his sweat filmed face. He clenched a shaking hand tighter about his glass. He gulped a few deep breaths, then looked up.

A dark figure was turning away from him and disappearing, weaving its way through columns into the depths of the embassy.

"Shit." Jack drew the back of his hand across his forehead. They had been watched. He looked about him, saw the area empty, and decided to follow.

The man moved quickly, stealthily, down the

hall and up a back set of stairs. He was older than Jack. Heavier breathing and the insistent creak of one kneecap as he took each step hid any sounds of Jack's pursuit. As he turned the corner upstairs, a hallway mirror flashed a fleeting portrait of his face.

Jack stumbled to a halt and caught himself. Then the gut-wrenching shock that had made him stop for an instant sped him along instead. This man he could not afford to lose, for he'd spent most of his waking life since the Sand Wars looking for him! Twenty-five years had aged Winton, but not to such a point that Jack could not recognize the man who'd condemned the Knights to Thrakian defeat and death on Milos.

Winton and Thraks. This time, he had the chance to make the connection. Questions embedded in his soul were close to being answered.

He hurried after his nemesis.

Two guards stepped out of an alcove at the top of the stairs. "Sorry, sir. This part of the embassy is private."

Jack looked at the WP insignia on their epaulets. He smiled tightly. "I seem to have made a wrong turn."

"The men's room is down on the first floor," one guard said. "Just outside the dining room."

Jack pivoted and returned downstairs. His fist had clenched involuntarily and he opened it.

One of the guards had been with the man who had brought Ballard's eye to them.

That left Jack wondering just who the enemy was as he reentered the dining room and took his seat at Amber's elbow. Kavin gave him a curious look from across the table. As he sat, he was aware of the violent trembling beside him, but he could not turn to her as a servant bent down with a plate.

"What's wrong?"

The Bythian High Priest sat across from her. He turned his light emerald eyes on Jack. "We were discussing a phenomenon of my religion known as the Holy Fire. Its appearance heralds the Third Age we talked of. My ancestors used a minor form of it to cleanse sins."

Jonathan, looking ill at ease next to Colin, laughed awkwardly. "Who is without sin?" he asked.

"No one," Hussiah returned. "Without the Holy Fire." He made that eerie copy of a human smile. "The Lady Amber strikes me as a curious one. In my people, curiosity is not an idle trait."

Amber got to her feet, the lines of her dress quivering with her agitation. Without looking once at Jack, she whispered, "Forgive me, your reverence. I . . . I cannot stay for dinner."

Colin answered, "Of course. Jonathan."

The bodyguard got up almost as quickly. Amber moved her hand over to Jack's hair, an intimate gesture that betrayed her trembling. She bent down and said in a low voice made husky by unshed tears. "Come see me later. Please."

One of the Thraks made a guttural noise. His companion answered it with a gnashing of face plates. Jack looked swiftly at them. When he turned back, Amber had gone.

Colin cleared his throat. "My apologies, Omnipotent One. Foreign travel can be . . . difficult."

"Indeed," said the High Priest. He looked at his plate. "Ah. Nando feet. What a rare appetizer." He picked up an eating utensil with relish.

CHAPTER 21

Amber let the night air hit her like a slap in the face. She took a deep breath to steady herself before she ripped off her headband and let her hair come tumbling down.

The walkways of Sassinal were empty this late. It made her suspect the Bythians even more of reptilian coldness. They were probably curled up inside their baskets of homes. She turned her head as a wheeled conveyance whirled past her, its rider pumping furiously. The Bythian never gave her a second glance. She was in no danger here on Sassinal streets, only beyond where surfas reigned at night. It was about the only advantage she could think of for a one-sexed race.

She closed her eyes briefly and tried to dismiss Hussiah's burning gaze that had speared her the moment he'd entered the embassy. How could he see through her like that? How could he know about the deaths that churned inside her? She could not even tell Jack something like that and yet this . . . this stranger, this thing . . . knew.

A low hanging branch slapped her lightly, emitting its fragrance and Amber's eyes snapped back open. She ducked under the tree's overhang.

He could not possibly know about her unless . . . unless he was like she was, born with the talent.

Amber kicked off her dress shoes. The cool, packed

197

dirt beneath her feet felt good. What made a High Priest a priest, anyway? Back in Malthen, she knew an old lady who'd lived between the cracks in the buildings and swore she could feel the angry earth beneath the hot permaphalt streets and claimed damnation and salvation on alternating days. And yet, she'd known an uncanny thing or two. A little chill prickled up Amber's spine.

Preoccupied, she brushed past the empty streets and thresholds and entered the Walker villa. She prayed that Jack would have the time to see her later that night. Somehow, she must find the way to tell him what she'd done.

Winton rubbed the scarring along the side of his face, feeling the eerie sensation of numb and too slick flesh under his fingertips. What would it feel like, he wondered, to be that heavily scarred all over? The eerie illumination of the multimonitored room played over his features.

The thought distracted him for a moment, then a sound tinned on one of his monitors. He tuned it in.

The Thraks were cleansing themselves in a privacy booth after their meal and before returning to their villa. Winton smiled. Dhurl's synthesizer made it nearly impossible for him to converse in the clicks, whistles and other sounds of the Thrakian vocabulary so he did not.

"It would be odd, would it not," the Ambassador mused as he rubbed his face plates clean, "if one of the Knights we faced tonight was the one we detained during the Sand Wars?"

His aide clicked.

"Of course not," Dhurl returned. "He escaped years ago. We have to assume our implantations were successful or else we would have felt the consequences of our actions."

There was a dry rustling Winton could not identify though he was now hunched over the monitor, listening intently. He'd begun to sweat in the enclosure. It filmed his forehead now, running into his brows. He clenched a fist. He'd known it. He'd known it! But which one? Storm was the obvious choice. Not adrift for years, no. Detained by the Thraks. What the hell did they mean by implantations?

He got no more answer than that, for the Thraks left the booth and his line buzzed dead. It was then he saw that his recorder had malfunctioned and he had no evidence to verify his accusation. Winton clenched his teeth viciously and sat back in his chair.

"Taking a late stroll?"

Jack smiled at Kavin. "I think I might."

The commander shrugged his own shoulders and smoothed back his hair. "Not a bad idea," he said. "Think I'll go with you."

Jack dropped a hand onto the shoulder nearest him. "No," he said, without explanation.

Kavin laughed gently. "All right. But don't say I didn't warn you if Colin doesn't let you past the first door."

"Who uses doors?" Jack returned as his friend walked off in the dark. Kavin twisted about, gestured good night, and went on.

Jack stripped off his dress jacket. He wore black underneath. He left the jacket lying on the front walkway where one of the junior officers would no doubt pick it up and return it to his room. He had business elsewhere and strode into the night, his mind busy. He never looked back or saw the figure materialize with sinewy grace to retrieve the jacket and stand holding it, before fading back into the tree lined boulevard with its find.

The embassy had darkened now, its paper lanterns dimming with the advent of late evening, its guests gone, its dwellers returning to their business and perhaps even to sleep. Jack stood watching it, his head tilted back. He adjusted a strap about his neck and prayed that the security shift had not changed.

He scaled the outer wall swiftly, swung into a second floor window, and paused until his eyes adjusted to the darkness. He was in a bedroom of sorts, spare, for it held no life or personality of its own. A few steps and he was at the door and out into the hallway.

A single man stood watch on the staircase. Jack smiled grimly. It was rare for his prayers to be answered so promptly. He was on the guard before he was heard, knee in the small of his opponent's back and forearm at his throat as he bowed the man down. The guard snarled for breath, his metal alloy teeth glinting in the half-dark.

"I remember you," said Jack softly. "Do you remember me?"

The man gargled. He twisted his head frantically for breath.

Jack tightened his hold a fraction. "You escorted an assassin to my quarters. You roughed up a young lady a tad more than your assignment called for. The assassin carried a gold eyepiece and a message."

The man froze in his hold.

"You remember," Jack said, pleased. "So do I." He applied pressure until he heard the snap, then let the body sag down upon the top stair. It was a pity, but the man wouldn't have had the answers he wanted anyway.

Jack stalked back the way he had come, hugging the shadows and dark alcoves of the second floor.

He found a recessed stairway and took it with a surety that was almost like following a scent. On the landing he hesitated.

A voice curled softly out of the darkness and about him. "You were expected."

A tiny light flared, its brilliance almost dazzling, as it dropped to the floor and an assassin stood there, his face creased by a tight smile. He stood balanced, weight lightly on the balls of his feet. There was no doubt in Jack's mind that the man was ready for him.

"I didn't think I'd make that much noise," Jack said.

"You didn't. But the house is full of small lizards. They're more efficient than netting and safer than insecticides. Your climb up the wall sent a wave of them scurrying to the corners."

"Sensitive creatures. What about you?"

The assassin's lip curled very slightly. "Do not make the mistake of baiting me, Captain Storm. I'm not a messenger boy any longer."

"Then you're merely a killer."

They both moved to their right a step or two. Jack felt himself grin as he anticipated the assassin.

The man paused, head tilted a fraction as though he listened to something. Then his attention came back fully to Jack. "Yes," he answered lowly.

"Who sleeps down that wing?"

"One of my employers."

"Then I suggest you move aside. I have business with him."

"No."

They moved as one. They closed, fists clenched. Thud, block, block, hit. They fell back. The assassin panted and Jack's ribcage ached as though the one blow that had reached him might have broken a bone. His knuckles smarted. He'd gotten the first hit, the assassin the last. The ones in between that each had blocked had been meant to be deadly.

Jack sucked in a low breath. The ache gave a sharp prick. He bared his teeth to hide his discomfort. "What happened to Ballard?"

"Ballard?" The assassin spoke through tight lips. It pleased Jack to see that his first blow had done damage.

"The man the gold eye belonged to."

"Ah. He survived. He was given a fee and let go. Did he not come back to warn his friends of treachery?"

"He has no friends," Jack answered. He ducked as the man kicked at him, heels grazing his temple, but before he could whirl and grab, the assassin was back in position breathing heavily. "You're hurt," Jack noted.

"And so are you."

"But not as badly. Tell me who hired you to bring me Ballard's eye and I might let you run."

The assassin showed his teeth. The tiny flare blazing on the corridor floor began to dim. "You're just a farm boy at heart," he rasped. "Go back to the fields. You're involved in things you have no idea of."

"Perhaps," Jack answered, "you'll tell me some of them before you die." He sprang. The assassin hesitated just a moment but it was enough, and Jack had his hands full as the flare went out, plunging them into night.

He knew it was a mistake, but it was too late to do anything but hang on. They fought desperately, rolling and grasping. Crimson blazed across the back of his head as they smashed into the wall. His eyes blurred with the intensity of his pain. He held on.

Nails raked along the side of his neck. He had a

moment to wonder if they'd been poisoned, but he held on.

Then the assassin stopped fighting and sagged in his arms, breathing heavily. Jack did not give in to the temptation to loosen his hold.

"All right, farm boy," the assassin said. "I was hired by a man named Winton to carry Ballard's eye. Pray you never meet him."

"I know him," Jack answered. "What about the attack on Colin of the Blue Wheel?"

"That was . . . from a different organization."

"What organization?"

"I . . . have my loyalties. Squeeze away. I won't tell you more."

"Do you have a target here?"

"Naturally."

"Who?"

There was a pause, accented by a rattle. Then the whispered answer, "You."

Jack felt the chill sweat trickling down his forehead. "Who?"

There was no answer, and he knew there would not be.

"The broadcaster Scott Randolph?"

"Ah. You recognized my handiwork there, too." A hacking cough. "The Thrakian League asked for that one."

"Why?"

"That is one question an assassin never asks."

Then he went slack in Jack's arms. Jack held him another moment until he realized the man was dead, and then let go. He stood up. He knew his faith in Amber had not been replaced despite the confession.

He looked up. Security here was not as it had been in the emperor's palace on Malthen, but there were still recorders and cameras whirling away in the corner. He pulled the strap away from his throat. It came away in streamers, having saved his jugular vein from the assassin's nails. He pocketed the synthesizer attached to it. The ambassador would have the assassin's confession on tape, but he would not be tied in to it by voiceprint.

But their death throe wrestling match had been heard and he had no time to get to Winton. Jack turned and ran down the landing to the recessed staircase, and was gone by the time the WP roused the household.

He stayed out of the way crossing the town to Colin's quarters. It seemed swirled in darkness and aroma and he hesitated. Then he decided that Colin was too good a friend, and went to the front tapestry and rang the bell strand hanging there.

It was Jonathan who pulled back the tapestry and glowered at him, the man's face rumpled in half-sleep.

"I'm expected," Jack said softly.

Jonathan let him in, saying, "His reverence told me you'd probably be by. He says to tell you that Amber's been upset for days and that he can't help. Maybe you can."

Jack ducked his head to enter.

CHAPTER 22

He wanted to tell her she was free, but he was afraid she'd smell the murders of two men on his hands, and so he decided to wait until morning to gift her with their deaths. Instead, he brought compliments.

If she'd kept looking at him, he might have been able to tell if she'd pinked with pleasure at that or not. But she wasn't watching; she was looking out at the courtyard as though drawn by it, sprawled on a pile of pillows by the low wall.

"Amber," he said, to capture her attention. "Look at me."

Her face turned. She used her hair to veil her thoughts from him, its strands sweeping down and over covering half her face. One soft brown eye watched him warily.

"I've found Winton. He's here at the embassy in some capacity. I've got him."

Her silence answered him.

"What have I done?"

"Nothing," she answered shortly, after a pause.

"Then what can I do?"

"Take me home. Take me back to Malthen, with its streets of concrete and permaphalt."

"Where you'll be safe?"

No answer at all this time.

"I'm going to burn Winton. I'll do it if I have to

go through Pepys or Colin or that damned Bythian High Priest."

"Or me," she murmured softly.

He could think of nothing else to do, and nothing that he wanted to do more. He crossed the room and knelt beside her on the pillows, and took her in his arms. Gently, he swept back her hair. A delicate perfume wafted up as he did so. She put her arms up and firmly pushed him back.

The expression in her eyes meeting his shocked him. "You love me," he said quietly, and was surprised to find a tremor in his voice.

Amber shook her head. "Dammit, Jack. It took you long enough to see it."

"I haven't been looking."

"No." She reached up and touched the side of his face where a very faint paleness swept into his dark blond hair, all that was left of a laser burn she'd treated long, long ago. Her touch was cool against his face. "And if I were looking, what would I see?"

A heat rose in him and he found it hard to answer, "The same, I hope."

A tear swelled in her right eye. "I'm lost," she whispered, "if I can't."

He hugged her close and her resistance collapsed, then she wove her arms about him and returned the embrace, tighter and tighter. He felt the swell of her body against him, the quickening of her nipples through the thin fabric of her caftan, and his own answering quickening. They kissed, tentatively, then deeply. He tasted the exotic sweetness of a Bythian fruit on her lips, then followed the curve of her cheekbone across her face to her temple, passing the saltiness of teardrops on the way.

Once having started to kiss her, he did not want

to stop, and he traced the contours of her face. He paused only when she let out a soft moan.

"What is it?"

She hugged him tight again, burying her face in the curve of his neck where it met his shoulders. That was all the answer he needed.

The pile of pillows shifted, covering the floor near the window, as they lay back. Jack fought for control, to move slowly, his hands finding, then holding the curves of her body. She answered, biting his lip gently, then moving away so that she could open his shirt and trace her fingers along his chest. "You're hurt."

"From this morning." She salved the assassin's bruise with the coolness of her fingertips. She opened up the curled hairs on his chest as though they were buds, and found his own nipples, and caressed, then kissed them.

They pressed close again.

Jack said then, "I love you," his voice thickening.

"You damn well better," she said, and took her caftan off, flesh like silk offered up to the touch of his hands. She quivered under his stroke then reached for the fastening of his pants.

Bare skin touching bare skin. The port wine dark sky without sheltered them in privacy. A house lizard skimmed the curtain without drawing their attention. Nothing and no one might have existed in this or any other world but the two of them.

Jack hesitated. "I can't hold off much longer."

"Now, then."

He moved over her. She tangled her fingers in his hair and drew his face close to her so she could see the expression in his eyes when he entered her. She felt a brief moment of pity for the Bythians who had no concept of what it was to make love, to merge with another being. The night perfume from the gardens made her light-headed and passion drummed her pulse faster. His eyes grew large and luminous, taking her in, even as she opened up to take him in. His eyes. . . .

His eyes opened wide in startlement. A convulsive ripple went through him. He gasped, as if in pain, and then slumped down upon her.

Amber froze. She blinked, then shrugged out from beneath his limp body. "Jack?" she whispered. "Jack!"

She touched him. All the fire was gone. Fear and nausea rose in her gorge. She bit it back and, with all of her strength, pushed his body over.

His eyes rolled back in his head, and a tiny rivulet of blood trickled from one nostril. There was nothing in his blank sight. She saw Colin's near-death mirrored in his slack form.

A rush of hot saltiness blinded her sight. Amber patted his face gently, then desperately. "Don't do this to me! God, don't do this to me! It's not funny, Jack!"

Then she rocked back on her heels. He hadn't done it to her. She'd done it to him.

She had killed him without a second thought.

Amber assailed the east-side wall, fingernails raking the stone, pulling herself up. She panted, blinked, squeezing a heated blurriness out of her eyes that would not dry away. She made the wall top and crouched there, an animal among others in the port wine darkness.

She'd dressed. She could not remember dressing herself, although she did remember pulling Jack's clothes back on.

Why did she bother with herself?

Amber wiped the back of her hand across her mouth. Her chin was wet as though she'd been drooling or frothing. She caught her breath and looked down.

Glowing yellow eyes met hers. She started a moment, gasping, then realized it wasn't the High Priest, but something on all fours that paced below her.

A surfa.

She feared for a moment. Amber took that fear and tore it out of her, physically, and threw it down.

The beast reared and snapped at the fringe of cloth torn from her overjacket. It growled and shredded the fabric, and its frenzy drew other beasts until she looked down into a boiling pack. They began to throw themselves at the wall.

She was not sane any longer.

If she had been, she would never have snarled back and leaped into their midst, her fingers curling like talons and foam dripping from her open mouth.

CHAPTER 23

Winton stood over the blood-splattered body with distaste written on his face. Distaste and a feeling of having been inconvenienced. The WP guard hesitated to approach him, but did, with surveillance record in hand.

"Have you played it back?"

"No, sir."

"Good work bringing it to me." Winton looked past the guard to the hallway, where the ambassador was beginning to lumber toward them.

"What is it?" he began officiously.

"Messy business, sir. I suggest you go back to bed. I'll have the grounds secured." Winton palmed the tape.

"Yes. Well. Of course you will. G'night, then." The bulky man turned and lumbered back the way he had come, leaving behind a faint scent of good bourbon. Winston aimed his handgun and shot, and the ambassador collapsed. He was dead before he hit the flooring.

The guard's eyes bugged out and he paled as Winton turned to him. "Put through a call to Emperor Pepys. Tell him an assassin got into the embassy and took out a guard and the ambassador before he was downed. Tell Pepys we need a new ambassador and that I suggest he appoint St. Colin of the Blue Wheel."

The WP guard gulped. "Yes, sir."

Winston made a noise of satisfaction. That little appointment would solve several of his immediate problems. He replaced his handgun in the hollow of his back.

"Get them out and get the stairs cleaned. And I don't want to find out about this on the grapevine."

"Yessir."

Winton watched the body being towed past him. He didn't like losing assassins. He waited until the detail was busy cleaning bloodstains off the rugs and then went to his office.

His eyes narrowed as he played the tape.

He could not identify the killer. There was a certain grace to the being—it could even be a Bythian. "Shit," he said. He would have to take Storm out himself. He considered that his quarry might be one of the other Knights, but he was not worried about taking them out. The Thraks, the Bythians, and the berserker infestation he'd introduced into the armor would do that for him.

"Jack never came back to the barracks last night."

Colin stood there barefoot, his open robe thrown over what passed for pajamas this far from home. He ran the palm of his hand over his face as though the gesture might awaken him more fully. "Storm," he mumbled, "has his own sense of time."

Kavin pulled himself up straighter. He did not have the friendship that Jack had with this man, and he was a little uncertain of how to tread here. But tread past that doorway he would, knowing as he did where Jack was going after the embassy dinner. "Sir," he said while listening to Lassaday and Rawlins grumble at his back, "you and I both know the two of them have little privacy to protect. It's important. We've got problems at Black Piss River and the Knights are going out."

"Again? You haven't even had time to set up a shop."

Lassaday returned from the too bright street outside, "Damn right, sar, if you don't mind my saying so. But the buckos around here seemed to be enjoyin' a fight."

"I've got a field team out there."

"Right. And we're going out to protect them."

Colin cleared his throat and let the three in through the door of his residence. As he did so, he glanced across the street and saw a figure ducking surreptitiously inside a threshold out of sight. Less sophisticated methods than he would figure, but the Walker villa was definitely being watched. He dropped the door tapestry down, turning his thoughts to matters at hand. "May I suggest a meeting with Dr. Quaddah, commander? The people here are fractioned . . . you're going to find armies as thick as the brush on the hillsides. It might help to know who had what in mind when they attacked."

Kavin paused. The sun through the windows glinted off his silver-blue hair. He smiled slowly. "Then I'd just have to be bothered figuring out who was right, wouldn't I? That's a moral dilemma I don't want to have to be in. No, I plan to just keep knocking them over their heads until they decide not to fight, period."

Lassaday shouldered in after his commander. Colin glanced at the younger one, Rawlins, who looked to be a couple of years younger than his captain, but then Storm had always had a certain amount of age in his eyes that had never shown on his face. The Walker shrugged.

"Amber's rooms are in that wing. The tapestry depicts a mountain scene with a sunrise."

Lassaday had already begun walking in that direction. The bandy-legged sergeant yelled back, "It looks like a sunset to me, sar, but I reckon this is it."

He paused outside the tapestry. Kavin joined him. He cleared his throat and called out, "Jack . . . Jack, we've got orders."

No sound from inside. In fact, this wing of the corridor was still in purple shadows, from the angle of the rising sun, and cool in its quietude. With another clearing of his throat, Kavin pulled back the edge of the tapestry.

His face blanched. "Oh my god."

Lassaday drummed his heel on the tiled flooring of the Bythian kitchen and looked about sharply as he munched.

Rawlins, however, sat pale and slumped. "It had to be the girl," the second lieutenant said.

"No signs of a struggle except one of passion—you're probably right, sar," the veteran said. "But I doubt it. I saw the two of them through basic training. A feisty little piece, she was, but she'd have died for Jack. No, I bet my nuts we'll be a time putting this one together. It's good the captain has the thick skull he has, or we'da lost him."

"Then you think she's been taken hostage?:"

"Maybe. Wouldn't put it past these snakeskins." Lassaday swallowed. "Good food, though." He shivered. "Heard you had those damn beetles eating with you at the table last night."

"Yeah. They put up a one-way privacy screen, though. It seems that's part of their etiquette. Gave me the shivers—they could have been sitting there flipping us off for all I could see. But we could hear them. Crackle, slurp, gulp." Rawlins' face paled even more at the thought. To save himself, he clutched at the glass in front of him. "Here's to Captain Storm."

"To Storm," Lassaday echoed.

"Isn't that premature," a weak voice at the doorway countered.

They shot to their feet. "Sir!" "Sar!"

Kavin helped Jack into a chair. "Since you two have had refreshments, why don't you go back across town and get the transport loaded. I'll be along presently."

Rawlins held himself very erect, his white-blond hair spiking straight up. "Will you be going out with us, captain?"

"In a moment. Get my field pack ready."

"Yes, sir!" With a snap, the cadet turned and left them.

Kavin poured a cool glass of fruit juice and pushed it in front of his friend.

Jack allowed himself to slump over the table, now that his subordinates were gone. He pushed the glass away.

"Drink it," Kavin said gruffly.

"I don't want it."

"I didn't ask if you wanted it."

Jack took a sip. The reddish pulp darkened his lips which had been little more than a purplish slash in his face. "Where is she?"

"We don't know."

"Then what happened?"

"We don't know that, either. I'm hoping you can tell us."

"No sign of a struggle in the room? What about outside, in the garden? Anything?"

Kavin shook his head. He sat down heavily opposite Jack, all humor gone from his face. His dark eyes were grim. "I think she attacked you. Fled in terror at what she'd done."

"She's not like that."

"I don't know what the hell she's like! But every

time somebody drops dead mysteriously at the palace, she's within earshot. You brought her out of under-Malthen, you tell me. My dossier says she was just a pickpocket and ran minor scams. You tell me if she's a trained assassin or not . . . and if she is, what the hell is her method?"

"If she is," Jack said quietly over his glass, unable to meet his friend's eye, "if she is, she uses psychic energy."

"Psychic—what the hell are you talking about?"

"Her mind. She can use her mind."

The commander rocked back in his chair. "To kill?"

"We think so. But she's under neurolinguistic programming and we don't know what her trigger is or who her targets are. She's like a weapon that's suddenly decided to begin discharging and wiping people out." And he hadn't had the time to tell her she was innocent of the other murders. "If she's not here, and she hasn't been taken, then she's run. She thinks she's killed me."

"I wonder why."

Jack winced at the sarcastic tone, but their gazes met. "Give me leave to go find her."

"I can't. I've got to leave a small detail here to finish assembling the shop, and the embassy's hollering—there was some kind of trouble there last night—" Kavin overlooked the expression on Jack's face at that last. "I've got someone out on a hoverscout now, seeing if anyone went over the walls." He deliberately did not tell Jack that the night sentry had reported a skirmish at the East wall where at least one surfa was dead and forensics was examining other remains to determine if there'd been another victim. He added, "Colin said the house is being watched. If we're lucky enough to pick up that agent, we might find out more."

Kavin bared his teeth slightly. "I think we could convince him to tell, don't you? But leave I can't give you."

"I won't take no for an answer."

"You're a soldier. This is your post. I can't make it any plainer for you than that."

Jack never dropped his gaze, but Kavin finally looked away as Jack said, "I'd go through hell for Amber."

They both heard the silvery ring of bells at the front of the villa. Kavin ignored it as he said, "You may have to. In the meantime, let our scouts do what they can to find her, you're in no condition." Kavin pushed himself abruptly to his feet. "I can't do any more for you than that. This is an ugly little world right now. For some reason I don't understand, these people seem intent on tearing themselves to pieces in suicidal frenzy. Amber's at their mercy, Jack." He paused at the doorway.

Colin came in. His skin tone had grayed and he suddenly looked much older than his years. He looked up wordlessly at Kavin as the commander took his elbow and sat him down.

"What is it?"

"Word from the embassy. There—there's been an assassination. The ambassador's dead."

Jack, who'd been on the verge of telling Kavin about his late-night foray into the embassy domain, clamped his lips shut tight and felt his own face drain of color. "What happened?"

"A guard died. The assassin was stopped, but not before . . . before he succeeded. I've been sent word from Pepys. I've been asked to step in." He looked at his hands, which he had been twisting together. "It's an honor, of course, but it—it changes everything I do here. All my plans, my investigations, my field work . . ."

Jack watched Colin become an empty shell, and then, just as palpably, fill again.

Colin straightened up. "I'll accept, of course. I'll have to temporarily." He looked from Jack to Kavin. "Any news of Amber?"

"Not yet."

Colin nodded. He got back to his feet and stripped off his blue robe. He looked down at Jack. "He's got me, my dear boy. Watch out or he'll have you, too."

Jack watched the saint leave the kitchen and prepare to make an announcement. Kavin's mouth worked but no sound came out. Then . . . "Amber," and the word was laced with suspicion.

"No!"

"How do you know what she did when she left you here?"

Jack launched himself to his feet. His head throbbed as if it would swell and burst. "No," she had nothing to do with it."

"You can't know that."

"I can, because I'm the one who went in. I didn't kill the ambassador, but the others . . . owed me."

The commander considered him, and though he said nothing, in the depths of his eyes Jack saw that he was not believed. Kavin hesitated another moment, then said, "Because of our friendship, I won't do anything."

Jack let out the breath he'd been unconsciously holding.

Kavin shoved his hand out to take him by the shoulder. "We have a different kind of war to fight, one that you and I are better suited for."

Jack nodded and let his companion lead him out.

CHAPTER 24

"Quaddah wasn't kidding. For every wind-worn hill out there, there's a platoon standin' behind it." Lassaday spat into his empty cup even as he glared out the transport windows. The hovercraft skimmed the terrain and the black, oily surface of the river system known as Black Piss River dominated the forward viewscreen. "I'd give my balls to know where these hissers come from."

Simultaneously, from all over the transport, soldiers yelled, "Who'd want your balls!"

The old sergeant flushed, clenched his jaw and said not another word.

Jack leaned close, eyeing the terrain intensely, looking not only for the field camp they'd come to rescue but for possible sign of Amber, though he knew it was impossible she'd come this far.

A crackle came in over the com lines, and Kavin sat up straight and homed it in. "Got 'em, finally," he said with grim satisfaction.

"Walker One, is that you?"

"Help someone, anyone . . . oh, my god. There's somebody there! They heard us!" Transmission broke up into a ragged cheering.

Kavin shook his head at Jack. "Amateurs," he mouthed. Jack found it in him to give a slight smile.

"Walker One, we're on a tight schedule. Bundle up so we can get you out of there."

"Ah . . . hello? Who is this?"

"This is Commander Kavin, of the Dominion Knights. St. Colin sends his regards and suggests you boys come home."

The com line crackled again. Jack frowned as he looked forward. Thin shreds of clouds stretched out over the worn hills. They seemed to carry the interference with them.

"Ah, commander, that's going to be harder than it looks. We're surrounded. Have been since this morning. Someone out there is really pissed at us."

At his back, Lassaday whooped at the off-color language. Jack shook his head.

Kavin fought to keep the com line open, despite the interference and the drift of the signal. "We'll take care of that. You just pack."

"But . . . there are ruins here. Any kind of battle will annihilate them. You—we can't be responsible for that."

"We hear you," Kavin said calmly. "Then we'll just turn around and go home."

"No! Wait a minute!"

The commander looked up at Jack. The laugh wrinkles moved about his eyes. He scratched a slender forefinger into his hairline.

"Ah . . . commander? We'll do whatever you want us to."

"Right. Then sit tight until you see us walking in to give you an escort." Kavin keyed off. He sat back in the form-fitting chair and looked at the control panel. "Why do you suppose the Bythians picked now to get upset?"

Jack shrugged. "Probably the ruins. Colin's used to poking around dead worlds, where nobody's going to argue with him."

"I wonder if they're big enough to set into."

"You wouldn't."

"Try me." Kavin played the instrument panel and brought up the target screen. It came up, not only with the field camp located on it, but the ruins. He frowned. "Not big enough."

"Better luck next time."

"Right. Okay, captain. Tell the boys we're going to kick ass."

Jack opened up the bulkhead to the cargo hold and leaned down, saying, "Suit up."

The half a dozen topside with them were already suited. They brought up Bogie and Kavin's armor.

"Who's driving?"

"I am," and Kavin smiled grimly.

They lost six Knights at Black Piss River. Twenty-two died, but six were lost from all accounting. Jack never saw where they went or what happened. He and Kavin thought it possible the overwhelming numbers of Bythians might just have carried them off and dissembled them elsewhere. He hoped not. Abdul was one of them.

Kavin put the hovercraft down in a lush green meadow, but Jack was busy reading grids. He stood up, his armor moving with him, but feeling alien and stiff. Bogie had been silent when he'd put it on. "That's not just a river system down there . . . it's a salt marsh, and a toxic waste site that's been reclaimed."

"What?"

"That's what accounts for the color of the sands in the riverbed. I don't think we want to be wading around in it too long, though the carcinogen count doesn't appear to be above normal."

"Shit." Kavin's voice was muffled, then he sealed his armor seams. "I didn't think barbarians had waste dumps."

"These do."

Lassaday offered Jack some stim-gum. His mouth was dry, but he waved it off. The grids showed enemy troops moving at an incredible rate.

"They're out there," he said, "like sand on a beach."

"Don't kill anybody," Kavin responded and raised his voice so the platoon could hear it down in the hold, "unless you can't help it."

Jack put his helmet on and sealed it as the hover bumped to ground. Forty-eight Knights got to their feet as the sides of the hover opened. Jack leaped out.

Battle armor is not equipped with stuns. Scouts and reconns are, occasionally, but battle armor's purpose is to destroy the enemy, not put it to sleep. So Jack was the only one of the forty-eight to even have a stun option. He did not think to use it, for as he hit the ground running, the Bythians opened fire, and they seemed to give no thought to the vulnerability of ancient ruins.

He found himself involved in two battles. Bogie screamed in dire pain inside his head, and the noise reverberated throughout the bones of his skull and the fillings of his teeth, even as he reacted automatically and opened laser fire. Jack reeled as a shell exploded next to him, sending grass and dirt sky high and hitting him almost hard enough to topple the armor. But he gritted his teeth, kept on his feet, and shook off the wave of Bythian suicide infantry who clung to him.

But inside, oh, inside, Bogie screamed again. Jack felt bile at the back of his throat and his heart pounded so horribly he thought it would explode.

"Bogie! What is it?"

No answer. No answer but the chill lance of psychic terror that stabbed him again, bringing with it a clammy sweat that poured off his brow and threatened to blind his sight.

Jack swung his head violently, then swore as the suit responded with like violence, out of control, but it shook the Bythians off him and, at his back, other suits of armor trod over their broken bodies as they advanced toward the flimsy prefab building that housed the Walker investigators.

He fought because his reflexes had been finely honed to fight and because the hundreds of Bythians he faced gave him no choice. Inside, he cried . . . a keening wail. Or was it Bogie? The pain of it made his nose run. He kept his com lines open to receive but not to send. He wanted no one to hear what he was going through, and it was bad.

Lassaday had fallen and dislocated his shoulder. He kept up a steady stream of curse words, most of which even Jack had never heard before. But the sergeant kept working, and the first ten Knights drove a wedge through the Bythian ranks, opening up a path to the Walkers.

Kavin grunted, "They're the bait—watch it boys. Once the Bythians find out they're not going to pull us down, they'll go for hostages."

Out of the corner of his visor, Jack saw Rawlins' dark armor jump the point of the wedge, power vaulting the last five meters to the field camp. Once there, he set his shoulders to the building and opened up a backfire.

Jack shivered. His flanking viewscreen blinked for attention. He licked his lips and the air shuddered in his lungs. He opened up his com. "Tanks on the ridge," was all he said before he signed off.

"Shit!" That was Abdul. "Going out, commander." The bronze suited figure split away, carrying five others with him. Kavin said, "The rest of you stay in formation. We need to open this wedge up. Anybody wants to retreat, let 'em go."

The Bythians fought as if they had not heard, or perhaps not believed, tales of the slaughter from the day before. Or perhaps the twenty-two Knights they were able to pull down gave them hope as the morning wore on. Jack only knew that they kept the wedge open and sometime after the sun rose in midheaven, the Bythians finally broke and ran . . . but not before leaving some four thousand dead and wounded behind.

A living corridor of Knights had been opened up between the hovercraft and the Walker field camp, and it had become obvious that the Walkers were going, regardless of what the Bythians did.

The smoky sky cleared gradually as did Jack's target screens. He toggled on, just as Rawlins whispered hoarsely, "They're pulling out."

Jack found himself on one knee without remembering how he'd gotten there. The chamois at his back was soaked with sweat. His running nose had dried and crusted on his upper lip. His eyes felt swollen and burning. He found the water nipple and took a brackish drink.

We won, Boss, Bogie growled in his ear.

"Yes."

He stood. His gauges were dangerously close to showing a red field. He'd expended an incredible amount of power on the Bythian army. He might not have made it till nightfall.

The Walkers ran from their camp, carrying only what they could hold in duffels, their faces pale, and their own eyes swollen. They slipped and fell more than once on the bloody pathway.

Jack sighed and pushed away the inquisitive spark of life that tried to touch his mind. He was weary.

*   *   *

Bogie retreated. He felt clawed and shredded, but triumphant. That *other* that had engaged with him existed no longer. He'd outlived it. Now he knew that it had intended to devour Jack. That it existed only to eat, live, kill, and die. He had no name for it and did not know if Jack, who nurtured him, had one either.

He only knew that it had come very close to killing him. Such a death, he sensed, was far different from sleeping the cold sleep.

And yet it made him aware that he was not yet living, either. Not dead, but not alive, and the time was approaching when he might have to take steps to realize his potential.

Those steps could be the death of his host. He sensed it. In many ways, Bogie was not that different from the microbe he'd killed.

The thought saddened him. Inside the chamois, he clung as close to Jack's body warmth as he could, for Jack gave him the only semblance of life he had experienced thus far. He was more than grateful. He might not yet have achieved flesh, but Bogie had regained most of his soul.

CHAPTER 25

"Twenty-two Knights dead, with another six unaccounted for," Kavin told the pale new ambassador. "And thirty-eight hundred Bythians. All because your field team wanted to look at a religious ruin that obviously meant a great deal more to the natives than the pile of stones it looked like!"

"We're on the same side, commander," Colin answered, with a great deal more color in his voice than he had in his face. "We had permission to investigate the site."

Jonathan cleared his throat, and Colin added, without looking, "We find out now that the Bythians are so divided as to be unable to grant such permission."

"Too late."

"It would be wishful to think that this came about because of Thrakian instigation."

"Yes." He stood, in ambassadorial robes that were much too big for him, and Jack decided he liked the old dark blue Walker robes better. "Gentlemen, we've put word out that the skirmishes have been isolated incidents. Violence engendered by offensive actions taken by the Bythians. It is possible they will believe us when we say we are not here to war on them, only to protect ourselves." He stepped down from the interviewing dais. "It's equally possible they won't."

Kavin saluted then. "Ambassador."

"Commander." Colin inclined his head and left the audience room of the Embassy.

Jack trailed behind, weary to the marrow of his bones. Even his teeth hurt, and with that vague thought, he remembered the second of the battles he'd fought that day. What had been happening? Had he gone mad? Or had Bogie? Or perhaps something had happened to Amber. He put a hand out and caught the man in front of him by the elbow. "Let me have a skimmer."

They stopped at the porch. Jack heard movements behind him ... WP guards and embassy staff, but he paid no attention to them.

Kavin rubbed the brow over his right eye as though it ached. "We haven't found anything."

"I need to look."

His commander paused for a long time as though searching for the words he wanted. Then, he said slowly, "I need someone to take a closer look at the sites on the printouts Colin gave us."

Unspoken: *Someone who might known a Thrakian sand crèche when he sees one.*

"I'm your man."

"Right. I'll tell Lassaday."

There were humans waiting on the steps when they came out, sitting in the sun, startling because of the lack of tattoos on their skin and their smell of sweat.

Kavin stepped over them as the small, compact old man looked up, "Captain Storm?"

"Yes."

"A word with you."

The man came from Merchant's Row. His prosperity spoke just as his bodyguard did not, both a kind of body language Jack understood. Jack looked up as Kavin hesitated. "You go on. I'll be there."

The silver-haired man nodded and walked out into the street.

The merchant rubbed his hands together. He had misshapen knuckles—arthritis—something Jack had seen on frontier planets, away from the frequent overseeing of medical care. Once begun, it was a difficult disease to remedy.

"What can I do for you?"

The merchant pulled a sliver of fabric from under his jacket. "I'm to give this to you. If you want to know more, you're to go to the Tavern of the Forked Tongue, Eastside." Even as he slipped the rag tatter into Jack's hands, the bodyguard got between them and slipped the merchant away.

Jack let them go as he peered at the fabric. He recognized blood at its edges. Then he held it close. A long, tawny hair was imbedded in the blood-stained rag.

Amber!

Jack looked up, but the two men had disappeared.

Amber stared the lizard down. It watched her through its clear inner eyelids, feet clutching a hot rock. Her stomach knotted painfully and she could hear it rumbling. She'd eaten only once—some kind of eggs, she'd no idea what—and her fever burned like wildfire throughout her body. But even though she still wanted to die, Amber had no intention of starving to death. This was the first lucid moment she'd had since diving headfirst into the pack of surfas. She could not remember what saved her—blue bolts of power had danced upon the back of her eyes and when she'd come to, she was stumbling around in the foothills, her only injury a livid wound on her left wrist. And now she was hungry.

"Come here, breakfast," she clucked.

The creature's tongue flicked out, tasted the air, and withdrew. She shuddered in spite of herself. Her fingers clenched the sharpened stick it had taken her half the afternoon to fashion. The lizard moved its head. Now. She had to strike now or forget it.

Amber lashed out. The sensation of the writhing, impaled body gagged her and she dropped her booty in the dust, where it wiggled to death. She swallowed, hard. "Oh god," she said, and grabbed up the stick again. "Please don't let it taste raw."

Amber had long since shed her overjacket, weapons belt (empty) and spare waterskin. She stood, trembling from cold and fever in the blistering sun, and watched a cloud boil up.

"Dear god," she said. "Let lightning strike me."

She watched the storm brew, and smelled the difference in the dry air. Her ears even popped once as the pressure changed. She leaned on her killing stick. Her feet hurt but if she took her shoes off, she knew she'd never get them back on. She was hot, so hot she could feel her skin sloughing off her, fried and cracked. Her skeleton ached and keened through the holes in her skin. *Still sane after all these years. . . .*

The bones of the earth rolled and crackled under her. Rock and stone, polished and jumbled by eons of wind and rain, stretched around her. She might be the only person in the world.

Amber sagged. The stick failed to hold her and she dropped to her knees. It fell away from her and bounced to a stop a boulder or two away from her. She knelt dumbly and stared after it. Should she get it or not?

She shook her head. Her lank and knotted hair

obscured the vision of one eye. Irritably, she tossed it back.

"Am I still sane?"

Her voice echoed and Amber laughed at her quavering tones.

"Probably not!"

The air thundered. The wind lashed down at her as the storm broke. But it was not water it held. It rained dust at her, gritty and searing, tearing at her until she huddled close to the earth and tried to pull her blouse over her face, just so she could breathe.

It passed that quickly, its fury meant to be spent elsewhere. She looked up and spat. Grit speckled her teeth and dry tongue. She would have cried, had she had enough body water to do so.

Amber retrieved her killing stick and began to stagger over another hilltop. Perhaps she would find water there. At the rounded crest, she stopped, and then dropped to her stomach.

A tiny river cut through the hills. She blinked rapidly. Green trees and brush hugged its banks, greedy to keep its water a secret. And someone else was there.

In the brush, she saw a uniform jacket. A man lay there, probably napping in the late morning sun.

Who the hell would be out here?

But she recognized the jacket as her pulse jumped wildly. That was Jack! She'd know that jacket anywhere.

Amber had slid halfway down the crest before she remembered that she'd killed him. She put her feet under her and crumpled at its base with a sob, pushing her filthy face into her hands. The river ran by close enough to smell, even through her dust-choked nostrils.

The Bythian wearing the uniform jacket stood up. The Omnipotent Hussiah smiled at her.

"Be welcoming, Lady Amber. I have been waiting for you."

She gulped down a sob and looked up. He'd shed his headdress and the Knight dress jacket looked ridiculous over his native blouse and trousers. His green eyes glinted.

"Get away from me!"

The High Priest tilted his head. "Our world is rigorous," he said. "Do not turn away help you will need to live."

"I don't want to live! I'm a killer." And Amber turned her face away in her shame.

The Bythian made that grimace of a smile. "No, my lady. I have been watching you. You have done much to make sure you do live. And all for a being who has lied to you."

She was pulled by his stare. She could not keep from looking at those hard emerald eyes. "Lied?"

"To you. And if we continue to let him live, he will be lying to all my countrymen."

"Jack's alive?"

"Did you truly think you struck him down? No. You shielded him even as you struck at him."

"How—how do you know. . . ."

The High Priest stepped forward until he towered over her, and she lay huddled on the ground looking up, up, until it felt as though her neck would break. "You think he will not have you if you are a killer?"

Amber stifled a groan.

"And I have looked into his mind. He will not. I am not pretending I know much of your offworld ways. But I can purge you. This gift I am offering you."

She thought wildly, grasped at what she had

heard Colin talk about, what the High Priest had talked about before. He looked down on her now and it was as if he tugged on her soul, tugged at it before tearing it out of her skin. "Can you . . . can you take away what makes me kill?"

The snout-smile stretched. "Of course, Lady Amber. That is why I am here." And the Bythian hand, gray overswirled with plum tattoos, reached down for her.

Hussiah watched from the mouth of the earthen cave as the hatchling purred in its sleep. He rubbed a weary hand over his second eyelids. He did not pretend to understand these beings, not at all, but in this one he'd finally found the tool he needed.

The off-worlders would be here, encouraging the hopes of those who wished for the Third Age, until driven off. To the east, Omnipotence Suh-he-lan had brought in the Thraks. Hussiah quivered as he thought of the hard-shelled beings. Unlike Suh-he-lan, he could look into their souls where he saw Bythians were no more than meat for the table platters. No. He would not deal with the Thraks. But neither would he deal with these others, these ho-mans. The God of All called. Much better for his fellows to be clasped to the breast of the God than to break themselves upon the stones of their world any longer.

Hussiah desired the peace of the God of All. He desired it for all of his fellows. He was tired of shedding another life, dividing his soul with it until he died/reborn. The world was old. As hard as they had tried to conserve it, the water was sparse. Mistakes from their past haunted them still. Toxic wastelands were still unreclaimed. No. It was better to go into peace than to try to carry on.

But the fellow known as Jack worried him. Yes.

The prophecy of the Third Age was written in that being's eyes. Hussiah had recognized it immediately, for was he not the greatest of all Bythian seers? He had himself written the prophecy of the Ages in a fever dream sent by the God of All.

Now he was going to defeat it. He was tired.

The hatchling stirred on the cave floor as though the frenzy of his thoughts touched hers. Hussiah stilled his breath and meditated until she quieted. In the morning, he would begin working with her.

When he was done, she would kill Jack Storm—this time successfully.

CHAPTER 26

It was almost the oldest political trick in the world, waving the bloody shirt. But it caught the attention of everyone in the shadowed, beery smelling pothole of a bar called the Forked Tongue.

At his back, a warm hand folded over his and a voice suggested, "Why don't you put that up, fella, and come have a drink?"

Jack twisted, used leverage, and the suggester was on the floor under the ball of his foot. Jack twisted the wrist in his hand a shade more, and the man went very gray and silent. Beads of sweat popped out on his upper lip.

"What was this?" Jack asked.

"I—I'm the one who sent you that. Don't damage the hand, fella. I need it for piloting."

Jack let the man get up. The pilot eyed him and rubbed his scarred chin reflectively.

"I meant to get your interest," he said.

"You've got it."

"All right then. Come to the corner with me and talk." The pilot called out, louder, "Wally—two beers!"

The bar went back to its din of noise.

Jack noticed that his newfound drinking companion walked with a profound limp.

"I'm Ted," the pilot said. He captured a second chair to put his leg up on.

"And you know my name. What have you to do with the Eastside merchant?"

"Him? I fly for him sometimes. We have a lot in common—we both want to save our skins when the snakes decide to kill each other off." Ted's voice dropped a little as the bartender came over and dropped off the chilled bottles. Dribbles of ice and sweat ran down their sides. Ted and the bartender looked expectantly at Jack.

Jack forked over a couple of silver pieces. The bartender smiled widely before pocketing one of them, pushing the other over in front of Ted with a finger accented by a split fingernail. He left the two of them alone.

Jack still had the blood-etched rag. He laid it down on the table. "Do you know where this came from?"

"A hellcat of a girl. She's alive, but the news doesn't get much better than that."

Jack opened a beer and tipped it up, savoring the drink down a raw throat. The pilot watched him warily before doing the same.

Jack took the rag back up and tucked it inside his uniform jacket. "How much do you want for the rest of the news?"

Ted smiled and leaned back in his chair. His jumpsuit was a nondescript gray, patched and repatched, and his dark chestnut hair was poorly cut and going thin. He'd seen much better times. "No, fella. It's not that easy. This is not an 'I give and you give' session."

Jack started to stand. "Don't waste my time."

Ted held out his hand. "It's no waste. Ever heard of the Green Shirts?"

Jack sat back down.

The pilot gave a lopsided grin. "I thought that

might get your attention. This is complicated, but I represent a group of concerned businessmen who want to be able to get the hell out off this planet."

"Now?"

"No, but soon. And I can tell you that I mean *very* soon."

Jack etched his initials in the frosting bottle. He took another drink, but a more cautious swig. He didn't want to expose his throat to the other man. "Surely such . . . businessmen . . . could catch the ear of the ambassador."

Ted let out a roar of laughter. He did not subside until his flushed face had returned to a normal color. He sniffed. "Maybe," he said, and wiped at a tear in the corner of one eye. "But the new ambassador is too holy to consider such things."

Colin. Of course. But what had this to do with Amber? "Why should I help you?"

"Because I know about the girl. And . . . because I knew about Claron."

Jack felt his jaw tighten, and a muscle twitch. The pilot saw it too, because he gave another gratified grin.

"I'm a bush skimmer, see. I did close terrain mapping for the mining companies. I did some reconn photos of some very interestin' phenomena there. That's why I got busted up and ended up here. I wasn't supposed to live, y'see, fella. But I did. So I have certain connections and one of them got ahold of me about a month ago and told me you were en route. That if I would be willin' to testify to certain happenings on Claron, you might be able to get me out alive t'do it."

"You saw sand crèches on Claron."

He nodded. "Absolutely. Of course, there weren't no reason to firestorm it, but just in case anybody asked later, I suppose it was better than nothin'."

"Not much," Jack muttered. "What's your price for Amber?"

"Oh, that's part of the package. I can tell you now where she is—it won't do you any good."

Jack smiled thinly, and Ted suddenly looked nervous. "It might," he said slowly, "do you some good."

"The girl's been picked up by the High Priest Hussiah. He goes into th' hills all the time. He's some kind of prophet or something. Anyway, he won't be giving her up until he's ready, but in the meantime, it's my guess she'll be okay."

"How do you know this?"

"My skimmer got caught in a dust squall not far from here. Just picked me up and set me down. I saw her and him go off. Came back to town and found out they thought she was dead, just bits and pieces, so to speak." Ted gave a tentative smile. "I thought one o' the pieces might catch your attention."

"Bush skim much around here?"

"Some." His eyes narrowed and he took on a canny look. "I won't be telling you anymore until I'm bunked in th' company of Dominion Knights and got my ticket home in my hand."

Jack finished his beer and stood up. "How will I reach you?"

"Don't worry. I'll be watchin' you." Ted saluted him with a fresh bottle of beer. "Here's to th' Dominion!"

"Right." Jack watched him empty the bottle in two gulps. *Here's to the Dominion which firestorms colonized planets without a thought to twenty thousand inhabitants just to immolate one Knight and one sand crêche.* He left the Forked Tongue feeling sick to his stomach.

*   *   *

"Let me sleep."

"No," said Hussiah. He pushed at the hatchling. He caught the fuzzed edge of her thoughts. She was susceptible now. Wearied but not too exhausted. He handed her the clay cup into which he had carefully sprinkled his drugs and stirred them into water. "Drink this."

Outside the mouth of the cave, another dust squall whirled past. The cave filled suddenly with grit and twigs. Hussiah merely brought down his second eyelids, but she blinded herself. He took her hand and forced the drinking jar into it. Too many fingers, that hand. Clumsy. "Drink."

She gulped it suddenly.

Hussiah smiled. It was the one thing he'd ever learned from off-worlders. The muscular grimace was an outward manifestation of satisfaction and pleasure. He enjoyed doing it as much as feeling it.

He watched her. He had some fear that the drugs might not work on the hatchling as they worked on his own people. Some fear, but not enough to keep from using them.

She blinked and swayed, then retreated into an open-eyed, catatonic state.

"You will listen to me and you will learn," the High Priest said. "I will teach you of the harshness of life, and the reward of death. I will teach you to be unafraid of death, and then you will no longer fear killing."

"When you no longer fear killing, the shell of your mind will be open to me. I will teach you to embrace the killing with *scah*, that is, honor and reverence, and you will be free."

"Free," Amber whispered.

"Yes, hatchling. First I will purge you. Like the sun that burns our eyes if we stare at it too long, life burns into our souls. You must forget everything."

"Forget," she said quietly.

Then he did to her what she had once feared he could do. He reached in and ripped her soul free of her flesh.

Hussiah smiled even more widely.

CHAPTER 27

Two weeks stuck in Jack's mouth like a bad taste. He sat in staging, eyes narrowed to focus on the grainy projection in front of him.

"Look at this tape. It's Black Piss River all over again. For every stick out there, there's an army, and every one of those tin soldiers is standing in line to take a shot at us." Kavin perched on the corner of a conference table. The slide holo was projected up against the flattest wall they could find in the villa, but there was still a distortion at one corner from a column.

"That's three engagements in fourteen days. They're taking massive casualties. We've pulled Denaro's bunch out of trouble once—" Jack frowned at that. The militant Walker had stepped in as soon as Colin became ambassador, evidently feeling that his talents were needed to spur the religious investigations onward. For his fervor, he'd earned a week's stay in the local infirmary. Jack waved a bypass on the stim-stick Lassaday passed around, but he took in a lungful of blue-gray smoke drifting on the air anyway. It burned the back of his throat and left him with an edgy feeling. The sun was barely up, tingeing the indigo sky. "We've even covered the Thraks once. One day we're the good guys, the next, the enemy."

Lassaday said, "And where are the hissers coming from? Or is everyone in the southern hemisphere a part-time soldier?"

"And why? With this many armies in the field, why can't we find a decent commander? It's suicide," said Kavin.

Rawlins spoke up. "It's like they're not coordinated."

"This is a civil war. One army isn't going to coordinate with another, looey." Lassaday snickered. "Besides, we're just here to protect his reverence's ass from getting shot off."

The cadet flushed to the roots of his towhead. "That's not what I meant. I meant each army operates as though each soldier in it is independent." He stood up and the holo covered him for a moment looking eerily like a Bythian skin tattoo. "See this placement. I took it out—" The cadet ignored the jeers and catcalls from the back of the room as though he'd been bragging unnecessarily. "I mean, sir, that I shouldn't have been able to. See this wing here. When the battery command here went down, they should have gone in to cover it—but they didn't. I walked in and took it out because there was no one in the way."

"Cowards." Travellini held the stim-stick, took a deep inhale, then released it. He smiled, a movement of thin lips that almost did not exist.

Jack stared at the screen. "No," he countered. "I think Rawlins is right. I've never seen one Bythian move to cover or help another."

"Every snake for himself?"

"Maybe."

Kavin dangled one of his long legs over the side of the table. "That could explain a lot. They cooperate, to a point."

"Maybe it's a religious taboo," Lassaday said.

"Possibly. We should get Quaddah in here to look at these films."

The room grew quiet. Not a Knight in that room was unaware of what a civilian might think of the slaughter depicted. But it could not be helped. Kavin reached around and snapped the projector off. "We have other concerns that need to be looked into, as well. I've got two men not responding in Quadrant 42 and I don't like having missing men."

"I'll go," Jack said.

The two eyed each other. "You've already been out there once."

"And I didn't find anything, but at least I can get out there and back."

Kavin smiled faintly. "There could be trouble."

"I'm going."

"I'll go, too, sir," Rawlins said.

"Not necessary. The skimmer won't hold but one armored man. All right, captain, you take it out. Let me know what you find."

Jack nodded. He and Kavin both knew he would scour the area that might have been covered by Amber as well. There had been no further word of her . . . it was as though the earth had opened up and swallowed her whole. It was no longer enough to know the High Priest had taken her in. He wanted her returned.

"And Jack—"

He paused at the barracks' doorway.

"Quaddah has sent word that the armies might be mustering whatever attacks they can because the dust storm season is closing in. We might be on the edge of it, so take care."

Jack saluted and left.

A skimmer was not Jack's search vehicle of choice—a hoverscout had more range and could carry him through bad weather, but a skimmer was better than nothing. He stood in the building converted to a garage and checked out the battered piece of equipment which looked as if it had been on Bythia since first contact.

A Thrakian sand crèche. The real thing, or manufactured by someone in case it became necessary to firestorm Bythia as well?

And if it was the real thing, Jack could not suffer it to continue, because it would become the germ, the seeding for the sands to come later if the Dominion left and the Thraks remained. Nor did he want Amber left in the wilderness anywhere near Thraks and their sand.

He shouldered the garage door and pushed the skimmer outside. Its engine coughed over on the second kickstart and Jack mounted it. As it rose into the air, he pushed back the landing wheels with the heel of his boots and revved it into cruise. He soared over the city wall. Beneath him, dark shadows to race the shadow of the skimmer. He looked down and saw the genetic horrors known as surfas keeping pace.

They fell back eventually, their black oily tongues panting out of crimson, gaping jaws. Their eyes glittered as though knowing he'd be back.

On the roads below him, the Bythians piloted their high-sided windsails down rutted roads used for centuries, wheels sunk into grooves as permanent as rails. Even the high sides were not always enough protection, so they ran their vehicles in caravans. The sail of each vehicle was dyed to match the tatto skin patterns of its holder, and Jack could always spot a road by the ribbon of prismatic colors billowing upon it. He made a low circle about Sassinal and its regions, then headed toward Quadrant 42.

*   *   *

Amber bowed low, touching her forehead to the ground. She drew her eyelids down and kept them down, knowing she ought to still be able to see through them, but she could not because she was different from her elder. Still, she obeyed.

"I will strike," Hussiah warned her. "Feel it."

She did. His body scent curled up inside her nostrils, carrying his aura and his intentions with it. Now, cool and meditative. Now, heating with the first tension of muscles. Now, the pungent scent of tingling nerves. And now—!

She dodged to her right, eyelids flung open, her hand curved into a rigid claw, and, pinned under it, lay Hussiah. Painstakingly, he turned his face to her and smiled.

"Now," he said. "You have become a warrior. Your mind is clear. You never need kill anything but that which you wish."

Amber returned the smile. She released her elder.

He held up a strangely tooled jacket and pressed it into her hands as she relaxed and coiled back. "This is your enemy now," he said. He took her hand and stroked it down the fabric. It was redolent with the memory of scent. "Know him. Remember him."

Jack programmed the skimmer. He paused for a moment. The Thrakian sand crèche that Colin's aerial surveys had unveiled was not all that much farther north than the Black Piss River. The scar on his right hand itched a little and he scratched the absence of a little finger and thought to himself that the itch was merely psychological. All the same, he'd like to be able to scratch that mental itch, too. Would he find sand or not, or just a patch of desert, maybe a dried out riverbed, in the green belt?

He'd hung Bogie up behind the pilot's seat. The Flexalinks shone in the bright morning sun. The armor danced with a life of its own and Jack swore the gauntlets brushed his shoulder at least once, just to touch him.

I remember sand, the armor thought, without letting Jack hear him.

Jack reached out to tap the keyboard and slow the skimmer down. The skimmer nosed into a spiral search pattern, cameras examining terrain and panning it before him.

"Be there, Amber. Be there."

The armor shifted behind him.

The dust storm hit him head on. The plastishield screen of the skimmer immediately pitted as Jack buckled down and sat tight in the pilot's seat. The cloud boiled about the vehicle, shredded apart and died down, that quickly. The skimmer nosedived, whined, pulled itself up and steadied.

The buffeting pulled Bogie off the equipment hooks and Jack found his hands full trying to keep the armor on the back of the skimmer. He lost control of the vehicle and it skewed around as he wrestled with the weight of the Flexalinks. Green forest treetops whipped below him and when Jack finally had the bike righted, he'd lost track of where he was.

Hovering, the skimmer came to a stop and the Black Piss River came up on the target screen. No blips moved. No heat screening came up other than the low grade of decomposition. The Bythians had never come back for their dead. Jack cruised north.

His rear view screen showed the dust storm cloud moving south at a rate that was difficult to track. The fore screen showed a structure with apertures at random. He studied it a moment before down-shifting the skimmer and bringing it in.

If he did approach the sand crèche, he wanted to do it on foot. Taking the skimmer over it would alert whatever Thraks were manning it.

He was wearing Bogie when he stepped away from the skimmer, helmet hooked at his weapons belt. The armor throbbed about him, humming with power. The breeze shifted and he caught it in his face and felt grit in his teeth. The hair at the back of his neck prickled as the sand-ridden wind brushed across him.

His mouth had gone dry. Jack unlocked his helmet and put it on. The less scum he got into the suit the better. The holo bathed him in its pinkish light. He'd taken his shift off and crimped on the leads about his torso. Power stung him at both wrists to let him know it was there.

"Computer tracking. Pinpoint artificial structure," Jack ordered. Screens flashed, and then his compass map came up, pointing the way. He strode in that direction, taking the landscape in leaps and bounds, unwilling to leave the skimmer down and alone for very long.

Bogie had stilled in his mind. He wondered, as he had over the last several weeks, if he'd gone insane when Amber left. At his back, the chamois he'd installed a generation ago for comfort and to catch the sweat that always trickled down his bare skin, hung close.

The brush here billowed as high as trees, cloudlike and thorny, pulling at him. It scratched harmlessly across the Flexalinks. Jack homed in on his target and waded through. He was in a hurry.

He plowed to a stop and then he had an inkling of a realization why the Bythians had attacked first, and in force, at Black Piss River. The stone ruins had been but a gateway to this massive and intact temple.

The temple was old. So old it was as beaten and rounded as the mountain peaks cupping the valley it stood in. So old, its stone was etching away into dust at the base of its columns.

But not so old that its bas-relief pictographs were worn away.

"Shit," he said, and his voice seemed to blare inside the helmet. He looked around, thinking that Colin might have been happier had he never come. *Be careful what you ask for, you might get it.*

Jack moved then, toward the temple. He made sure his scanning cameras were recording as he passed among the friezes and columns. He did not have time to read the religious history engraved there, but knew he had to have a record of it. As he moved through the roundabout of stone and marble, he kept the altar in view.

So fascinated was he by the temple that he tripped and fell over the leading edge of the sand crèche that was steadily engulfing it. Jack spat out a pungent word, then rolled over on his elbows. Sand scratched deeply into his visor. He stared at it, face down, almost without recognition. Then the chilling realization brought him to his feet.

Colin's interesting "rock structure," ancient temple, and sand crèche were one and the same.

Now Jack *knew* why the Bythians had fought the Dominion encroachment so fiercely. The Thraks had already been here, and done the ultimate desecration.

Jack grimaced as he kicked aside a Thrakian larva squiggling through the hip-deep sand in the valley beyond the temple. He gagged. The Thrakian hivelike structure in the center was buried almost to its spirelike tip, and the sand spilled out of it.

Nowhere were there guards ... other than the six suits of battle armor arranged about it, on their feet, still and motionless.

Abdul. And the five others missing for the three weeks since the battle of Black Piss River.

Jack's skin crawled. He keyed the com on. "This is Captain Storm. Rise and shine, boys. We have a skimmer and it's time to move out."

Low, static crackle answered him.

No one responded. Was the armor empty? Who had taken them out, six of the emperor's finest, and left their empty apparel here? Were they an offering? Had the Bythians taken them like so many scalps?

Or had the Bythians hoped the invincible Knights could take out a sand crèche?

They must have because Jack saw no adults anywhere. He waded along the outer edge of the beige and pink grit. He found a piece of chitin, empty and hefted it in one gauntlet. Laser fire scored the edge.

There had been a battle here, then. The Knights, victorious to the last. Then, nothing. The crèche still existed. Soon it would be checked on. Jack knew they would not leave it unmonitored for long. Sand was being manufactured, young grown.

So why then hadn't Abdul called home ... called for back ups or a lift out.

Why was there no sign of life in the armor?

He clenched his teeth against his fear, knowing he'd have to approach the suits and lock visors, or even remove a helmet, to examine them. Dust and gravel crunched beneath his boots. Unpleasant memories made him flick the sound on high, the mikes picking up and amplifying the tiniest sound.

Something growled.

CHAPTER 28

Jack ground to a halt. He swallowed hard.

The nearly imperceptible noise came from the armor nearest him. Its black and green Flexalinks winked obscenely in the sun's reflection. He faced it directly and brought his gauntlet up.

He could not be awake. Or alive. Perhaps the skimmer had gone down and he was now as much a part of the Bythian earth as the rocks and gravel.

Maybe he'd taken too much mordil and still lay in the barracks, thrashing in sleep that was supposed to be drugged dreamless, aching for Amber.

Anything.

Because this was one of his nightmares come to life.

"Come on, you son of a bitch," Jack broadcast. "Come and get me."

The armor crackled apart like an eggshell, Flexalinks exploding in a shrapnel about them, the power of the eruption kicking up a cloud of sand. And *it* reared out of the leavings of what had been a man, then a host, then nothing but a few gnawed bones and stringy ligaments.

The berserker saurian roared. Its crest came up as it leaped out of the armor, and behind it, Jack heard echoing awareness from other suits. He aimed the gauntlet and opened fire before the towering beast could tackle him. Nothing fought worse or faster than a Milot berserker, armed or otherwise.

He hit his power vault, somersaulting over the head of the beast. Teeth that could rend his armor flashed below him, snapping at his heels. He fired wrist missiles at his fellow Knights as he jumped, knowing that the armor harbored nightmares beyond belief.

Two exploded in flame and smoke, but another one crackled open. The berserker lay curled inside, immature but waking. Jack hit his power vault again and lasered it from midair. When he landed, the first berserker was waiting for him.

It bowled him over. Circuitry fused from the impact. His rear camera blinked out for a second. Jack lashed out, his laser searing everything in a semicircle around him, sizzling into a puddle on the ground. It hit him again and the blow made Jack gasp.

Get up, boss.

Bogie reached him. Winded, Jack lay inside the cradle of the suit's gadgetry and technology, temporarily helpless. He managed a twitch, which the holo picked up and translated into a powerful kick and the berserker roared. Green-yellow blood squirted from its hind leg.

The berserker picked him up and threw him. He crashed into the skimmer, sending it rolling. It burst into flames and Jack staggered out of range of the explosion.

The berserker bounded after him and picked him up a second time.

Jack fought a dizzying moment, then realized what the beast had done. Had fracking picked him up, inside full armor. He swallowed fear and air. One of the leads had come loose and his armor's right leg was dead because of it.

"I can't move. I've lost power."

?

The sentience had done it before, on Lasertown.

"Power my right leg, Bogie. I don't have time to replace the lead."

?

"Dammit, Bogie. Hear me . . remember." The ground twirled beneath him. He'd never last a crushing fall.

No, Boss. It is you who cannot hear me.

His mind flooded with Bogie's voice, and he shrank from it. even as it reached out to embrace him.

Let go. Let me in. You fear me worse than the ones we fight.

Sweat and blood trickled down the side of his head, and he knew Bogie was right. Whatever Bogie was, a part of him or a parasite, he feared it worse than the beast racking him over now. And whatever Bogie had been, it was a powerful, mature voice flooding him now. Jack forced himself to lay still within the armor, blanking out his thoughts, reaching for Bogie like a drowning man reaches for land.

Jack kicked out with his left leg. Hesitantly, his right kicked. It was odd, almost as though it was numb. His leg moved because the armor did. The berserker staggered under the weight of the armor. Jack began to kick furiously.

It dropped him.

Jack rolled. He got his left leg under him. Awkwardly, the right followed. He straightened up and stood dead center as the creature charged him. He put his gauntlet up. The berserker bent over, snapping, fearsomely carved ivory scissoring inside a cavernous jaw. He fired right down its gullet.

Even then, he took two more vicious blows before it died.

Jack staggered over to the last two suits. The men inside were dead. He fired them anyway, afraid of what might be feasting on their flesh inside the suit. He lasered down half the thorn forest to make a bonfire to consume the sand crèche and the armor. Without knowing what caused the infestation, he dared not bring the dead back.

Then he wrenched his helmet off and was violently ill on the grass outside the temple archway.

CHAPTER 29

He remembered thinking that he'd lost too much blood. He was dizzy and light-headed as he stood, watching the funeral pyre of six Knights, their armor and their nightmare destroyers, and a Thrakian sand crèche. The heat washed against him, white-hot, hotter than an ordinary fire, fueled perhaps by the alien sand and machinery that made it. He put his helmet on against the heat and stood watching it, watching the blue-white flames dance until the night was its darkest plum.

Tired unto death, he staggered back from the bonfire and found the remains of the skimmer. It would not yield enough scrap to make a wastebasket, let alone take him home. He stood looking down at it in a stupor.

Let me take you, Bogie said.

"You'll have to," Jack answered him. "I can't make it otherwise." He yielded all, surrendered all, to the armor.

In the far, faraway years of a long ago Earth, his Amerind ancestors celebrated the medicine walk, a spiritual walk of the soul, to find truth and gain knowledge. Storm walked that pathway now, his soul linked with that of an even more ancient beast.

They began in the dawn, as the dust season hit,

and only an armored man could have hoped to make it through.

The Bythians gathered to watch the suit of All Light striding through their lands. The armies had pitched their camps, dug in, sheltered themselves from the storm as best they could. The first would be bad, a warning of the season to come, then there would be a few weeks of peace, and then the season would begin in earnest.

This storm caught most of them by surprise, out on the land, fighting for their beliefs, whatever they might be. They would wait it out and then return home, to their mills, farms, looms, shops, ordinary lives, until a more favorable time in which to wage war.

But the suit changed all that. The Holy Men knew now why their forecasts had been incorrect. The God of All had wanted them trapped in the dust, in the sterility of the grit and the storm, to see the being walking through it.

The more bold of the Bythians, first eyes closed against the stinging wind, walked out to meet the being. They would greet it, offer fruits and vegetables and water. He would stop. If they were very lucky, he would remove his helmet to drink the water and accept their offering. Then they would gasp at the strangeness of his features and bow their heads respectfully to the ground until he left them.

Many Bythians had never seen a human, never wanted to. A few had seen the Thraks . . . insolent creatures who walked upon their lands as if they already owned them. There was no doubt in any Bythian mind that the Thraks intended to, one day. The only doubt was whether it would be with or without the Third Age.

And so the Bythians did what they had never done in their lifetimes, which were incredibly long. They left their sensible shelters from the dust and followed after this being with the suit of All Light, to see what he would lead to. This was a time of prophecy.

Hussiah heard the rumblings in the land. He left his cave and stood in the wind, where he could feel the gritty edges of the storm to come, and he listened.

Then he turned and said to the hatchling, "It is time."

"Time?"

"The Holy Trial you've been trained for is upon us. Come with me." He left the cave and valley without a second look.

Dhurl received the scouting report with considerable distress. "The entire crèche destroyed? What happened?" His synthesizer crackled, bleeding out at the scope of his annoyances.

His aide bowed low on his spindly chitinless front legs. "I'm sorry, Ambassador. We had been out of communication with them—our attention had been diverted to placing our ship in orbit and cloaking it there—when we reestablished a link, there was no answer. We skimmed out to see what the problem could be and found all destroyed."

"No. No. You guaranteed me that temple was a holy spot—that the Bythians would not dare to attack it, no matter what the consequences.

"The temple still stands, your eminence." The groveling creature strove to keep its features in a mask of contrition, but one plate or another kept sliding off into abject fear, its truer emotion.

"This is disaster. This will set us back years." Dhurl turned away from the subordinate for a moment.

"We found only this at the site." The aide crept forward, dropped the artifact, and then backed into its former position.

Dhurl picked it up. His faceted eyes recognized the Dominion insignia immediately. He dropped the equipment plate. "Those chitinless Knights!"

"How—how could they have known?"

"It matters not how. Knowing this, they will soon put other pieces of the exoskeleton together. We have only one recourse before us now." Dhurl drew himself up to the limit of his height. Warrior genes made for taller Thraks, but for a diplomat, he was impressive. His mask reasserted itself and when his aide looked up to see this new expression, he let out a short rasp and quailed back to the flooring.

News filtered into the Forked Tongue almost quicker than anywhere in Sassinal. Ted was meeting his merchant employer and making arrangements to smuggle in a few barrels of forbidden thread from the holy city of Tharb, in the northern hemisphere, when he got the word. They dropped their beers abruptly and made their way to the Dominion barracks in the South Quarter.

A young, white-haired boy with eyes of limitless blue stood sentry at the door. "Captain Storm?" he said in response to their urgent inquiries. "He's out on patrol."

"Patrol my ass. He promised to make sure we got out of here when the time came, and I'm here to tell you, it's *here*."

The young man looked at them in blank astonishment. "What are you talking about?"

"Take me to your commander, fella. I don't want t'be telling this twice."

Rawlins chewed it over, then went for Kavin on the run.

Kavin sat on the edge of the conference table, frowning slightly. "I don't see how the Triad Throne or the Dominion can be held to any private commitment Captain Storm made, whatever it might have been." He held his chin high, as though offended by the smell of the two men sitting in front of him. He might have been. Nervous sweat ran off the two of them, the arthritic merchant no better than his hired smuggler.

"Then let me put it to you this way: when that curtain of dust lifts, we're going to find about twenty thousand Bythian free soldiers sitting outside those gates."

"Bythians don't travel during dust storms."

"Not if they can help it, but this one's been prophesied."

"As what?"

"As the beginning of the end of the Second Age and the dawn of the Third Age, or the end of the world. Either way, you and I don't want to be in town." Ted swallowed convulsively in his effort to be persuasive.

Kavin sucked on a tooth for a second. He looked at Rawlins. "When's Storm due back in?"

"He's overdue now. Early reports indicate he was caught on the leading edge of a small squall up north." But Rawlins' eyes flickered slightly and Kavin thought he read more trouble there than he heard in Rawlins' voice. Why hadn't Storm called in himself?

Kavin felt a queasiness roll over in his stomach.

What if the Thrakian sand crèche had proved out? There were sixteen kinds of hell and trouble brewing in one of those. He stood up. "What can we expect from the Bythians?"

"Prophecy time. They've been looking forward to this for hundreds of years. There will be a Holy Trial . . . three champions . . . one survivor . . . if any survive. If one does and some religious mumbo jumbo occurs, we're talking Third Age. If not . . the Bythians will annihilate themselves and anyone else living on the planet."

Rawlins let out a low whistle. "Lieutenant, go get Sergeant Lassaday for me," Kavin ordered.

The towhead left, a little reluctantly.

As soon as his footfalls faded, Kavin pointed at Ted. "You're not here because of Holy Trials. You're here to save your ass. Why do you think Captain Storm would have any interest in you?"

Ted licked his lip apprehensively. He glanced dartingly around, saw no help, and decided to plunge in. "I know why Claron was burned off. I'm a bush skimmer, see. I did some mapping for the free miners. It's a long story, goes back to the Sand Wars."

Kavin sat back on the conference table edge. "I've got time. Tell me."

The pilot took the liberty of propping his bad ankle up on the table. "I wasn't always stove up like this. I made a good living as a bush skimmer. Then I found something I shouldn't have. A Thrakian sand crèche on Claron. Now Claron was a new planet, just opened up for colonization. Damn Thraks shouldn't even have known about it. You heard about the Sand Wars?" Ted eyed Kavin. "Maybe. You'd a just been a pup, like me, but maybe. Anyhow, I was lookin' for somebody on Claron. A Knight."

"The Thraks were supposed to have wiped out every Knight there was in the Sand Wars, 'cept maybe one or two who went AWOL, but those kind didn't go AWOL. They were elite, you know?"

Kavin nodded his head briskly. He knew.

"Well, someone in the Dominion found out the Thraks honor ferocity among their defeated. They'll take in one or two of their best enemies. Honor them. Convert them if they can. Subvert them if not. And put 'em back where they'll be found. There was supposed to be one of those Lost Knights on Claron, and I was supposed to keep my eye peeled for 'im while I was skimming."

"I didn't find the Knight. I did find the sand crèche. I reported it. Next thing I knew, the warships were comin' in overhead, firestorming the place. It was a nightmare. Nobody was meant to get out of there. Nobody. I made it, only because I was out skimmin' and had camped so far out. I barely got singed. But then the agent I was working for visited the evacuation camp and tried to make sure I would never talk about what I'd found."

"But you talked to Storm. Why?" Inside, Kavin found it difficult to breathe. His guts were clenched just below his navel. He knew why. Storm had been on Claron. Storm knew what sand crèches were. But he also knew that Storm wasn't the lost Knight they were looking for. He stood up.

"Because I worked for a lot of people. I got here, thinkin' I was out of trouble." Ted gave an ironic laugh and shook his head, thinning hair ruffling. "The Bythians are the hardest working people I know—at dyin'. See, they only have one life. They renew themselves. The Bythian you meet today is the same snakeskin that was around two hundred, even a thousand years ago. And they're tired. They fucked up this world once, cleaned it up, went back to simpler ways, but inside, they're tired. Most of 'em don't want a Third Age. They've seen it all. So dying is a gift to them."

"I don't want to be here and get a surprise package like that. But I'm stuck here, so my contact gets ahold of me and says, the Dominion Knights are on the way. If you want out, go to this Knight and tell him what you know. He'll see to it you get out. So I did. And he promised." Ted stopped talking. He took a look at his companion. The old man huddled as if very cold. Ted patted his knee comfortingly.

Kavin rubbed his temple where a vein had started throbbing. It had become very clear to him that this scroungy bush pilot and his lover could give evidence that the Dominion needed. He looked at Ted. "Can you identify the agent?"

"Sure. His name's Winton."

The commander took it in. He knew the name, too. The secret head of the World Police. Winton was here on Bythia now, working undercover at the embassy. Kavin had had word of him. Pepys trusted Winton, but sometimes appeared afraid of him. The emperor had asked Kavin to keep an eye on him. Now the commander had two very fragile shipments and he had to make sure they were returned to Malthen.

Rawlins reappeared with Lassaday.

Kavin took his veteran sergeant into a corner. "We're going to be evacuating personnel as soon as we can verify this man's story. I want him to be one of the best preserved bundles we intend to ship out. He's going to be Dominion evidence. Guard him with your life if you have to."

"I'll lose my balls before I'll lose him, commander."

"Right." Hiding his smile, Kavin turned back. "Gentlemen, Sergeant Lassaday will be taking care of you."

Rawlins waited for him. The commander motioned to him. "Let's go take a look from the top wall and see what we can see."

CHAPTER 30

Kavin lifted the night glasses. The wind blew fiercely, whistling down over Sassinal's walls as though it had personal vengeance in mind. The EP suiting they wore was already filling with fine grit. He'd be full of dirt before he got back to the barracks. Rawlins lay flat on the wall, anchoring him about the ankles so that he could stand up to look out.

In the wind and the dust, heat was cut down considerably—but he could still see the red-black smears in the darkness. Bythians *were* massing out there—by the hundreds and soon, probably, by the thousands.

The Dominion commander's thoughts hesitated as he did a long, slow sweep of the horizon. He'd miscalculated when they'd come to Bythia. He knew now that he should have tolerated the poor attempt to hit the shuttle bringing them in and that by attacking back, he'd set off a global confrontation. He knew now that he'd given the splinter groups a common enemy—and one that they were not afraid to attack. He'd failed Pepys and more ... he'd failed those vaguely remembered codes of his brother, the man whose footsteps he'd spent his whole life trying to follow. He knew now that merely wearing the suit, and resurrecting others to wear the suit had not been enough.

He wished Jack had come back. He had no one to talk to about his shortcomings, but he had often felt that Jack would have understood. But Jack had been missing for a day and a half, and the probability that he would not make it back was extremely good.

The Bythians wanted to die. No doubt about it. Their religion told them a better life lay beyond. He'd given them the means to quit this planet and they were eager to take it. He could not comprehend that. Another failing.

With a sigh, Kavin lowered the glasses. The EP visor shielded his face somewhat, but all he saw now was a fierce and murky cloud shifting with the violent wind. Early evening weather reports said the wind would be dying out during the night.

By morning there would be thousands of Bythians instead of hundreds. He was certain of it.

By morning, the three hundred Dominion Knights he had left to command would be up to their gauntlets in bodies.

Unless a miracle happened.

He got to his knees, unable to stand in the wind any longer. Rawlins pulled himself up until they braced each other shoulder to shoulder. Kavin passed the young man the night glasses.

Rawlins took a look, but his exclamation of surprise was grabbed by the howling storm and lost. Kavin tapped him on the shoulder; together, they climbed down the wall and stood in its lee, somewhat out of the fury.

"What are you going to do, sir?"

"Prepare the shuttle for evacuation. And prepare the rest of us for one hell of a fight."

Amber staggered in the wind. She was stung in a hundred places or more from the sharp pebbles

and rocks blasted aloft, bleeding or bruised, she
knew, and she could not see. She kept her eyes
closed. She had pulled down her headdress so that
it would bandage her eyes against the storm and
had added a pull-down veil across her nose and
mouth. She followed Hussiah's form as he'd taught
her—by scent and by heat, but her senses were yet
unreliable. The moment she'd been trained for was
near. She would champion death for Hussiah and
his followers. Her victory would mean that the
gates had opened for his people and that the God
of All beckoned them to join him. She would face
two other champions but only one would be of
consequence.

He would be wearing a suit of All Light—as
opposed to the darkness and sweetness of peaceful
death as such a one could be. The enemy. The
Deceiver.

*. . . a battle armor of Flexalinks, with an honor-
able man inside of it, calling her . . .*

Amber blinked inside her mummylike wrappings.
The stray thought passed through her, as cutting
as the wind from the storm they braved. It passed
through her, but not without leaving marks of its
passage, just as the stones had left cuts and bruises.
She knew him. . . .

If he was mad again, he'd come a long way to
find himself. He had the impression of multitudes
following him, trailing him through the most hellish curtain of circuit destroying grit he'd ever run
across. Whenever he staggered to a halt, to empty
the catch bag or hope he could find water, a Bythian
had appeared bearing gifts. One or two had spoken halting English. They'd thanked him for cleansing their temple. That, Jack understood. The rest,
he did not. They called him Champion and other

names and he knew only that he might very well wring Colin's neck when he made it back to Sassinal. He'd thought to ask of Amber. He'd been told that a human hatchling lived with the High Priest. That must be her. Perhaps she'd come out to greet him also, and he could take her in his arms and let her know that everything would be all right.

But in the whirling curtain of sand, he could not make out forms. His sensors were screwed, clogged, target screens only half-functional, his long range com out for the count . . . but his own senses told him he was being followed as he took the long strides across Bythia to Sassinal. Once he'd staggered to a halt and dropped, only to find a Bythian carefully pulling off his helmet, administering a wet rag to his lips, pulping a fruit for him to eat, a tent draped about the armor as if he were being laid out for a funeral, and the dust skimming around them as though the Bythian had had the power to part the storm. Perhaps he had had . . .

None of which would explain what had happened to Bogie. What had happened to Bogie, the sentience told him, had been an awakening. Gone was the childlike fighter of his acquaintance. In its place, a grim but adult being aware of the struggle to live, to remember, to grow. . . .

And a Companion. A companion more intimate than a lover. Bogie remembered Milos and the Sand Wars vaguely. He would help Jack search for the truth of his background.

There would be no more endless dreams with recurrent loops of nightmares. He now had a Companion to walk with him through his psyche.

Unless, of course, he was mad.

In which case, the dual conversation was moot.

*   *   *

Rawlins woke Kavin in the morning. The first thing he noticed was the eerie, muffled, total silence. The bells and wind chimes that had gone insane in the wind, some even smashing themselves to bits, had stopped.

He went to the wall and saw that others were there before him. Most of them were Bythians, but he saw St. Colin with that militant, macho son of a bitch Denaro at his side.

Jonathan, the bodyguard, stood at the wall's base and rolled worried eyes at him.

Rawlins gave the commander a boost up and Colin moved over to give him room to stand.

"Jesus."

Colin coughed and Kavin added, "Sorry, your holiness."

"Quite all right. I think."

Nothing could quite describe the sight. Thousands upon thousands of Bythians sat on the plains and roads approaching Sassinal. The grassy plain had been stripped by the storm, but it was far from barren. Headdresses waved like pampas grass, the ground became a sea of costumes and tents, accented by the prismatic, tattooed skin of the beings sitting there. A fragrance hung on the air . . . dark, mysterious, excited.

Not all were warriors. No. And Dr. Quaddah, who stood on the far side of St. Colin, excitedly babbled that some of these aliens had come from the Northern hemisphere, across an ocean, to sit in front of Sassinal's gates this day. There were no signs of the gate scavengers. Kavin's stomach rolled. How fortunate could he be.

"What are they doing?"

Colin shrugged. Quaddah rubbed his brown, wrinkled face and said, "Waiting."

"For what?"

"Everything and nothing."

Kavin curled a lip at his enigmatic answer. Colin slapped him on the back. "Where's Jack?"

"He never made it back in from patrol."

"What?" Colin stared at him, mild brown eyes huge with shock.

"All he had was a skimmer. We think the storm's edge took him down."

"What in heaven's name was he doing out there?"

"Looking for Amber." *And Thraks*, but Kavin could not tell the man that. "I need to send a patrol out to search, but—"

"Not until you know what's going to happen." Colin sighed heavily. It was obvious the older man understood.

"What are you doing up here? I sent word out last night we wanted to evacuate the embassy this morning."

"I have . . . other duties." Colin indicated his robes. He'd gone back to wearing his Walker blue over-robe.

Kavin made a sound he hoped was noncommittal. He gazed out over the sea of Bythians once again. They were not moving. He touched Colin's elbow. "Let's go have a drink and talk this over."

Colin inclined his head, saying, "I think I could use one."

They left the wall.

Because their backs were turned, they missed the last two figures to join the ocean of Bythians. The High Omnipotence was given a corridor to walk through until he reached the nearest gate in the wall, his apprentice moving discreetly behind him, and they both sat. The corridor remained open as though they'd opened up a permanent breach in the ranks.

It was doubtful either Kavin or Colin would have recognized Amber anyway.

"I want you to go with me to the Thrakian Embassy," Kavin said, when they were far enough away from the wall with its many ears.

"Why?"

"I consider it part of my duty to convince them evacuation is necessary."

"They'll laugh in your face, if Thraks laugh," Colin answered. "They will probably view our leaving as voluntary ceding of this world to the League."

"If they live that long."

Colin shrugged. "It's a futile mission."

"But necessary. I've got to get them off, too, if for no other reason than to make sure Bythia stays neutral territory. Otherwise, I'll have botched up this whole assignment and Pepys will have my balls." Grim as his statement was, Kavin heard the echo of Lassaday in his words, and fought to keep from smiling.

The Dominion Embassy was closest, and it was there they walked for their drink. Bythian servants were stripping down the tapestries to pound the dirt out. They walked through without a challenge. Colin frowned.

"That's strange. The WP should have a guard up."

"Out gawking at the snakeskins. I'll send a couple of Knights over."

Winton materialized out of an inner corridor. "That won't be necessary, commander. I have everything completely under control."

Winton was a square, heavily muscled man just out of middle age, but not past his prime. He'd been lasered across the temple . . . it widow-peaked his dark hairline in a sinister fashion. Kavin did not like the head of the World Police, never had. He didn't like the clandestine activities that Winton appeared to dabble in, he didn't like the fear/respect in which Pepys held the man, and he didn't like the *man*.

"Still hiding in corners, Winton?" Kavin said lazily, not bothering to hide his dislike.

"Some men choose corners," Winton answered. "Others, armor." He bowed his head to Colin. "Ambassador. Ambassador Dhurl sends his regards and requests that you join him at the Thrakian Embassy. He would like to speak with you."

Colin stiffened. Then he sighed. "I suppose I must."

"I'll go with you," Kavin offered.

"That won't be necessary," Winton interjected. "The Ambassador's safety is still my responsibility."

The two men measured one another, then Kavin gave way. He had enough bad marks to earn Pepys' disfavor without getting on the bad side of the WP, also. He inclined his head and left.

Winton watched the commander go. He smiled thinly. He had also intercepted a low frequency message from Storm and knew the captain was within a few kilometers of Sassinal. Winton had no intention of warning him about what lay waiting for him.

He would not have to kill the Knight. Thousands of Bythians sat waiting for the chance to do so.

All he had to do was finish off Dhurl and Colin while he had them together.

The shock waves of his actions would bring Pepys and the Triad Throne toppling down.

And the Bythians would take care of the Thrakian subverted, lost Knight for him.

CHAPTER 31

"Rawlins, I want you to report to the Thrakian Embassy. Tell them you're St. Colin's assigned bodyguard."

The young man's face blanched. "I—what?"

"You heard me. Dhurl has invited Colin for a little confab. I'm willing to bet it's more than a friendly discussion about the current situation, and I don't like the idea that his holiness is going in there without friends."

"Yes, sir. Right away, sir."

"How's the evacuation?"

"We have two hundred personnel shuttled out to the staging area, sir. The craft is being readied."

Kavin nodded. The transport was far enough out of town that even if the Bythians rioted and swarmed the city, there should be no problem getting a lift-off. Getting the saint and his people out there, and the remainder of the Knights . . . well . . . one thing at a time. "Good work."

"Yes, sir!" And Rawlins' smile was like a beacon. "And we heard from Captain Storm, sir. He's walking in."

"What?"

"Yessir."

Kavin returned Rawlins' smile. "That I want to see. Is he on the com?"

"No, sir. His suit's not functioning one hundred percent. He's had some trouble, I guess."

"Well, your assignment's been changed. Don't go guard Colin, go and get him. I'll meet him at the front gate. With any luck, we can get Storm inside and take the hovercraft to staging."

Rawlins snapped off a last salute. Kavin watched him streak out the barracks' door. He made a few minor adjustments to his dress uniform, added a weapons' belt, and made his way to the wall for the second time that morning.

Rawlins hesitated outside the Thrakian Embassy. His skin crawled at the thought of seeing where the bugs actually . . . lived. The thought of running into one of them eating . . . slurp, gulp, burble, without a privacy screen, churned his stomach. But he had his orders, and so he approached the gate.

Only one house in Sassinal was gated. But it raised the hair on the back of Rawlins' young neck that the fencing was not guarded, and it swung open eerily to a push of his fingertip.

He half-pivoted on the ball of one foot, ready to go back. But he thought of Kavin . . . saying St. Colin might be there without friends. Rawlins wasn't a Walker. He didn't even like Walkers. But he knew both his commander and his captain held the man in high esteem.

So Colin must be worth something to somebody somewhere.

He swallowed and went through the gates, half expecting to get a Thrakian bullet through the chest, or have his legs lasered off below the kneecaps.

The front door, which was a real door, another oddity on Bythia, was also unguarded. Now that sent more than the hair up on Rawlins' neck, it made his testicles crawl.

He leaned inside the doorway cautiously as the door opened to a push of his toe.

Bile rose in his throat and he gagged as he saw the half-crushed body of a Thrakian guard inside the doorway. Ichor ran across the flooring from under the sable chitin.

"Christ."

Then he choked. Where was Colin?

He vaulted the Thrak. The movement took him skidding down the front corridor. He stopped, turned carefully, listening. . . .

Voices . . . down the right wing.

Rawlins did not walk. He sprinted down the corridor and when he came to the doorway, he did not stop, he threw himself into the room.

So it was his body Winton's rifle fire caught instead of St. Colin's.

With a grunt, Rawlins thudded into Colin, bowling him over, and the saint cried out, as the projectile slug plowed into his side, scouring his ribcage with wildfire and pain.

Winton stood hunched over in the room. Dhurl and his aide lay fallen at his feet. Ichor stained the tiles, pooled, and ran together with the crimson tide that issued from Rawlins.

Winton paused a moment. Coherent thought returned to his dark eyes. Colin saw his glance flicker toward him, and, grasping Rawlins' body in his arms, closed his eyes. *Don't let this boy's sacrifice be in vain*, he prayed.

Breathing hard, Winton clenched his weapon. He knew the bullets had probably torn through both bodies. Projectiles were hard to come by. He had a few left in the magazine. He wanted to save them for Storm . . . just in case.

He turned and ran from the embassy.

Rawlins moaned. He tried to sit up, palm over the hole in his gut. "Sssaint . . ."

Colin moved out from under the boy. His ribs smarted and his over-robe was scored, but the norcite interwoven fabric had taken most of the damage. Rawlins was a different matter. Colin laid his hand over the boy's.

"Don't cry, son. Just lie still."

He prayed again. He prayed to be filled with love and power, not his, never his, himself only a channel . . . a miracle to be repeated.

Rawlins quivered in shock, unable to stop trembling, legs icy—were they even his—heels pounding the floor, teeth chattering, the only warm spot in his own body his stomach where his guts pushed up and out, squeezing between his fingers, blood pumping out. . . .

He ceased moving.

Colin stayed where he was, until the tremendous warmth flooding his arm from the shoulder down flickered out, then was gone. For a moment he felt on the verge of tears and terribly bereft.

Then, under his hand, Rawlins took a deep, sighing breath. His eyes fluttered and he looked up.

"Sir?"

"Lie still. You'll be weak. But you won't die. I'll send help." Colin shambled to his feet, and felt his age, his years, his fatigue.

The boy lay his head back on the tile, and slept.

There wasn't a Thraks alive in the embassy to hurt him, so Colin did not hesitate to leave Rawlins there. He had to get to the wall, to the Eastside gate, to stop Winton from whatever further madness he planned. He had to work at making his legs obey him, and he staggered from the embassy like a very, very old man.

Rawlins never heard the click, slide, click, slide of insectlike legs and chitin across the tile.

Mortally wounded but alive nonetheless, Dhurl plucked off the Dominion weapon belt from the boy. He hoisted himself up.

The Thraks eyed the human on the flooring. This one ought to die for what the other had done, but Dhurl's time was limited. He, too, made for the door and the gate.

Jack pulled up on the crest. He could hear himself breathe and, worse, he could smell himself sweating. As the gray-purple dawn edged up the sky, he could see the wind had finally gone, taking the dust storm with it. He reached up and took his helmet off, and hooked it on his belt.

There was an ocean of beings on the plain below him. Jack headed down the crest, wondering if he saw dead or living Bythians. He rubbed his eyes. The rear cameras had been out on the suit. He wondered what was at his back. He turned and looked behind.

Windsails billowed against the horizon. Hundreds more Bythians followed him on foot.

"Shit. I might have known," he said.

Colin set you up.

"Maybe. Or maybe they're just coming in for water and supplies."

Bogie laughed, a deep, booming sound. Jack massaged his forehead wearily. *At least they're not fighting. I calculate the Eastside wall to be the best approach, there's a natural corridor there, and the power vault will carry us out of range after two short bursts clear the way . . . *

"Save your tactics, you bloodthirsty half-life."

Saving.

"If you want to be good for something, locate

Amber. She's supposed to be sitting in the hills somewhere."

There was a pause, then: *Amber is the second form sitting in front of the gate.*

"What?" Jack broke into a run.

Bythians moved aside for him like a boat keel sunders a tide. He did not care that his suit made him a moving juggernaut. He yelled, "Amber!" and heard his voice cut across the noise of the murmuring Bythians like ice cracking on a clear winter's day.

She got to her feet.

Or it was supposed to have been her, but he slowed, digging in his bootheels for traction, staring at the veiled and headdressed creature that got sinuously to its feet.

Dust and cloth covered it from head to toe. It was Amber's height. It could have been Amber.

Jack slowed to a walk, unaware of the commotion beginning at his back as the Bythians got to their feet, and fragrance filled the air, thick and pungent, their trilling voices beginning to rise.

"Amber?"

She moved her arms out from her cloaking. Only her eyes stared out from her face, all else was covered by the dust, her thick hair hidden under a Bythian headdress that was, bizarrely, a cobalt blue feathering which repeated the blue tattooing of her skin.

Her skin!

The bastard had gone and tattooed her to match the Bythian skin patterns.

"Amber!"

She blinked, nothingness in her golden brown eyes.

Jack halted in front of her, his heart pounding in his throat.

"Jack! Jack!"

He looked up to the wall, saw Kavin standing there. Stunned, he looked back to Amber.

Before he could do anything else, the Bythians erupted in a roar of sound as the High Omnipotent Hussiah got to his feet also. His whistle cut through the din of sound.

He looked at Jack and repeated what he had just said. "It is time."

The gates opened up and three hundred suited Knights moved out onto the field. The Bythians grew deathly still.

Jack pushed past Amber. "Get 'em out of the suits, Kavin, for god's sake. They're infested!"

Kavin elegantly climbed down the wall to a point where he could jump, then landed lightly on his feet. "What's wrong, Jack?"

"I just spent the last two days in hell wondering if I could get back here in time. The suits are carrying a parasite . . . a parasite from Milos. You might have heard about it—maybe not. But the thing lives off heat and sweat, incubates, then it attaches itself to a live body. Then, it . . . consumes it. It's called a Milot berserker, and I ran into six of them out there . . . the six guys that were carried off from Black Piss River. I don't how or why, but I do know what—and every minute that armor is worn, is a minute closer to one of the worst deaths I've ever seen."

The Knights stood and looked at one another. Lassaday was the first to shuck his armor.

"Son of a bitch," he said. "I heard of 'em. Thought they was one of the craziest rumors to come out of the Sand Wars."

"It was no rumor, sergeant," Jack answered him.

"Then ask him how he knows." A strange voice cut through the air.

Jack put a hand out to Amber, who stood in his way between his view and the now open gate. He moved her aside ever so gently.

Winton smiled grimly at him.

It is time, Hussiah had said. Jack felt his heart slow and steady. He took a step forward, a step forward through time and space, headed for an ancient enemy.

It was Hussiah who stopped him.

"This is our time," the Bythian High Priest said, his eyes glittering with emerald fire. "You are a Champion."

He trilled his words out to the thousands of Bythians surrounding them. They responded with a flood of noise.

Amber uncoiled then, awareness coming into her eyes, taking off her cloak and veil, dropping them into the dust at her feet.

Hussiah took her hand. "This is our Champion."

He translated a second time.

Jack looked back to where Winton had stood. Bythians jostled him, he could no longer see his enemy. He clenched his jaw.

Then silence fell as the broken body of a dying Thraks reared in the open gateway.

Dhurl had studied his Bythian history well. As he crept close to the Eastside gate, he smelled the moment about to happen. His face plates shuddered and he assumed a mask despite the trail of ichor he left behind him.

This world had to be theirs.

There were three champions prophesied.

All he had to do was provide one to take the Thrakian side.

Intelligence reports had come through, finally.

He knew one of the Knights had been theirs. It was time to take advantage of long ago implants.

He gained the gateway.

"Halt!"

The sea of Bythians surged and fell silent. Hussiah stood with his arms raised, and he turned also.

He did not try to contain the aroma of disdain as the Thraks took the gateway. It was injured, he saw with pleasure.

"What is it?"

"I demand the third," Dhurl said. "For the Holy Trials."

"You are a temple desecrater!" Angry trills nearly drowned out Dhurl's rasping reply.

The Thraks paused and said again, "We did not mean to desecrate your grounds. We were raising our young there. Raising a hatchling to be our Champion in your Holy Trials, in the shadow of your Holy place."

Hussiah did not believe the Thraks for a moment, but he translated. There was a murmuring, then another Holy Priest rose. Hussiah eyed Suh-he-lan with disdain.

"I support his demand."

Hussiah decided nothing would come of it. Who could the Thraks choose who would defeat either Amber or the Suit of All Light? He shrugged and turned back.

"Choose."

Dhurl rose to his greatest Ambassadorial height. He looked across the assemblage of Knights.

Winton stayed within the gateway, in the shadows, doubly pleased. The Bythians had not torn Jack apart. So he would get his second wish—the chance to see Jack exposed as the traitor he was, and Winton himself would destroy him. He cocked the rifle.

Dhurl tore the synthesizer out of his chitin. It made a substantial hole and caused him a substantial amount of pain, but it was just one small irritation in his mortality. If he would die, he would die in his native voice.

He clicked. It was a windy, husky noise, for the synthesizer implant had ruined what passed for a Thrakian throat. But it passed. He made a series of clicks and whistles, painstakingly, for the Knight who was meant to hear them someday.

Kavin saw Winton tense. He knew the WP commander was up to something. He saw the man's feverish, intense stare focused on Jack. The muzzle of the rifle was pointed. He calculated the line of fire.

Jack, again.

Then, as Dhurl spoke, he *knew.*

Winton had pegged Jack Storm as a lost Knight. Would kill him here and now, no matter what the circumstances, even if it ruined whatever other ambitions the man might hold.

He saw Colin appear at Winton's elbow. The saint was bowed and grayed. But he did nothing, as he lifted his squared chin and looked out over the assemblage of Bythians.

Still looking for your damned evidence, Kavin thought. This was a religious happening, and Colin was bound not to interfere.

But Kavin wasn't. A stinging warmth came to his eyes as he stepped out, knowing the Thrakian message fell on deaf ears, all of them—except his.

"I answer Dhurl. I will be the Thrakian Champion."

*   *   *

"No!" screamed Winton. "You can't be! It's him, I know it is, it's Storm!"

He raised his rifle and set himself.

Kavin turned. "No, Winton. I'm the one. I was just a boy when the Thraks picked me up, but they were impressed that a child would try to operate a suit. They had me for . . . years. Then I escaped. And one of the first things I did was start killing Thraks wherever I could find them, Treaty or no Treaty. I'm your goddamn, fucking lost Knight."

Jack said, "Scott Randolph was murdered because of you."

"Probably. The Thraks didn't know I'd been deprogrammed. They didn't want the broadcaster exposing their plants." Kavin moved slowly, deliberately, into Winton's line of fire.

His face went livid. "Goddamn, I'll kill you anyway!" He surged forward firing.

Kavin threw himself that last hand's width of distance between Winton and Jack.

Jack caught his body even as Winton threw the rifle down and ran.

His friend sagged into his arms. Jack looked down, uncomprehending, at the holes in Kavin's torso. Then at his own armor, where the slugs had just flattened like so many useless tokens.

The norcite covered armor.

Jack picked up Kavin and cradled him. Humor flickered in half-open brown eyes.

"Why did you answer the call?"

"Because Winton expected . . . you to." Kavin coughed. Blood-flecked foam speckled his lips. "I . . . couldn't let a friend take the blame . . . for me. I never told you . . ."

Jack looked up, anguished. "Help me! Help him!" He looked at the girl who stood closest to him. "Amber. . . ."

She turned eyes without recognition or pity on him.

Kavin shook his head. "Let me go." He coughed again. "There's so much I meant to tell you. . . ."

Jack knew there was no hope. He held his friend close. "I know. I was a Knight, too."

"I knew it!" The triumph in Kavin's voice was there, if weak. "Did you know my brother?"

"No . . . but your brother died fighting for my brother on Dorman's Stand."

"Good." Kavin smiled.

Colin sagged at the gate. He went to his knees, breathing like a torn vacuum hose, unable to dredge up the strength he'd had earlier. He saw the death and could not defeat it this time. He put his hands over his eyes. Across the gateway, Dhurl gave a gurgle and toppled over. A foul stench drifted into the air.

Kavin tried to form a last word and settled for clutching his friend's hand.

Jack's eyes filled. Lassaday came forward, his face red. "Let me take 'im, captain."

"No." He looked for Winton. But he did not fight as Lassaday and Travellini gently took the broken body from his hands.

Around him, the Bythians had fallen back in shocked dismay. Hussiah felt his guts twist. He drew in a great, sucking breath of air. He told his people what had just happened.

Many of them cheered.

As for himself, he felt only a great weight settling on his chest.

The Third Age had just begun. One Champion had brought back a quality into the world that had been missing from the Bythians for many a century—the ability to put another's life before one's own.

"Kill him," he ordered Amber. "Show him to be the Deceiver he is."

Amber pulled back, hearing her teacher's voice. Her time had come. She sensed the heat of the bodies around here, smelled the aromas of anticipation and victory.

She was preparing to strike when something grasped at her, something not of this earth, *in her mind.*

Amber, it said. *We love you. Come back.*

Her throat tightened. She could not breathe. She looked at the Deceiver towering over her in the suit of All Light, bright as the sun that could burn out her eyesight.

She remembered. "Jack—"

No. Jack was dead.

Amber, hear me. We love you. We need you.

She threw back her head and screamed. "Jack!"

He was going to find Winton and rip his still beating heart out of his chest. He was going to take his gauntleted hand and tear flesh away until he found that blood-pumping organ, then take it and—

The scream seared his mind. He looked down at his blood-stained armor and looked up and saw Amber throwing herself at him.

He caught her.

He was alive again in her eyes.

"Oh, god," he cried and held her. He tore the Bythian headdress off her hair. He kissed her. She clung to him, crying. He held her as tightly as he could, Bogie's senses making the armor a second skin, and he said, "I've got to go after Winton."

Hussiah danced in agitation. There must be only one Champion. One! And then he realized his folly. He had heard rumors . . . and not understood them. But the humans were only half a sex. It took two of them to be complete. Unwittingly, Hussiah had delivered to Jack the balance of his being.

Before she could answer, the ground around them burst into flame.

With a scream of their own, the Bythians, en masse, fell to the dust and put their heads to their earth as the Holy Fire erupted about the two Champions.

Amber let go of Jack. The fire passed around her. She felt its cool flame licking at her. It surrounded Jack and only Jack.

A skimmer grazed their heads. Lassaday looked up. "I bet my balls he's going to get off-planet."

"How?"

"We started evacuating last night. The transport's half-loaded now."

Jack's eyes narrowed. His dark blond hair was illuminated in the eerie flames. "I'm not losing him this time. The suit'll carry me!" He strode away, and broke into a run, taking the ground in earth-eating leaps. The Holy Fire burned after him.

Amber put her hand to her mouth.

Instead of char, the flame left a verdant streak. It plowed the dying plains around Sassinol with life.

She thought of Claron. If only he could see what he was doing!

Hussiah took her by the elbow. "Come," he said. "We must see!"

She looked at the Bythian High Priest. "I failed you," she said.

He shook his head. "No. I be failing myself. I

was not strong enough to see the fulfillment of my own prophecy. But the Third Age has begun. Come! I must see the Holy Fire!"

Red field. All his guages showed red fields, but Jack did not slow. He let his momentum carry him after Winton. Just let him get close enough!

He caught him at the crest. The bush skimmer coughed and hesitated, dipping low, and Jack raised his gauntlet. Laser fire clipped the rear thruster, and the skimmer gyroed.

It came to earth carrying its reluctant rider. Winton jumped off and hit rolling. Jack let him get a few strides head start. Then he power vaulted, overleaping the running man.

He pivoted and smiled as Winton ran into his grasp.

Even as his head tilted back and his bones popped from the strain of Jack's hold, Winton gasped, "You're a traitor. You're infested. You *know*—"

"That's right, Winton. I know you ordered us to die on Milos."

The man stopped struggling a moment. His eyes narrowed in memory. "Milos . . ."

"Why?"

Winton's lips worked, too dry to spit, but he tried. "You should have died on Milos. If you had half the guts you should have had, you would have! No one was meant to survive Milos. Infested. All of you were infested! And Regis had to be gotten out of power. It was the only way."

"Who were you working with? Who told you to sacrifice the Knights?" He applied a little more pressure with his gauntlets.

"Who do you think?" Winton sneered. "Pepys was always right there, waiting for Regis to make a mistake."

"And Claron?"

Winton's sneer became lopsided under Jack's grip, but he got out, "All your fault, Jack. If you hadn't been there, I'd have found another way to deal with the sand crèche."

Jack squeezed tighter, and Winton died an ugly death.

The Holy Fire died with him. As Jack dropped the body at his feet and looked around, he saw the flames gutter. As it died, he looked back and saw the acreage behind him where the flames had fanned out and spread.

Green shoots pointed skyward. Trees rippled and branches hung low with leaf and fruit.

Jack closed his eyes in sorrow. He knew, for the barest fraction of a second, he might have had this miracle for Claron as well as Bythia, but he had killed. The Blue Fire crept up his armor and curled in the palm of his gauntlet, the very crumb of a miracle.

Hussiah gained the crest with Amber. He lifted up his hand and let her go to Jack. Holy Fire sparked the gap between them, and then the High Priest held the fire in the palm of his hand. He looked to Jack. "I will take it to the rest of Bythia," he said. "Your part is done." He turned his back on the two of them and went back the way he had come through tree and brush, the bruised fragrance of his passage drifting back to them, his hand upheld like a torch.

Lassaday chewed his stim-gum with relish as the transport shuddered and shifted into top speed. "I'm gonna miss those snakeskins."

"What on earth for?"

"What for, kid? Well, for one, they made one

hell of a good beer." And the sergeant rubbed his palm over his bald head. "And because we had to leave th' commander back there with 'em."

Colin sat back in his chair. The cold sleep bays had not all been readied yet, and he waited with the handful of others. "I think, sergeant," the prelate said, "that he died the way he wanted to."

"With honor and not because the Thraks had a hold on him," Amber said.

"Th' only way to go," Lassaday agreed.

Jack had a faraway look on his face.

"Jack—" she began, but the intercom interrupted her. "Gentlemen . . . and ladies . . . it's going to be a rough ride back. We've just gotten word the Thraks have declared war."

A tiny muscle flexed in Jack's jawline. How could he pull down the emperor and commander of Dominion defenses if they had to go to war against the Thraks?

"What are you thinking?" she whispered.

He looked down, and considered her eyes. He smiled and pulled her closer. "I was thinking, first things first."

DAW

NEW DIMENSIONS IN MILITARY SF

Charles Ingrid
THE SAND WARS
He was a soldier fighting against both mankind's alien foe and the evil at the heart of the human Dominion Empire, trapped in an alien-altered suit of armor which, if worn too long, could transform him into a sand warrior—a no-longer human berserker.
☐ SOLAR KILL (Book 1)   (UE2391—$3.95)
☐ LASERTOWN BLUES (Book 2)   (UE2393—$3.95)
☐ CELESTIAL HIT LIST (Book 3)   (UE2394—$3.95)
☐ ALIEN SALUTE (Book 4)   (UE2329—$3.95)
☐ RETURN FIRE (Book 5)   (UE2363—$3.95)

W. Michael Gear
THE SPIDER TRILOGY
The Prophets of the lost colony planet called World could see the many pathways of the future, and when the conquering Patrol Ships of the galaxy-spanning Directorate arrived, they found the warriors of World ready, armed and waiting.
☐ THE WARRIORS OF SPIDER (Book 1)   (UE2287—$3.95)
☐ THE WAY OF SPIDER (Book 2)   (UE2318—$3.95)
☐ THE WEB OF SPIDER (Book 3)   (UE2356—$4.95)

John Steakley
☐ ARMOR
Impervious body armor had been devised for the commando forces who were to be dropped onto the poisonous surface of A-9, the home world of mankind's most implacable enemy. But what of the man inside the armor? This tale of cosmic combat will stand against the best of Gordon Dickson or Poul Anderson.
                                                      (UE2368—$4.50)

DAW

DAW Presents the Fantastic Realms of
JO CLAYTON

DAW

THEY WERE THE ULTIMATE ENEMIES, GENERALS OF STAR EMPIRES FOREVER OPPOSED— AND WORLDS WOULD FALL BEFORE THEIR PRIVATE WAR...

IN CONQUEST BORN
C.S. FRIEDMAN

Braxi and Azea, two super-races fighting an endless campaign over a long forgotten cause. The Braxaná—created to become the ultimate warriors. The Azeans, raised to master the powers of the mind, using telepathy to penetrate where mere weapons cannot. Now the final phase of their war is approaching, when whole worlds will be set ablaze by the force of ancient hatred. Now Zatar and Anzha, the master generals, who have made this battle a personal vendetta, will use every power of body and mind to claim the vengeance of total conquest.

☐ **IN CONQUEST BORN** (UE2198—$3.95)